"Diego," she called softly. In that instant, he would have gladly renounced ten years of revolution for ten minutes in her arms.

"What?" he said harshly, trying to disguise the knot of emotion in his throat.

"If you're going," Melinda pressed on, refusing to make room for disappointment, "could you at least let me have a drink of that wine?"

He tried to set it on the ground for her to retrieve after he had achieved a safe distance between them, but the bottle refused to remain upright on the craggy slope that led to the stream.

"It's open," he said gruffly. "You'd better come and get it, or it will spill."

"I don't have any clothes on," she reminded him. As if he could have forgotten.

"Where are they? I'll bring them to you."

"In that case"—she smiled—"you might as well just bring me the wine."

He could think of no excuse and he could not tell her the truth: that he was more afraid of her, and what she could do to him, than a whole squadron of government troops. . . .

Books by Leah Laiman

Maid of Honor
For Richer, for Poorer
For Better, for Worse
To Love and to Cherish

Published by POCKET BOOKS

MAID OF HONOR

Another Summer of Love

OF

HONOR

LEAH LAIMAN

POCKET BOOKS

New York   London   Toronto   Sydney   Tokyo   Singapore

This book is a work of fiction. Names, characters, places and incidents are products of the author's imagination or are used fictitiously. Any resemblance to actual events or locales or persons, living or dead, is entirely coincidental.

An *Original* Publication of POCKET BOOKS

POCKET BOOKS, a division of Simon & Schuster Inc.
1230 Avenue of the Americas, New York, NY 10020

ISBN: 0-671-53404-1

First Pocket Books printing July 1995

10 9 8 7 6 5 4 3 2 1

POCKET and colophon are registered trademarks of Simon & Schuster Inc.

Cover art by Punz Wolff

Printed in the U.S.A.

MAID
OF
HONOR

✑ 1 ✑

A reverential hush had fallen over the crowd. There was the possibility of history being made, but more than that, the sense that something beautiful was unfolding before their eyes. Like balletomanes watching Barishnykov or fight fans ringside for Ali, strangers smiled at each other with the born-again fervor of a casually congregated group who suddenly realize that they have been randomly chosen to bear witness to a divine revelation. It was the first test run of a D'Uberville VT-12, a quarter-of-a-million-dollar racing machine that was going to revolutionize the world of driving. And they were watching a master at work.

At the start of the second lap, the car picked up speed.

"Look at her go," whooped Eddie Gravino, the car's second engineer, watching from the circuit's control booth. "The VT-12 comes on cam at 3500 rpm. She's gonna rocket." His commentary was as much for himself as the half-dozen people within earshot, but they leaned forward to catch his words, evangelicals eagerly waiting for the prophet to interpret their visions.

"Oh yeah, baby, shift her down," Eddie encouraged, even though there was no one to take his instruction. "That's it," he enthused, as if his command had been obeyed. "The go pedal's down hard now. The tachometer's got to be over the 7300-rpm redline. Listen to that engine sing!"

To the uninformed, Eddie's ethereal chorus was a mind-numbing roar, as the car circled into its third lap, clocking speeds over 186 miles per hour. But even an ignorant ear could hear the change as the mechanical multivoiced choir under the hood suddenly seemed to lose its perfect pitch. The zooming bass was replaced by a high-pitched whine, which seemed either the cause or result of the car veering first to the left, then sharply to the right. In less time than can be measured on the average man's watch, the D'Uberville had rolled twice, righted itself, and careened into the retaining wall, flattening its aerodynamically beaked nose like a can in a compactor.

Eddie was out of the booth before the sirens went off, but there were already people running across the track. The air was filled with the acrid scent of burned rubber, but the smell of panic was even stronger. He wanted to scream, to cry, but he forced his legs to keep moving. It was his fault. He shouldn't have let Sam drive. The boss would kill him—no, he'd kill himself —if Sam was . . . He stopped his thoughts. He couldn't think that way. And then, he slowed and smiled. He didn't have to. Sam was getting out of the car and walking away, pulling off her helmet and shaking out her famous cascade of copper curls as people closed in on her.

Everyone was talking at once, but the minute she saw Eddie, Sam zeroed in on him, launching into a litany of flaws on the car she'd designed herself and spent the last sixteen months perfecting.

"She understeers on the skidpad. The front tires were grinding down to carbon, and I couldn't feel a damn thing. Then on the drag strip, the throttle linkage stuck wide open and the rev-limiter didn't kick in. That's what did me in. We're going to have to fix that."

"I guess I don't have to ask if you're okay," Eddie grinned, relieved.

He pulled out the notepad that he'd started carrying from the day that Samantha Myles Symington had appointed him her second in command. He'd learned the hard way that when Sam had something to say, she expected you to get it the first time. Of course, he'd heard about her, knew people said she was some kind of automotive genius, but he hadn't really believed it. As far as he was concerned, she wouldn't have been there if she wasn't the boss's wife. And Andrew Symington wouldn't have been the boss if his father, Forrest, hadn't had a paralyzing accident just in time to resurrect the younger couple's fading ambitions from their own failed enterprises. Besides, nothing a woman had to tell Eddie Gravino about cars could be that important. On the first day, she'd given him some instructions that he'd considered less than crucial and put on the back burner. It had almost cost him his job, and he never made the same mistake again.

3

He was already writing. "We can make the adjustments on the second car. When do you want to try it?"

"As soon as you make the adjustments."

"Don't you think maybe you've had enough for one day?"

"Can you make the changes today?"

"Yeah, I can. But . . ."

He sensed her focus faltering and followed her gaze to the edge of the crowd, which was parting as though at some unheard command. It was neither the fact that Drew Symington signed their checks nor his patrician aura of authority that made the people around him pull back. Unlike his father, who had always maintained his distance from the workers on the line, adopting the noblesse oblige attitude of his wife's truly aristocratic family, the heir to the D'Uberville Motor Company fortune was generally warm and approachable. But today, fury emanated from him like white heat, and it simply made good sense to move away from the fire.

The two-year-old girl in his arms, with her mother's red hair and her father's blue eyes, was laughing and clapping her hands. "Mommy made bang," she repeated over and over, delighted as much by the phrase as the act. "Mommy made bang."

It was hard not to share in the child's glee, and Sam laughed, too, stretching out her arms to her happy daughter. But Drew wasn't even smiling as he handed Moira over to Eddie. "Take her, will you, please, Eddie?" he asked, and Moira allowed herself to be turned over without resistance, having learned from her first experience with all things sweet that Uncle Eddie always had a special treat waiting for her in his shirt pocket.

"Drew," Sam began carefully, still not quite sure just how angry her husband was. "It wasn't as bad as it looked, and I won't have the same trouble with the next run. Right, Eddie?"

Eddie nodded as best he could with Moira's little hands gripping his neck while she waited impatiently for him to unwrap the lollipop she'd found right where she'd expected it.

But Drew wasn't looking at Eddie for confirmation. "There's not going to be a next run. Is there, Eddie?" he said.

Eddie sighed and looked from husband to wife as they stared defiantly at each other while addressing him. Even though they worked together every day, the Symingtons rarely had public disagreements. But when they did, there was hell to pay for anyone caught in the middle.

"Come on, boss," Eddie pleaded, "You know I can't stop her."

"I can," said Drew. And with that, he picked up his wife, threw her over his shoulder, and marched off the track, equally oblivious to his wife's outraged cries and the suppressed smiles of the people who cleared a path for them.

"How could you?!" Sam demanded, incensed, when Drew finally put her down in the well-equipped trailer kept for her convenience adjacent to the track.

"How could *you?*" he countered, equally enraged. "You promised."

"I promised I wouldn't take any unnecessary risks. This was necessary. And it wasn't a risk. How could I find the flaws if I didn't drive the car?"

"Use a test driver like everybody else in the business. Do you think the Fords turn themselves into crash test dummies?"

"Number one, this wasn't a crash test. It was a drive test. I just happened to crash. Number two, we're not producing Fords. The VT-12 is a really special car. It's going to change the way cars are made at DMC, maybe the way cars are made everywhere. I can't build it if I can't drive it."

"Then you can't build it."

"What are you saying?" asked Samantha, and Drew heard the fear in her voice. For a minute, knowing how much she loved making this car, he felt sorry for her. Then he remembered his own fear as he had walked into the stands with his baby daughter just in time to see his wife smash into a wall. His anger left him as quickly as it had come.

"I'm saying," he faltered, hearing the tremble in his own voice and doing nothing to hide it, "that I love you beyond all reason. That I can't live without you. That Moira needs you. And that no car in the world, revolutionary or not, is worth losing you."

"Oh, Drew," Sam sighed, coming to him. "Do you think I don't know that? Do you think I don't feel the same way? I swear to you, you're not going to lose me on a track. You have to trust me on that."

Drew looked at Sam. It had been four years since they'd been married, five since he'd first spotted what he'd suspected to be an imaginary nymph skinny-dipping at the Millpond and known that if she were real, she'd be his. They'd lost each other more than once in that time, sometimes through the treachery of others, sometimes through their own foolishness. But they'd never completely let go of the cords that bound them together, and they'd always managed to follow those lines back. Loving each other had never been difficult, but learning to trust that love sometimes seemed the hardest thing in the world.

He let his hands slide through the silken tangles of her hair and pulled her to him. She could feel his desire rising as he kissed her on her eyes, her cheeks, and finally, her lips. She flushed with her own need as he unzipped her overalls and helped her step out of them. He caught his breath, still aroused after all these years at the sight of her near perfect body that was so often hidden in her shapeless work clothes. She was pulling off his clothes, her ardor matching his, and they sank to the floor, ignoring the sofa they frequently used for the very same purpose. He closed his eyes as he propelled himself into her, feeling the familiar warmth of her body envelop him. He'd been here many times before, but each time was newly discovered delight. Sometimes, they would make love with their eyes open, watching and responding to each other's passion. And sometimes, like today, there was no need to see. Their bodies moved slowly, sinuously, totally in synch, until they both stopped, sighing deeply, satisfaction complete, as their souls touched.

There was a knock on the trailer door, and they hastily separated themselves.

"I left the baby with Eddie," Drew groaned, assuming the engineer had tired of playing baby-sitter and had come to deliver his charge back to her parents.

"What are you two doing in there? Open up. It's the middle of the day, for God's sake. Have you no decency?"

Sam looked at Drew and gasped. It couldn't be.

"Come on, you guys. Don't you know better than to keep a movie star waiting?"

It was! Sam began a frantic search for various portions of her clothing that had been scattered around the trailer in her haste to get naked with her husband. "Oh my God, Melinda! I can't believe it. Hold on. I'll be right there."

She grabbed for the door, then paused for a second to look at her husband. He was disheveled, but he was dressed, and Sam wasn't waiting any longer. She flung open the trailer and fell into her sister's arms.

"What are you doing here?"

"Come at a bad time, did I?" Melinda laughed, taking in their flushed faces and Drew's belated effort to tuck in his shirt.

"No, of course not," said Sam, involuntarily straightening her own clothes and feeling herself blush.

"We just had no idea you were coming," said Drew, coming to the rescue as he gave his sister-in-law a welcoming hug.

"Nobody did. It's the only way I can get around now without having a hoard of paparazzi trailing after me. I skulk around like a wanted criminal. Isn't it glamorous?"

Sam looked at her little sister and laughed. At the moment, she looked like anything but a movie star. Her hair was tied back into a ponytail, and a shapeless hat was pulled low over her eyes. She had no makeup on, and her jeans were at least a size too big. But even in disguise as a normal person, there was no denying the legacy of beauty she shared with her sister. Neither Melinda nor Samantha ever made an issue of their looks, but the fact that they were genetically endowed with a lot more of what everyone wants and very few get was obvious to everyone but themselves.

Sam knew Melinda's complaints were halfhearted at best. Not so long ago, Sam had been working on the line at DMC and Melinda had been private secretary —and then much more—to Forrest Symington. Now, just a few short years later, the diabolical senior Symington was incapacitated, she was married to his wonderful son and building a new car for DMC, and Melinda had become an Academy Award-winning actress. As kids, fighting imaginary forces, they had dubbed themselves the Myles Militia. They weren't engaged in many battles these days, but their loyalty and devotion to each other still held true.

"God, it's good to see you," said Sam fervently. "How long are you here for?"

"Just the weekend. I got the part in the new Elgar Franz film. We start a three-month shoot in San Domenico next week."

"Congratulations," said Drew, genuinely pleased for her. He knew from Sam that she'd been lobbying for the part for months.

"That is just great," said Sam, who enjoyed her sister's triumphs as much as her own. "Uh . . . where exactly is San Domenico?"

"In the Caribbean," answered Melinda authoritatively.

"I know that," Sam went on in mock exasperation. "But where exactly?"

Melinda hesitated. "Somewhere south of Cuba you make a left or something, I think. Oh, I don't know. I just get on a plane and it takes me there. But it's supposed to be very beautiful."

Drew laughed. "You girls certainly know your geography."

"Oh, it's Mr. Rand McNally," Sam teased her

husband. "And I bet you could pinpoint it on a map with your eyes closed."

"As a matter of fact," Drew smiled confidently, "San Domenico is an island of approximately two hundred and ninety-three square miles—"

"Approximately!" laughed Melinda as Drew went on without stopping.

"—That lies in a section of the Caribbean called the Bartlett Deep. Their primary cash crop is sugar cane with a little coffee and cocoa thrown in. The highest point on the island is—"

"He's making this up," said Sam with conviction.

"No, I'm not. I just know these things."

"Yeah, sure."

"Okay, so we once considered expanding DMC operations to Latin America. I had to do a study."

"Which explains why you are the only person outside of San Domenico who actually knows where it is."

"You should apply some of that knowledge to your own business," said Melinda, still kidding around. "When I was coming in, I saw that heap of scrap metal stuck to the wall of the track. Didn't seem like a good place for it."

"Tell that to your sister," Drew said, knowing he had an ally.

"What? You were in that?" Melinda looked at Sam incredulously.

"It looks worse than it was."

"Jesus, you could have been killed."

"That's what I said," chimed in Drew.

"No, I couldn't have," insisted Sam, on the defensive from both of them.

"Are you crazy? You've got a child to think of."

"That's what I said." Drew was enjoying this.

"I know that. I wasn't in any danger."

"Who are you kidding? I saw the car, or what was left of it. Don't you think it's time you stopped acting like Evel Knievel?"

"I didn't say that," appended Drew, "but I should have."

"Okay, lay off you two. We don't need to talk about this anymore. Don't you want to see your niece?" Sam deliberately changed the subject.

Mention of Moira got them on another track, as Sam had known it would, and Drew went off to fetch her. Sam picked up the phone.

"Who are you calling?" asked Melinda.

"Everybody!" responded Sam. "It's not every day we get visited by movie stars," she added, only half joking. "We're having a party!"

2

Sam loved nighttime at Belvedere. Standing on the terrace outside the master suite, she looked out over the formal gardens. Dozens of tiny lanterns were hung from the exotic trees, their shimmer making magic of mere beauty. She remembered a time when she had been intimidated by this place that was now her home. How forbidding its gates had seemed, how frightening its patrician facade. But her child had been born here, albeit by accident, and her husband before that. There was a history here to which, even though it was not her own, she would be forever tied. Her mother-in-law, Mathilde D'Uberville, whose family money had bought all this, had readily ceded the reins of the household to her. The staff now moved at her command. Still, there were moments during the day, when approaching the rolling green grounds and the white columns spread sentrylike across the wings of the mansion, she felt like a fraud, a poseur playing at being mistress of the manor.

But not at night. At night, Sam belonged. Somehow, cloaked in the shadows of darkness, the estate seemed smaller, more manageable. The golden glow of interior light softened the forbidding frame of the mansion and made it warm and inviting. Cicadas played their one-note symphony under stars augmented by the garden's twinkling spotlights. And Samantha Myles Symington was at peace in her home.

Below her, Sam could see and hear her tiny daughter, gurgling with mirth as she ran away from her father who pursued her with a lumbering walk and a menacing "I'm going to get you." Moira was wearing embroidered peach silk pajamas sent by her aunt Melinda directly from China where she had gone to make her last film. Drew was in his tuxedo, although he hadn't bothered to tie his tie yet, and as he caught Moira in his open arms, it dangled temptingly in front of her, until, unable to resist, she grabbed it and ran away again, giggling delightedly. Nothing ever amused her so much as her own mischief.

"I guess this is what's meant by having it all."

Sam jumped, startled by Melinda's voice. "I didn't hear you come in," she said, kissing the air in the vicinity of her sister's cheek. "You look gorgeous."

"So do you," said Melinda.

The sisters studied each other appreciatively. Hollywood had taught Melinda how to use her assets. In spite of her own disparaging jokes, she *had* acquired an aura of glamour. She was wearing a simple white silk charmeuse dress with high neck and long sleeves but cut so perfectly on the bias, that it brushed every voluptuous curve of her body from neck to ankle, showing nothing but revealing all. Her dark chestnut hair was brushed straight and gleaming down her back, with only a single swoop of curl allowed to fall over one softly shadowed hazel eye. Her full mouth was stained a bright ruby red, the only slash of color in the chiaroscuro of her look.

Samantha, though less dramatic, was just as beautiful. Things had become less rigid since she'd taken over as mistress of the manor, with dinner often a picnic in the kitchen in jeans instead of the formal attire once the requisite of every evening's meal. But tonight, in honor of her sister and acknowledging the presence of her mother-in-law who had just returned from an extended trip to Europe and relished the niceties of aristocratic custom, Sam had pulled out all the stops. With only an hour to shop, she had chosen a deceptively simple suit by Armani. The jacket, a shimmer of closely knit metallic threads secured with just one button between her breasts, melted into the gleaming folds of the pants. She'd left her hair to its own devices and the copper curls reflected the light of her suit and warmed her skin with a golden glow, setting off her startling green eyes.

"Aren't you going to ask me?" Samantha asked her sister when they'd finished admiring each other's outfits.

"Ask you what?" Melinda replied, all innocence.

"As if you didn't know. Don't you want to know if he's coming?"

"No." She paused. "Is he?"

Before she could answer, the door slammed open and Sam was distracted by what had rapidly become her favorite sound in the whole world: the pat-pat-pat of little chubby feet running toward her. Moira always ran.

"Aunty Minna, Aunty Minna," Moira sang, racing toward them. "Daddy catched me. But I ran away. And I catched his tie." She looked back at the door where her smiling father sauntered in behind her and, dimpling with mischief, proffered the triumphal object to her beloved aunt.

"Maybe Mommy should take that and dress Daddy," Sam said, plying the wrinkled black satin from her daughter's tiny hand.

"Mommy dress Daddy," laughed Moira nodding, thinking it quite a good joke.

"You look so pretty, Moira. Like a Chinese doll," said Melinda, bending to appreciate her at her own level.

"Me not doll. Me girl."

"Well all you girls take my breath away," said Drew, losing himself for a moment in his wife's eyes, as she drew close, passing the tie around his neck.

"Uh . . . Is anybody here yet?" asked Melinda nonchalantly, not daring to look at her sister.

"My mother, your parents, Ian and Sarah, a few early guests. All wondering where the hostess and guest of honor are."

"Is . . ." Sam began but stopped as Melinda elbowed her in the ribs.

"We should just go down," said Melinda, taking Moira's hand and leading the way. She didn't really need to know. If he came, she'd see him. And if he didn't, it would be just as well.

* * *

"So how was your trip, Mathilda?" Diane Myles asked, trying to make polite conversation until the kids came down.

Mathilde D'Uberville Symington smiled politely and said, "It was *merveilleux.*" She had long ago given up trying to get her daughter-in-law's parents to pronounce her name correctly. Even though they had shared the occasional holiday meal and each family birthday dinner, the strain had never quite dissipated between them. For any other woman, the fact that first Diane and then her daughter Melinda had had an affair with Forrest Symington would be deeply troubling. But Mathilde never much cared where Forrest displayed his manhood, as long as it wasn't near her. It was the fact that Diane and Harvey Myles were so irredeemably lower class that disturbed Mathilde. At least, Mathilde thought, allowing herself a little self-aggrandizing joke, the Myles children had married well: Samantha to Drew and Ian Taylor, the son that Diane had given up for adoption (mistakenly assuming that he had been fathered by Forrest and not her own husband), to Drew's sister Sarah.

From across the room, Mathilde watched Sarah and Ian, heads close together, completely absorbed in conversation with each other. She sighed. There was a time when she would have insisted that it was bad form to speak exclusively to one's spouse at a social function. But things were different now. Mathilde no longer presided over Belvedere, and her own spouse was, thankfully, no longer a consideration. Since his accident, the only one who even tried to interpret the droolings from his wheelchair was Buddy, his keeper. Drew had taken over his father's post as CEO of the D'Uberville Motor Company, and his wife, instead of building her position in the Woodland Cliffs aristocracy, was building cars. Sarah had left a proper but ugly marriage to a socially prominent businessman for an untidy, loving one to a simple school teacher, whom she had once feared was her brother. In fact, the entire Symington family had moved beyond scandal and into soap opera. And surprisingly enough, Mathilde D'Uberville Symington didn't mind one little bit. Traveling around Europe, stopping in at friends in Majorca, resting at her family's chateau in the woods of Annecy, she felt freer than she had in her entire life.

As if to remind her that freedom had not come easily, a hush fell over the guests as Forrest Symington was pushed into the room. His head lolled on his shoulder, and his arms dangled uselessly by his side. Without being able to meet anyone's eyes, he knew that everyone was staring at him.

"Fuck you," he screamed, though all that could be heard was a gurgle. *"Fuck you all, you shit-eating voyeurs. What the hell are you gawking at?"*

"He's saying how nice it is to see everyone here," Buddy interpreted, as he always did when Forrest tried to grunt some communication.

"You fucking asshole," shouted Forrest. *"That's not what I said."*

But, of course, it was useless, and Forrest knew it. Although his mind had remained clear and active for the four years since he'd been pushed (accidentally they said, but Forrest didn't believe it) by Harvey Myles into the unremitting whirl of machinery at the plant, his language had remained unintelligible. Buddy was the only one who ever tried to talk to him, and even Buddy had no idea what he was saying, which was, more often than not, an expletive directed at

Buddy himself. And since it was Buddy who fed, clothed, cleaned, and propelled him, it was just as well that Buddy had no idea how much Forrest loathed him.

There was a smattering of applause as Melinda Myles entered the salon, holding her little niece by the hand. Moira, assuming that the clapping was for her, as it so often was, returned the greeting with the curtsy that *Grandmere* had taught her just that morning. Mathilde smiled. Thank God genetics had worked in their favor this time. The child would do her D'Uberville heritage proud.

"Will you look at that?" crowed Harvey. "They're turning her into a little princess."

Everyone laughed, and Moira, suddenly confused, turned shy and hid behind her aunt's legs.

"Come to Grammy, punkin," said Diane, holding out her arms, and Moira ran to her, knowing there lay safe haven.

As usual, Drew went to greet his father first. They had had their differences through the years, but since the accident, Drew had become aware how tenuous life's ties were and could bear no grudge.

"How're you doing, Dad? You look fine."

"I feel like shit, you fucking idiot," yelled Forrest, who did not share his son's magnanimity. *"Thanks to you and your fucking low-life bitch of a wife and her whore of a sister."*

"He says it's really nice to be with the family. That always makes him feel better. Right, Forrest?" Buddy translated.

"No, you asshole. You got it wrong as usual," grunted Forrest. But Buddy had already pushed him off to the side, ostensibly so no one could trip over the

wheelchair, but Forrest knew it was to keep him out of the line of vision and the forefront of thought. *"Vultures,"* he wanted to shout at them. *"You're all vultures feeding off my carcass."* But the guests had gone back to their chatting and laughing. They'd all become inured to the sight of the once great Forrest Symington, off in a corner, grunting to himself.

Even though it was her long-ago affair with Forrest Symington that had introduced Melinda to the possibilities of a better life and sent her running from the flats of Oakdale to the hills of Hollywood, she didn't even notice the flurry of activity around the old man. She'd heard a familiar laugh when she'd made her entrance and been happily upstaged by Moira. The minute Moira had let go of her legs, she turned to find Jack Bader smiling at her with the same mixture of love and pain she knew was reflected in her own eyes.

"You look great," he said, knowing it was no surprise.

"So do you," she answered, meaning it.

In the few years since they'd seen each other, Jack had changed. His gold-streaked ponytail was gone, replaced by a short stylish haircut that seemed to emphasize the clarity of his steely blue eyes. Although he'd always had a well-toned body (in part to neutralize the effect of a ponytail on his assembly-line colleagues), he now looked leaner, tougher. He had always been handsome, but now he had character. And he took her breath away.

He must have felt the same about her, because for a few moments, neither one of them said anything. Understanding each other still, as they always had, they let themselves indulge their eyes without any attempt to disguise their mutual captivation.

"You cut your hair," she finally said, wanting to reach out and stroke the silken down at the nape of his neck.

"It got so everyone accepted the ponytail. It didn't seem so important anymore." He shrugged with a self-deprecating smile.

"It suits you. You look grown up."

"You look like a movie star."

"Listen to us," she laughed. "We sound like we haven't seen each other since grade school."

"We didn't know each other in grade school," he pointed out, but he knew what she meant. They were talking as though there was distance between them, when the truth was that even if they hadn't been in each other's company, they had never left each other's hearts.

He took her by the hand and led her onto the terrace. He didn't want to talk. It was clear they had nothing new to say to each other, and they'd been over the old territory too many times. She had her career as a film star, he had his as a union lawyer. She would never come back to Oakdale, he could never see himself in California. He loved her, but he could not live his life for her. She loved him, but even he understood that she would be a fool to give up her future for him. They were irresistible forces impeded by immovable objects, and as far as either one of them could see, nothing was going to give. But here, under a cloudy sky, with only half a moon, all he wanted to do was hold her.

"Are you still happy here?" she asked him, although small talk seemed wildly inappropriate for the two of them.

"It's a relative term. I'm busy. I like what I do. I get

lonely sometimes, I guess, but then, who doesn't. How about you?"

"Same," she said. "I understand now what you tried to tell me about all the Hollywood hype. But, in the end, it's the work that counts. I stay for that."

"It's good work, too."

"Have you seen my movies?"

He looked at her with a half smile that said, You must be kidding. "Hasn't everybody?"

"It's not everybody's opinion I care about."

"You still care what I think?" asked Jack, pleased even though he knew, in the long run, it wouldn't matter.

Now it was her turn to look at him like he was crazy. "What is it about us, Jack?" she asked plaintively. "Why can't we make the connection? Do you think it's just bad karma?" He knew she was only half kidding.

"More like bad geography, I'd say," he answered, his regret evident.

They looked at each other forlornly. She wanted to kiss him, but she knew it would make her cry.

"If you ever . . . ," he said.

"If you ever . . . ," she said.

They smiled ruefully at each other. They both knew that for the two of them there would be no ever, but it was nice to hold on to the dream. And then, unable to stop himself, Jack took Melinda in his arms and kissed her the way he knew he shouldn't. She felt his heart beating near hers, and it made her cry as she had known it would, but she kept her lips pressed on his.

There was the sudden sound of applause, and they broke apart, startled, both assuming that their embrace, inevitable as it was, had somehow brought them to public attention. Then they laughed, embarrassed and relieved to see that no one was even looking at them. All the guests were focused on Representative Roy Stromberg, a Symington family friend who was the six-term congressman from their district. They moved back into the salon to hear what Stromberg was saying.

". . . and even though some of you may think that this has to do with the fact that the Symingtons have been great supporters of mine over the years, and I admit, they've put a penny or two in my campaign coffers, anyone who's ever driven a DMC knows this contract was awarded strictly on merit."

There was more laughter and applause. "What's he talking about?" Melinda asked Jack.

"I have no idea," said Jack.

Melinda looked to where Sam stood, congenially nestled in the crook of her husband's arm. But though both of them were smiling, Melinda knew her sister well enough to know that whatever the congressman had said, it wasn't all good news to Sam.

"Uh-oh," said Melinda.

"I hear you," said Jack, who had noticed Sam's white-knuckled grip on Drew's arm.

The congressman was proposing a toast, "To Drew Symington and DMC and to a government contract that's going to make him so rich that it will force his taxes and, I hope, his campaign contributions, sky high."

There were calls of "Hear, hear" and "Congratulations" as well-wishers crowded around the couple.

"When were you going to tell me?" hissed Sam at her husband between smiling thanks to her guests.

"I swear to you, I didn't even know it was official.

The bid went in a year ago and I never really took it seriously. Roy told me it was looking good this afternoon, but you were with Melinda. I had no idea he was going to make an announcement."

Before Sam could respond, Roy Stromberg was upon them, pumping Sam's hand, smiling into her face, congratulating her on the great job her husband was doing.

Drew tried to head him off but, with a sinking sensation, realized it was too late, as he heard Stromberg say, "If you need help finding a place in Washington . . ."

"Washington?!" Samantha looked at Drew, aghast.

"Not forever, honey. Just to set up the new plant. You know we're not going to be able to keep the military supplied with vehicles with just the Oakdale plant going. Not if we want to keep on making civilian cars."

"How long?" Samantha got right to the point.

"Not long. Maybe a year, two at the outside."

"A year or two? Are you kidding?"

The shock in her voice was enough to let Stromberg know that maybe it was time to circulate among the other guests. With a quick pat on the back to Drew, he hurried off. He'd been in politics a long time and had been through a similar situation himself when he moved his family from Woodland Cliffs to Washington. But, in the end, the siren song of the big pond attracted even the most entrenched fish. And when it came to power, there was no bigger pond than Washington, D.C.

But it was different for Samantha Myles Symington than it had been for Mrs. Stromberg. Sam couldn't have cared less about leaving Woodland Cliffs and its stifling society. She'd miss her family in Oakdale, but she wouldn't miss the pretentious pandering of the would-be elite. She had grown to love Belvedere and the comforts it offered. But she realized that many of the people who called on her there wouldn't even look at her if she was still just Sam Myles and not Mrs. Drew Symington. Outside of her family and a few select friends, the only thing she really cared about was her work. And if she went to Washington, that would have to stop.

She forced herself to stay calm, even though she wanted to scream at her husband that he was being mean and unfair.

"I can't move the DMC VT-12 operations, you know that."

"I know," said Drew quietly, and she could tell he was fully aware of all the implications and what they meant to her.

"Tell me the truth," she said. "Did you get this contract to make me stop working on the car?"

"Sam, I swear to you. I put in the bid just because Roy told me to, not because I thought we'd get it. I didn't think it would happen at all, let alone now."

"But you wouldn't be sorry if I never finished the VT-12, would you?" she asked accusingly.

He was getting angry. "Don't make it seem like winning a hundred-million-dollar government contract is a nefarious plot to thwart your dreams. It's not like that. You're right. I get upset when you do dangerous things. And since you've started testing the VT-12, you've been doing a lot of dangerous things. Call me crazy, but I don't like it. But I never said you had to stop doing it."

"What *are* you saying?"

"I'm saying there are choices to be made here, and we should be making them together."

"As far as I see, you've just arranged it so I have no choice," she said, not giving up.

"Not true. If I accept the contract, I have to go to Washington to fulfil it, there's no question of that. But I can turn it down."

"That would be stupid," admitted Sam.

"I agree. I could go to Washington and you could stay here, and we'd find a way to get together on weekends or something. Lots of people do that."

But his voice was forlorn even mentioning it, and she knew he was already thinking about the nights he wouldn't be able to see Moira asleep in her crib.

"No," she said quietly. "I wouldn't want that for Moira."

"What about for you?" he asked taking her hand.

"No," she said. "Not for me either." She put her arms around him and felt the tension leave his body at her touch. Holding him, she knew he would never deliberately set out to sabotage her career, and now, she couldn't destroy his.

"Oh, Drew," she sighed, "I love you. We've spent too much time separated already. The VT-12 can wait. My guys can keep doing research over the next year, maybe improve the technology. The delay could make it a better car," she added, convincing herself as much as him.

"We can set you up with a complete communications hookup, teleconferencing, the whole deal. We can make it so that you can see those graphs before they even draw them."

She laughed. "That might be going too far. Mind reading could be considered invasion of privacy."

"The only thing you couldn't do," he added solemnly in the interest of full disclosure, "is drive that brute around the track every day. And I'm not sorry about that. And neither is Moira."

"Hey, I already said I'd go to Washington. Lay off before I change my mind."

3

Sam and Drew rented a house in Georgetown, fully furnished, sight unseen. They had been told it was one of the lesser houses designed by William Thornton, the English-born architect who had designed the U.S. Capitol. But there was nothing lesser about its appearance. It was small but utterly charming, with a delicate spiral staircase linking its three floors. On the ground floor with its impressive arched entry was a grand salon decorated in the distinctive style of Sister Parrish, which was both elegant and comfortable. The walls were covered in an apple green shot silk, with overstuffed sofas and chairs in complimentary Colefax and Fowler chintz patterns. The dining room had a huge mahogany table that looked like it could seat a small regiment. A long hallway led to a large guest suite at the back of the house. Down a few steps from the ground floor was the only completely nonperiod section of the house: a state-of-the-art kitchen. Beside the kitchen was the obligatory maid's room, cheerily decorated in bright chintz patterns, which gave the room a sunny demeanor, that counteracted its basement location.

On the second floor was the master bedroom with a large bay window and another smaller room that might have been a dressing room or study. But Sam had insisted it be converted to Moira's room so she would not have to worry about stairs if she were to climb out of her crib in the middle of the night and come looking for her parents, as she had taken to doing lately. The owners, hearing her concerns, had thoughtfully provided a crib and passed on their permission for Sam to redecorate the room as a nursery after they moved in. The third and smallest floor had been turned into a spacious, single room: a wood-paneled library with its own fireplace, which looked as though it would be the most inviting space in the house on dreary winter evenings. And on Thirty-first, just north of Q Street, steps away from Montrose Park, its location couldn't have been more perfect.

"It's not Belvedere," said Drew, worried that Sam might find the small house a little confining after their years in the mansion.

"It's better," sighed Sam, absolutely in love. Then realizing she might have hurt her husband's feelings by disparaging his ancestral home, she amended, "I'm sorry. I just meant, it's *ours*. Nobody else lives here. There aren't any relatives in other wings. It's just us, and it's all we need."

"You don't have to apologize. I know exactly what

you mean. I think this is going to be the best thing that's ever happened to us."

They left Moira sleeping in her stroller, exhausted from the trip, and wandered happily through the rooms, examining the closets, testing the furniture. They were delighted with the dual air of history and comfort that permeated the house. Their predecessors had left the place in perfect condition and spotlessly clean. Just how clean Sam didn't appreciate until they got to the kitchen, which seemed almost sterilized. Staring at the empty cupboards, without even a box of crackers to brighten the void, reminded Sam they had not eaten anything all day except some bad plane food.

"I'm starving," she complained.

"Me, too."

"Are there any grocery stores or supermarkets around?"

"I don't really know. The only place I ever stayed in Washington was at the Watergate, and my knowledge of the city was strictly on a need-to-know basis. We'll have to reconnoiter in the morning."

"What about now? Do you think we could find a pizza place that delivered?"

"Maybe. If we could find a phone book," Drew said, then changed gear. "Wait a minute. We're not going to have cold pizza at home on our first night in the nation's capital."

"It doesn't have to be cold. There's an oven. And a microwave."

"Unacceptable. Do you think you can find a dress in one of those suitcases without unpacking everything?"

"I'm sure I can. But why do I want to?"

"Because I'm taking you to Jean-Louis, the most brilliant restaurant in Washington."

"Really? How do you know about it?"

"Because it's at the Watergate, of course."

She laughed. "It sounds wonderful, but did you forget. You're a father now. We can't just leave your little bundle of joy sleeping by herself in the foyer."

"I didn't intend to. We're taking her with us."

"Won't they mind? I mean, if it's really elegant, they don't usually cater to the family crowd."

"I'll call Jean-Louis."

"As in the name of the restaurant?"

Drew nodded. "Jean-Louis Palladin. He's the chef —and owner."

"You know him?" Sam asked, surprised, as usual, to be reminded that her husband had had a whole—very privileged—life before her.

Drew had the grace to be a little sheepish. "Like I said. I only stayed at the Watergate, and I only went where I needed to go. Which means, I ate there a lot. But it was no hardship, believe me. You'll see."

Standing in the restaurant's glass-walled corridor, eyeing the display of what appeared to be hundreds of wine offerings, Sam was glad that she had decided to wear her black velvet suit and the emerald and diamond earrings Drew had given her for their first anniversary. It was awkward enough to appear in Washington's most prestigious restaurant with a sweetly snoring baby in a stroller without being under-dressed as well. She hadn't missed the maître d's eyebrows shooting up into his hairline when he'd seen them enter.

"He's new," said Drew after he'd given his name and the maître d' had retired somewhere to "check." "He doesn't know me."

"From the look on his face, I don't think he wants to either," said Sam. "We can still go get pizza."

But before Drew had a chance to reassure her, he was engulfed in a Gallic hug by a man in a white jacket with curly hair, large horn-rimmed glasses and a bushy moustache.

"C'etait trop longtemps, mon ami."

"Je sais." Drew switched easily into French. Then turning to Sam, he said, "This is why I've been staying home so much. My wife, Samantha. Sam, this is Jean-Louis."

Samantha reached out her hand to shake, but Jean-Louis just used it for leverage as he pulled her into a hug only slightly less exuberant than he'd delivered to Drew.

"It is wonderful to meet you. *Elle est plus, plus meilleure que les autres,"* he addressed Drew before turning back to her. "He was too good a catch, I was worried, you understand. But you . . . you are perfect."

Sam laughed, flattered and warmed by his obvious affection for her husband. She started to respond, but Jean-Louis already had his head in the stroller and was making quiet sounds of divine adulation at the angelic napper.

"Also perfect," he announced, coming up for air. "I cannot stay. I have fish waiting for the grill. But I kept you a table in the corner. The stroller will fit in back. *La petite* won't be disturbed."

"This is so nice of you," Samantha said, touched and a little overwhelmed.

"For Drew," Jean-Louis shrugged as if to say, It's nothing. "And now for you."

The dining room was small enough to be called intimate, and Sam was captivated by the mirror panel at eye level that made it possible to cruise the room without actually appearing to.

"Oh my God," Sam said after they'd settled into their space, with Moira still sleeping soundly in the stroller backed against the wall, "isn't that Henry Kissinger over there?"

"Ugh. Don't let on that you've seen him. I don't want to have to go over and say hello."

"Do you know him?"

"We've met a couple of times. Maybe he won't remember me."

"Well, I'd like to meet him."

"That's just because you don't know him."

The menu was prix fixe and six courses long, and once it arrived, Sam wasn't interested in anything else. To start, they were served a complimentary nugget of smoked salmon followed by a quail egg nestled in toasted brioche with a garnish of ossetra caviar. Then came chestnut soup with chestnut and truffle quenelles floating on top. There was duck foie gras and a loup de mer poached with herbs and fennel and served with julienne of pumpkin sauteed with cardamom and cumin. Roasted noisettes of Texan venison followed and, at last, dessert: a tarte tatin, its apples caramelized to perfection, wearing a light veil of melting creme fraiche.

Stuffed but happy, Sam sipped her café filtre and with her free hand softly stroked the brow of her unbelievably cooperative daughter.

"That's one good baby we've got," Drew sighed, just as satisfied as Sam.

"Maybe we shouldn't push our luck. She didn't have any supper either. She could wake up hungry at any moment and make us very sorry we overstayed our welcome."

"I'll get the check," Drew said, but as he motioned for the waiter, his hand caught someone approaching from behind.

"Sorry," he apologized without really looking.

"Drew? Drew Symington?"

Drew turned to face his victim. "I can't believe it. I'm in Washington one night, and you show up. Honey, this is Senator Amos Kilmont. We were room-mates freshman year at Harvard. Amos, this is my wife, Samantha."

Sam knew who Amos Kilmont was, of course. During the last election, he had managed to get himself quite a bit of press coverage, and Drew had mentioned that they'd been friends once but had lost touch. She knew that Kilmont had won the election in the face of tremendous opposition by the Republican sweep, and it had cost him a small fortune. But by dint of the fact that he was one of the few incumbent Democrats who had held on to his seat, he was considered a power to be reckoned with on Capitol Hill.

"I know what you're doing here, of course," Amos said to Drew after warmly clasping Sam's hand and pronouncing himself thoroughly pleased to meet her. "My esteemed colleague, Roy Stromberg, got himself a little pork for his district and you're the pig."

Sam was ready to be affronted by Amos's mockery, but Drew just laughed. "Hey, don't forget I got you your first DMC right off the line, and you told me then it was the best damn car you'd ever driven."

"I was young," said Amos.

Sam could see that their jocular insults were just the way these two interacted, but she couldn't resist a defense of the company she knew so well. "Nobody makes a 150-bhp balance-shaft-equipped version of the twincam 2.3-liter Quad 4 like we do, and that's exactly what the army needs."

Amos did a double take, then looked at Drew. "Is she kidding?"

Drew beamed. "I'm afraid not."

"You taught her this?"

"She taught me. Samantha is Sam Myles, the—"

"Are you kidding? The Mylometer Sam Myles?"

Sam laughed. "I'm flattered. Did Drew put you up to this?"

"No way. That's one damn good invention, lady. I thought it was made by a man."

"I'm surprised you even know about it," Sam said with self-deprecating honesty.

"I'm on a couple of committees. One of them is the Industrial Economic Committee. This year, we're doing a lot of talking about cars and pollution. And I have to tell you, one of the primary reasons I supported Roy Stromberg on his decision to award you the contract was not because Drew here got me my first car, which got me my first lay"—they laughed, but Amos went on—"but because DMCs are fitted with Mylometers and we're looking for everything we can to bring down the government's contribution to the pollution level."

There were a couple of puffs of sound from the

stroller. Sam smiled apologetically. "Our baby," she explained, seeing Amos's look of shock.

"I'm ashamed to say I didn't even notice. You don't usually see babies dining at Jean-Louis."

"Problem is," Sam said, rocking the stroller vigorously, hoping to lull Moira back into sleep, "this baby didn't actually dine. And I have a feeling she's going to want to very soon, and she's going to let us know. Very, very loudly."

She looked at Drew. He was already signing the check. "Amos," he said, "I'm going to be around. We'll be seeing each other." He got up to pull Sam's chair out for her.

"Wait a minute," said Amos urgently. "I know I'll be seeing you, and I don't care that much. It's your wife I want to talk to."

"Don't you have one of your own?" Drew asked with mock belligerence.

"Yes, but she doesn't know anything about cars. Seriously, Sam. We can use your help. I want you to work for me. Be an advisor for my committee."

Sam was taken aback. "That's very nice of you, but I really don't think . . ."

"No." Amos was insistent. "I am not being nice. I'm imploring you. That committee is stale. It needs fresh blood, fresh ideas. I know you've got them, and I've got the power to implement them. What else are you doing in Washington?"

"Well, I . . ."

"It's not a bad idea, honey," said Drew, grateful that something could develop that would alleviate his guilt over taking Sam away from her beloved car design. "You should at least look into it. Maybe go to a couple of meetings. If it doesn't work out, you wouldn't be obligated. Right, Amos?

"Absolutely. Your country needs you, Sam. More important, those damn Republicans are going to take over the committee if we don't come up with something impressive fast. I need you, Sam."

Sam was intrigued. As beautiful as the house on Thirty-first Street was, the thought had occurred to her that in its quiet residential quarter, it seemed very far away from the things that mattered. She was used to being a part of something that was happening. Much as she loved her home and her child, enforced domesticity frightened her.

"There's Moira," she said, not offering an excuse but awaiting a solution. Right on cue, the baby started to snuffle. Sam resumed rocking, pushing the stroller back and forth.

"Answered prayers," sighed Amos, raising his hands heavenward.

"We've got to go, Amos," Drew said, taking the stroller from Sam and maneuvering it toward the door. "Let's see what we can work out."

"I've already got it worked out for you," Amos persisted, following them to the door.

Moira had now begun to cry in earnest. Sam picked her up and cooed to her, quieting her long enough to tell Amos that she would call him as soon as she'd looked into the day-care situation.

But Amos was having none of it. He grabbed a piece of bread out of a basket that was being transported by a waiter to a nearby table and handed it to Moira with a smile. The little girl grabbed it, stuffed it in her mouth, and smiled right back. Sam and Drew laughed. Amos wasn't a politician for nothing.

"What I'm trying to tell you," Amos went on, now that he had their undivided attention, "is that I've got a nanny for you." Sam's eyes lit up, and it was all the encouragement Amos needed. "She's my niece, Natalie. My sister's daughter. She's nineteen, just came from North Dakota a month ago. She's been staying with us, which is fine. But you know, we've got the big house back home and just the small apartment in Washington. Betsy's starting to feel a little cramped with a teenager always underfoot."

"Gee, Amos, I'd like to help you unload your unwanted relatives, but it's not exactly what we had in mind."

"Touché, Drew. It's not what it sounds like. Natalie's the oldest of six kids. She's been taking care of her sisters and brothers since she was ten. She's smart, she's fun. She'd make a great au pair. Believe me, if Betsy and I had kids, I wouldn't be sending her away so fast."

"We could meet her," said Sam hopefully. "What do you think, Moira? Want to meet a new friend?"

"Fwend," said Moira, enthusiastically munching her bread.

"Sure," said Drew. "Why not?"

"There's a pretty maid's room in the house we rented, but it's kind of in the basement. Do you think she'd mind?"

"Are you kidding? She shared a room with two sisters her whole life. She's thrilled sleeping on a pullout sofa in our den."

Moira was reaching her hand out to Amos for more bread. They all laughed. It was definitely time to go.

Amos handed Sam his card. "Call that number, and

just tell my secretary when you want to see Natalie. We'll get her there."

On the way home, they found a 7-Eleven and bought some coffee for themselves and some cans of tuna, bread, cereal, milk, and bananas for Moira. They gave her a banana in the car on the way home, but she was fast asleep again with her face squished into the peel by the time they got to Q Street. Giggling, they cleaned off her face, took off her clothes, changed her diaper, and lay her in her crib without her ever waking up. Then, dog-tired, they climbed into their own bed in the room next to hers. Too exhausted to make love, they nestled together like spoons. Feeling the breath of the man she loved stirring softly against the back of her neck, Sam remembered Amos's off-hand comment. Answered prayers. *Indeed,* she thought and then closed her eyes and thought no more.

Limousines had become routine for Melinda Myles, but brass bands and full color guards were another matter entirely. So it was quite a shock to emerge from the low light and the recirculated cool of the airplane into the bright, hot brilliance of the San Domenico sun and be greeted by a somewhat military rendition of "Hurray for Hollywood." Melinda blinked a few times and adjusted her sunglasses before looking down at the tarmac to confirm with her eyes what her ears had surmised. There was, indeed, a brass band complete with banner overhead boldly stating "Welcome Melinda Myles, Number One Actress in the World."

"That Elgar," Melinda said to herself, laughing, as she carefully stepped down to the asphalt, which shimmered with waves of afternoon heat. "I wonder what he would have done for Meryl Streep."

She saw him then, getting out of the requisite black town car, which had stopped just beyond the band. He was tall and intense, with a shock of black unruly hair that looked as though it had been introduced to a comb but had never quite learned to get along with one. Still in his twenties, Elgar had been anointed filmdom's latest boy wonder after making two crude but wildly successful independent films. Since his previous films had been postmodern nihilistic low-budget comedies, it was only natural that the studios award him with a big-budget period drama. To his credit, Elgar had hesitated before accepting the plum assignment. But the lure of big money, big names, and big story had been overwhelming. Add to that the appeal of a torrid love story between the wife of a landowner and one of his workers set in an American colonial outpost (for which San Domenico would substitute) at the turn of the century and the deal had been irresistible. And the advance press and foreign sales figures for *Native* had shown that, so far, he had not made a mistake.

Elgar hurried to the foot of the stairway to meet his leading lady.

"Elgar, you are too much," said Melinda as she took his outstretched arm and descended the final step. "A bouquet of flowers really would have been sufficient."

"Hey, I didn't do this," Elgar responded, nodding affably to the horn section who could barely keep blowing while they ogled the American movie star.

"Who did?" asked Melinda, not believing him. "My agent?"

"Nope. *El presidente.*"

"Give me a break," Melinda laughed. "I've heard of stroking, but this is above and beyond. If you think this is going to make it easier for you to cut my lines, you can forget it."

As the driver held the door open for them and they slipped into the backseat, the band switched to a brassy "You Are My Sunshine" in four-four time. Elgar and Melinda looked at each other and burst into gales of laughter, which they tried to stifle at least until the car had pulled off the runway and out of sight of the band.

"I wish I could take credit for it," said Elgar when they were in control again. "But it really was *el presidente.*"

"The real *el presidente?* Jorge Alvarro?" Melinda asked incredulously, still convinced there was a major gag involved.

"That's the guy. I'm told he's got a copy of *Lovers and Killers,* which he screens on a regular basis."

Melinda cringed at hearing the popular name of her first film. The writer-director, Prescott Wills, her mentor and lover, had called it *Desperation,* but after his death, the studio had recut and retitled it. Still, it had won her an Academy Award, so she couldn't very well complain.

"You're not kidding, are you?" she asked, although she still wasn't sure. Elgar had a reputation for youthful high jinks on his sets.

"Cross my heart and hope to die. The president has the hots for you. I was even told that you were the only reason he let us film on the island. Not to mention letting us use his personal army as extras."

"This is unbelievable," Melinda giggled. She'd grown accustomed to unwarranted admiration from strangers over the past few years, but she envisioned her fans as star-struck teenage boys and housewives, not heads of state. She had seen pictures of Jorge Alvarro shaking hands with the president of the United States; she had read stories about him on the front page of the *Times*. She was too modest to find his interest in her reasonable, but it was flattering nonetheless.

"He wanted to meet you at the airport himself, but he had a cabinet meeting. I told him you'd understand. But there's a reception tonight at the presidential palace."

Melinda smiled to herself. This was the life she had been born for and the sight of the Reef Hotel as they left the cane fields behind and entered the expanse of manicured lawns confirmed it. Looking for all the world like the plantation home it had once been, the Reef appeared charmingly but deceptively simple. A three-story white stucco villa with red-tiled roof, it had yellow-striped awnings shading the balconies that adhered to almost every window. There was no grand entranceway and no need for one. The palm trees and lush tropical flowers that framed the building exuded an air of true luxury that only nature could bestow.

As the car pulled up to the entrance, the doorman rushed to assist them. Dressed in plain white shirt and white pants, his beaming smile was his real uniform. Melinda knew she was going to like this place.

Inside, her room was large and spare, with cool tile floors and clean whitewashed walls. But her bed was an old iron four-poster, with a canopy made of yards of muslin. When she stretched out on the crisp white sheets, she couldn't remember ever lying on a more comfortable mattress.

"Get some rest," Elgar said after he'd made sure that her luggage was delivered and had tipped the porter well. They were going to be there for a long time, and he wanted to make sure that the staff knew to keep his star happy. "I'll pick you up for the reception around seven. We scout locations tomorrow, so you'll have the day off to get adjusted. Shooting starts the day after that, but you'll get a call sheet from the A.D. with all the details. You'll see Tommy tonight. He's invited to the president's, too."

Melinda was pleased to hear it. Tommy Kray was going to play her husband in the film, and they would have many highly emotional scenes together. Unusual as it was, because of their differing schedules and the fact that they could both command "play or pay" deals, which would commit them to a project sight unseen, they had not yet met. But, of course, like everyone in Hollywood, their reputations had introduced them to each other.

Melinda nodded and thanked Elgar, letting him kiss her cheek and pecking him back in return. It was a routine response, but Melinda sensed that even though they'd never met before the auditions and had since only had a few dinners together, they really did like each other and were going to get along well.

The minute Elgar had left, Melinda slipped out of her clothes and into the soft silk robe thoughtfully provided by the management. She lay down on the bed, luxuriating in the comfort, aware how much she needed the rest before having to bathe and dress for her audience with the president. It hadn't taken her long being in the spotlight before she realized that even first-class travel was exhausting. She was already drifting into a pleasant dream when there was a knock on the door.

"Could you please come back later," she called out, assuming it was the maid come to offer to turn down the bed she was already in.

"Open up, babe," was the response. For a moment, Melinda was puzzled. It didn't sound like Elgar. Then, it struck her. Jumping out of bed, she pulled her robe a little tighter around her, ran her fingers through her hair to fluff up the flat spots from her aborted nap, made a hurried appraisal in the mirror, and opened the door to her leading man.

Tommy Kray had never been conventionally handsome, but he had an urgent sex appeal that made itself felt through his smoldering screen image, and Melinda had been anticipating their meeting a little nervously ever since she'd heard he'd been cast. In fact, allowing herself the occasional daydream, she had even considered the possibility that the two of them might strike some incendiary spark in each other and wondered if it would be good or bad for the film. Clearly, Tommy must have had much the same thoughts, because he was standing in front of her, wearing nothing but a pair of torn orange sweatpants and carrying a bottle of champagne with two glasses.

"We meet at last," he said, stepping around her before she even had the opportunity to invite him in.

"Yes, we do," said Melinda, knowing she sounded like an idiot but too taken aback to think of a clever rejoinder. He sauntered across the room, then turned around, letting his eyes move slowly up and down her body, obviously appreciating what he saw. Annoyed as she was at his rude examination, she took the opportunity to do a little evaluating of her own.

His hair, longer than she had ever seen it in the movies, was pulled into a loose ponytail at the back and looked like it could use a shampoo. His skin, expertly buffed by professional makeup artists for the screen, appeared rougher in person, with the occasional scar testifying to a losing bout with teenage acne. His long black lashes curtained heavy lids that hung at half-mast over wide, dark eyes. His mouth was full, almost pouty, and he had drawn it into a smile that seemed more ironic than inviting. There was no question that his was not the face of the usual matinee idol, but as far as Melinda was concerned, that was good. She had met her share of pretty boys and, much like pretty girls, found them to be boringly similar. Tommy Kray was different, and she couldn't deny he exuded pheromones like a wolf on the prowl.

"Day after tomorrow," he began, putting his free arm around her neck and leading her to the edge of the bed, "we've got to look like we've been married for ten years. We got a lot of catching up to do."

He sat on the bed, forcing her to come down with him, and a feeling somewhere between irritation and indignation started to make its way from the pit of her stomach to the back of her throat. Tuned as he was to the shifting winds of animal attraction, Tommy sniffed the change and turned a high-beam smile on her. Devoid of all nuance, open and warm, it immediately made her question her quick response and rethink her reaction. He sensed this, too, and laughed while he poured champagne into her glass, never once removing his arm from around her. Melinda laughed, too, still not quite sure what she should make of this man.

A moment later she had her answer.

"We don't have much time," Tommy said. "Let's not waste it."

Locking himself to her with the crook of his elbow still folded around her neck, he pressed his lips to hers, forcing his tongue between her clenched teeth to begin an avid exploration of her mouth. And in that moment, Melinda developed a perfect understanding of her costar. Tommy Kray was an asshole.

Shock turned to outrage as she pushed against him only to feel his grip tighten. Somehow, he had managed to put down his glass, and she felt his hand roam over her body, easily finding its way inside her robe, stopping to cup her breast as if to weigh it for heft. Barely able to breathe, let alone move, she realized she still clutched her champagne in her hand. Letting her grip relax, she felt the glass wobble and tip and hoped that its contents would find their mark somewhere in Tommy's lap. It took a moment for the bubbling liquid to soak through his sweatpants, but at last the sticky wetness spread over his skin.

"What the . . . ?" he puzzled, pushing her away to examine the source of his discomfort.

"Ooops," smiled Melinda, jumping out of his reach. "Sorry."

"You bitch," he said, rejecting her apology. "You did that on purpose."

"Did I?" she queried innocently.

"What the fuck's wrong with you?"

"Maybe," she said evenly, struggling to keep her rage in check, aware that she had to work with this man in the most intimate of conditions, "I just don't like being pushed into anything."

"Grow up, baby. We're going to get naked in front of thirty people in a couple of days anyway." He moved toward her, backing her into the wall. He was smiling again, but there was menace in his eyes. "Don't you think it's better to get the preliminaries out of the way, know what we're dealing with here?"

"I know what I'm dealing with all right. Get out of my room."

He looked at her incredulously, as though he couldn't believe he was being rejected. He made a move toward her, and her heart beat with fear. Flashes of tabloid news items, stories she'd dismissed as gossip and publicity, streaked through her mind. Tommy Kray arrested in a brawl, fined for trashing a hotel room, brought up on charges by a woman who claimed he beat her. Was she going to be the next headline?

But as suddenly as he had approached her, he changed course. Picking up the bottle of champagne and his own glass, leaving hers where it had fallen on the floor, he headed toward the door.

"If we don't have personal chemistry, how do you think it's going to show up on that screen?"

"I don't know about you, but I intend to *act*. It's what we're paid to do."

"Fuck you," he said unceremoniously as he walked out. "I tried, but you are one uptight bitch."

It wasn't until she'd picked up her glass and hurled it at the closing door that she realized just how angry she was. It splintered on the tile floor, and she cursed softly under her breath, upset at both Tommy Kray and herself. She'd let an idiot get to her, and now she'd have to watch where she walked in her bare feet

46

for the next few days. She was deeply disappointed that this place, which had seemed so inviting, and her happy anticipation of the next few months had become tinged with dread.

Elgar was apologetic when he came to Melinda's door around eight o'clock. "I thought maybe I could get you and Tommy together before the president's reception, but he left a message that he would meet us there."

"Actually, I've already made his acquaintance."

"I don't like the way you say that."

"Well, he's an asshole. You know that, don't you?"

"He's a good actor."

"Maybe. But he's an asshole."

Elgar had been afraid of this. Since Melinda Myles had won an Academy Award, she was box office gold, and the studio had been glad to have her. But he'd had to fight for Tommy Kray, who after a promising start, had gotten himself a reputation as "difficult." It was only the fact that he was still exceedingly popular in Europe and would help the foreign presale that made them finally acquiesce. Even though Tommy's agent had promised he'd behave, Elgar knew he was taking a chance. But there was a danger that emanated from Tommy, probably in direct correlation to his surly brand of machismo, that Elgar knew would be magic on the screen.

"What happened? Did he . . . uh . . . come on to you or something?"

"You could say that," Melinda responded dryly, letting Elgar know by the tone of her voice that it had not been pleasant.

"I'm sorry," was all he said. He had hoped Tommy's reputation had been exaggerated; now he only hoped it had not been underestimated.

He sounded so disheartened that Melinda took pity on him. She understood why he had insisted on Tommy for the part. She had thought it brilliant casting herself when she had first been told. It wasn't required that making a movie be as much fun as summer camp, she reminded herself.

"Don't worry." She felt obliged to encourage her young director. "It's not going to affect the performance. It could even make it better. I mean, I leave my rich husband for a poor lover in the movie. Maybe a little friction isn't such a bad thing."

He kissed her for that, sweetly and sincerely. This was only his third film, his first big-budget studio production. He had a feeling that even though Melinda was not much older or more experienced than he was, he was going to rely on her a lot to get him through. Even better, he was certain she wouldn't let him down.

The black town car was waiting for them, and they sat in back, talking of other things until they drew within sight of the presidential palace. Still vaguely reminiscent of the fortress it had once been, it stood on the edge of an escarpment, its palisades looming over the sea that lapped at the beach below. But in the intervening years since it had served as a sentry for its people, all manner of architectural adornment had been added to its functional form. Terraces and balustrades embellished its facade; turrets and minarets extended its reach; elaborate lattices of filigreed wrought iron encased its entrances and balconies. And all of it, citadel walls included, was painted a tutti-frutti pink whose bright blush even the soft glow of tropical moonlight could not mute.

"It looks like it's made of spun sugar," said Melinda, aghast and enchanted at the same time.

"Or a Disney production that got out of hand." Elgar started to sing, "When you wish upon a star ...."

Melinda laughed. "You're right. It must be like living in fantasyland."

But as the car pulled under the vine-covered portico and a military officer dressed in impeccable regimentary white opened the door for them, they were quiet. Even on an island the size of San Domenico it was no small matter to be invited for an audience with the president, and they were both young enough and not yet jaded enough by the fame and fortune that Hollywood tends to bestow prematurely on its anointed to be excited.

Stepping into the pink marble antechamber of the palace, Melinda was glad she had worn the most elegant dress in her collection: a strapless sheath of white satin gathered at the base of her back into soft folds that fell to the floor in rivers of gleaming fabric. In the hollow of her throat lay a single, small heart-shaped diamond. Nothing else was needed. Surveying herself back at the hotel, aware of the curve of her naked back, the roundness of her breasts crowning in front, she had almost taken it off again, remembering Tommy Kray's crude advances and not wanting to encourage more of the same. But then she decided she would not let his cretinous machismo posturing dictate her conduct. If the president had gone out of his way to meet a movie star, she should at least have the grace to look like one. As she took Elgar's arm and moved toward the receiving line, she knew she had made the right decision.

From the pictures she had seen of San Domenico's president in the news magazines, she had thought he was taller. But dressed in the formal white military uniform favored by leaders in the tropics, his chest covered with an array of medals, there was no mistaking which one was *el presidente.* He saw her approach and left his place in line without hesitation, stepping forward to take her arm, bowing slightly toward her escort, silently asking polite permission for something that could not be denied. He turned to look at her, capturing her eyes with his own, and she understood in a visceral way she had not known before the meaning of charisma. His gaze conveyed interest, appreciation, even esteem for her but beneath lay awareness of his own unquestionable position and authority. He was handsome in the way that men of ultimate power are handsome, but his real appeal lay in the contrast of his smile, which was warm, disarming, and utterly without guile.

"Miss Myles," he said graciously, abandoning the reception line and leading her directly into the ballroom. "Welcome to San Domenico. I know your work and I am an admirer."

Melinda was flattered and awed at once, focusing on the president, but conscious of the marble floors and frescoed walls lit by half a dozen crystal chandeliers that streamed their rainbow incandescence on the assembled gentry. "I haven't been here long enough to be very informed I'm afraid, but from what I've seen so far, I'd have to say the same. But, of course, you live in paradise. There isn't much to not admire."

"You are right," he beamed. "San Domenico is next

to heaven. Better even than heaven if I can be permitted a small sacrilege. Because here, you *live*. I hope you will permit me to show you what I mean while you are in our country."

"I would be honored," Melinda said, meaning it.

While speaking, the president had led her past the tables set with gold-rimmed china, through one of the dozens of open french doors, and onto an arbored terrace. She took a breath and then another deeper one, sighing with delight. The air was perfumed with night-blooming jasmine that hung in fragrant clusters from the bowers overhead. He plucked a sprig of the delicate white blossoms and tucked it into her dark hair, which she had tied simply at the nape of her neck with a narrow velvet cord.

"It suits you," he said, admiring his handiwork with the innocence of a child. "It makes you look like you belong in paradise."

Melinda was charmed. "Thank you . . . uh . . ." She realized she didn't know what to call him. She was tempted to say "Your Excellency" but decided that designation was probably used only in B movies about banana republics.

She stammered and became flustered. "I'm sorry," she finally admitted. "I don't know what to call you."

"Jorge."

"I can't call you that."

"Why not? It's my name."

"But you're the president."

He laughed. "Yes. But I still have a name. If you will allow me to call you by your given name, then you must call me Jorge."

"Of course you can call me Melinda. But somehow it doesn't seem right . . ."

"On the contrary, it would not be right to refuse me."

She was touched by his warmth, by the unaffected way in which he made her feel there was no difference in their stations.

"Thank you, Jorge. You are very kind."

"And you are very beautiful, Melinda."

A discreet chime sounded, once then twice. She looked at him quizzically.

"The signal that the reception line is completed. The guests can go to the tables."

"Ah. Should we go in?"

"Only when you're ready." She hated to leave the fragrant air of the cool night, and he sensed it. "No need to rush. Dinner cannot start without me. They will wait." He laughed almost diffidently, as though he could not help the power he wielded, and she found herself liking him for that as well.

As he led her to their places, she took her first good look at the room. It was a grand ballroom in the old style, with graceful columns leading from the marble floor to the frescoed ceiling. Large round tables with elegant place settings and elaborate centerpieces of fresh orchids and jasmine had been placed around the edges of the room, with the band situated at one end and a small dais at the other. Jorge had seated her on his right at the head table on the raised dais. Theirs were the only two empty chairs left in the room. She noticed Elgar and Tommy, who had thankfully not made his presence known to her, sitting with the producer, Bill Finnegan, at another table surrounded by animated San Domenicans. Tommy had already selected the most beautiful woman among them and had his head practically buried in her bosom. Not surprisingly, the woman didn't seem to mind; in fact, she appeared to be relishing the moment. Melinda sighed. It never ceased to amaze her what people would put up with if it was connected to someone famous.

The president made a signal, and one by one, the others seated at the head table introduced themselves to her. She listened attentively, smiled in acknowledgment, but it was impossible to catch everything they were saying to her. At the foot of the table sat a striking woman, blond hair carefully sculpted and piled high on her head. She wore a blood red dress, exposing an expanse of white bosom, and a ruby and diamond necklace that reached almost into her cleavage. While the others warmly waited their turn to speak to the American movie star, she ignored Melinda so studiously that Melinda felt even more singled out than if she had been scrutinizing her under a microscope. When her turn came, the woman said nothing, and the conversation passed around her as though it dared not include her.

Melinda was intrigued. "But who . . . ?" she began as other voices filled the silence she left hanging.

"Lucia, my wife," Jorge Alvarro said shortly, and Melinda understood. Paradise has its dangers she reminded herself, and if she wanted to survive, she'd best keep her hands off forbidden fruit.

It was easier said than done. Throughout dinner, the president spoke only to her. And when the band that had regaled her at the airport appeared after dessert, substituting their military meter for some rather good dance music, Melinda could not find a way to refuse as he led her to the floor. She looked around and saw that Lucia was pressed close to a military officer with enough stripes and medals to be a four-star general. Tommy was swaying with a raven-haired beauty enclosed in one arm and a stunning redhead in the other. Even Elgar was on the floor, laughing with a pretty San Domenican. In the arms of the courtly gentleman who was the most powerful man in San Domenico, she could dismiss her after-noon encounter with a puerile, self-centered actor and his ugly attempt at conquest. Dancing with Jorge Alvarro on the sweet-smelling terrace of his pink palace, under the benign light of a tropical moon, she could believe, once again, in romance.

When the music stopped, she felt vaguely sorrow-ful, like Cinderella watching the clock tick its way toward midnight. He sensed that as well.

"I can ask them to keep playing," he offered.

"No," she responded quickly, realizing that, in-deed, he could ask anything and it would be done. "It's late. I'm still a little jet-lagged. Maybe I should call it a day."

"You do not work tomorrow," he said to her, capturing a glass of champagne for her from a passing waiter.

"No," she answered, then wondered, "how did you know?"

He smiled his deferential smile again. "It is a small country, and it is mine. I know everything. At least, they let me think I do."

She laughed as he had intended, and she saw he was pleased to have amused her. "You're quite remark-able," she said, feeling that even though he was president, she could say anything. "Not only can you laugh at yourself, but you don't mind if others laugh as well. I always thought a man in your position would be quite—"

"Egotistical?" he finished for her.

"I was going to say sensitive," she teased. "But I suppose it's the same thing. I'm so used to people who are jokes taking themselves seriously that it's refreshing to find someone who must be taken seriously able to joke about himself."

He raised an eyebrow. "They do say that politicians and actors are very much alike."

"Not you, Mr. Pres . . ." He gave her a stern look. "Jorge," she amended. "Maybe in the United States, where anyone who can afford to buy several million dollars' worth of publicity can aspire to public office. But I get the feeling that it's different here."

"By necessity. If I even had several million dollars, I would use it to feed my people, not my ego. San Domenico is poor; we have many problems."

Melinda looked around her. It didn't seem poor. He followed her eyes as they swept the ballroom with its elegant guests, the waiters with their trays of champagne, the expansive gardens surrounding a fairy tale palace.

"I did not build this," he explained. "I inherited it from a long line of corrupt rulers. They were imperialists who came from across the ocean, raped the land and its people, both literally and figuratively, and left it ravaged. When San Domenico declared itself free and sent the oppressors home, I was appointed by the judiciary to try to salvage what was left. But it's a difficult task. We have very few natural resources beyond the beauty of our island. It is my duty to preserve that and what little elements of luxury we have, to encourage the tourist trade. It's our only hope for the future. That's the reason we preserve the opulence of the palace. Not for me. I don't need this. I was raised in a two-room shack. I could go back there tomorrow and be happy. But the world would not accept a president who lives in a two-room shack. And then, I would not be serving my country. You've heard the expression You have to spend money to make money? It's true of countries as well as people."

"I'm sorry. I didn't know any of this. I'm ashamed to admit that I couldn't even find San Domenico on a map before I came here. As I'm sure you know, education is not considered a necessity for an actor, and I'm afraid mine is sadly lacking. I'm completely ignorant of your history."

"Please, don't apologize. I've had college graduates and heads of state who know as little as you do. I'm aiming to change that with a strong tourist campaign. If you would consent, I'd like to make you my hamster."

"I beg your pardon?"

"My hamster. The little animal in the rodent family who is used for testing."

"Oh, you mean guinea pig," she laughed.

He laughed with her. "Excuse me. Here I was priding myself on my perfect English, trying to impress you."

"But your English is perfect, and I am terribly impressed. And I'd love to be your guinea pig."

"Good. Then tomorrow, on your day off, I will take you to tour the sights. And you can tell me if you think I'm on the right course to turn our little island into a . . ." He hesitated and she nodded encouragement. ". . . A hot spot. Is that correct?"

"It's correct language. But I'm not sure it's the correct thing to do. From the little I've seen, San Domenico is so beautiful, I would hate to see it destroyed by hordes of tourists."

"I would, too. But tourists bring dollars, and without that, we cannot survive."

"Then I'm glad we're here. Hollywood studios are notorious for spending money, and I have a feeling they're prepared to drop a bundle here on this one. That should help a little."

"A lot. But I must confess"—his eyes smiled into hers—"this is one thing I did not do for my country. I did this for myself. I wanted to meet you."

"You're flattering me," she said, knowing it was only partly true. He had made it sweetly and abundantly clear that he relished her company. But she didn't doubt for a minute that no matter what his personal interest, he had carefully considered every dollar and every opportunity an international film could bring to San Domenico. And that was how it should be.

Elgar appeared at her side. He exchanged pleasantries with the president, then asked her if she was ready to return to the hotel, explaining that he had an early call to go location scouting even if she did not. The president suggested he could escort her home in his own car. For a moment, she considered his offer. The night was magic, and she wanted it never to end. She breathed in the perfumed air and turned to look at the garden behind them. Something red gleamed through the dark shadows of the bushes. She thought it was the moonlight, glinting on a dewy hibiscus blossom. She focused and was shocked to find eyes staring back at her through the night and knew then it was no flower.

Lucia was watching. Even Cinderella knew when it was time to leave the ball.

"Thank you, Jorge. But I really am very tired. It's been a long day."

"Then I let you go. Until tomorrow." He kissed her hand, nodded at Elgar, turned quickly on his heel, and walked into the palace without a backward glance. She wondered if he had seen Lucia, too.

"Jorge? You call him Jorge?" Elgar was assailing her as she lay her head back on the seat of the car.

"He told me to."

"Oh, baby. Princess Grace, the Sequel."

"Cut it out, Elgar. He's married."

"So what? He's president for life. He can have whatever he wants. And if he wants you—"

"Stop," she insisted.

But alone in her bed at the Reef, staring at the muslin, draped like clouds above her head, she indulged herself. Acting had turned her life into a fantasy. What would it be like to make the fairy tale real?

4

"That was nice, people, but we're going to go for another take," the assistant director shouted over the noise of the extras. "Can we keep it down, please?"

It was the fifth time they had shot the scene, and Melinda knew it wasn't working. She took a deep breath and tried to rethink her lines as one of the grips adjusted a reflector to keep the light from bouncing off the window of the house they had built for their set. The sun was hot and high, and she could feel herself perspiring in the long skirt and tight corset of her period costume. A makeup artist ran out and quickly blotted perspiration from her face before dashing back into the shadows so they could start shooting.

Up until this point, the work had gone remarkably well. Since the incident in her hotel room, Tommy Kray and Melinda had managed to avoid each other. As usual, they were shooting the film out of sequence, and they hadn't been called on to work together much yet. When the crew wrapped for the day, Tommy went off with his own entourage, several of whom had joined him from L.A., plus an ever-changing array of San Domenican women who always appeared to be listening attentively even though no one ever seemed to actually be speaking to them.

Most days, when work was over, a car would pick up Melinda and whisk her off to join *el presidente.* Sometimes he would introduce her to another pristine beach or glorious waterfall, of which the island seemed to have an abundance. Sometimes they would dine at her hotel. But most often, she would go to his quarters in the presidential palace, where he would have arranged a private concert, a sumptuous meal, or some other entertainment to divert her. She always left at an unfashionably early hour so that she would get enough sleep before her usual six A.M. call and be prepared for the next day's difficult work. Occasionally, she would see the president's wife coming in or going out, always with a group of animated friends that usually included the general that Melinda had seen her dancing with on the first night. Lucia never acknowledged her presence, but more than once Melinda had felt the woman's eyes boring through her from behind after they had passed each other. Only once had she mentioned it to Jorge.

"You must not mind Lucia. She has her life; I have mine."

"Whose choice is that?"

"Mutual understanding. And benefit."

"She's a beautiful woman. Don't you love each other?"

He smiled indulgently. "You are very naive. Love is not an issue in a marriage that has been arranged for a higher purpose."

"I don't understand."

"Lucia is not originally San Domenican. Her father was the governor before independence. My father was the head of the opposition. Several deals were made to end the occupation. Our marriage was one of them."

"That's dreadful!"

"No, just practical. As you said, she is a beautiful woman. She makes an excellent first lady. I understand your country has also had presidents who are not entirely immune to this type of situation."

"Touché," Melinda answered and determined not to speak of it again. After all, she was only a guest in his country and it really was none of her business. At least, not until he made some kind of romantic overture that would force her to confront the situation. She'd been the other woman once before. She had no desire to be in that position again. Still, she was grateful that in spite of his obvious interest in her, Jorge had never approached her in the guise of anything but a friend. Because, the truth was, she wasn't sure she'd have the strength of mind to reject him. He was handsome, strong, gentle, erudite, and unaffected. He wined and dined her, shared the beauty of his country with her, and asked for nothing but her company in return. And if, in the end, he wanted to make love to her, it would probably seem the most natural, maybe even wonderful, thing in the world.

Meanwhile, she still had several weeks of Tommy Kray to deal with. The scene they were working on was the first really dramatic moment together they were called upon to perform. Tommy, as the husband, was accusing his wife of having an affair, simply because, racist that he was, he could not believe she would have an affinity for the natives otherwise. Melinda's character, who was indeed having an affair but knew that her husband had no evidence of it but was simply reacting out his own hatred toward the native people, had to overcome guilt at her own transgressions to express her anger at her husband's offensive prejudice. As tricky as the dialogue was, the emotions they had to display were even more complicated and often at odds with the words they were speaking.

"Listen, guys"—Elgar had them in a huddle—"I need you to be more . . . there. It's not your line delivery that's bothering me. It's what's happening in the eyes. Do you know what I'm saying?"

Melinda knew exactly what he was saying. She looked at Tommy, whose gaze was fixed at something somewhere over her left shoulder. It was exactly the problem she'd been having with him all day.

"Maybe," she started slowly, trying to be diplomatic, "if you started out really trying to connect with me, and I kind of couldn't bear up under the scrutiny and turned away, you'd have some motivation to build up your anger. What do you think, Tommy?"

"I'm not having a problem with my anger," said Tommy, dismissing her.

Melinda smoldered. She had seen him do other scenes, knew that he was capable of magnificent work. She knew he was holding back, and it had to be by design. The scene was really the wife's, but she couldn't play it well without a proper foil. Tommy wasn't going to let her have the satisfaction of looking good.

Elgar saw and put a restraining hand on her arm. She let him take over. "Your anger is too controlled, Tommy. She's supposed to owe her allegiance to you. She's supposed to do what you want her to do, think what you want her to think. That's a wife's job, and she's not doing it. You think she owes you, and she's betrayed you. You're very pissed off."

"I've got to have something to react to," Melinda added quietly and then knew instantly she had made a tactical error.

"You want something to react to? Fine, baby, I'll give you something to react to."

She tried to recover. "I just meant—"

"Let's go," said Tommy, unwilling to listen.

"Tommy . . ." she tried again. But he was already on his mark.

"Elgar, let's do it if we're going to do it, man."

She looked at Elgar, helpless. He squeezed her hand and gave her a small nod. "It's okay, Melinda. This could work for us."

She found her mark and stood there, waiting for her cue. Her breath came shorter and her heart beat faster as she turned herself into the angry, frightened wife. She hardly heard the director say, "Action!" and Tommy was upon her, speaking his lines, his eyes blazing. He was into it this time, and for a second, she felt the thrill of knowing it was all working before she lost herself in the character.

"You stupid woman," he hissed at her, his voice as quiet as before but somehow this time really menacing. "You have destroyed everything with your treachery."

As before, she looked at him and turned her eyes away. But before, it had been because she was following the script direction. Now, it was because she felt burned by the fire in his relentless stare. They were engulfed by a wave of hatred. It was no longer clear whether it was Tommy and Melinda or a Victorian husband and his wayward wife, but it did not matter.

Elgar held his breath. This was the scene as he had dreamed it. The cameraman zoomed in on Melinda's face.

"It is you who can destroy," she said, sitting down as Elgar had instructed her to do but feeling truly shaken, "with your posturing and provocation. You know nothing and think you know all. You are the savage, not me or these people whom you disparage."

"Savagery sometimes befits the circumstance," he said, venom in his voice. Melinda looked up at him, startled. This was not the line in the script. He was ad-libbing, but since he was still in character and no one had called "Cut," she did not move. Then, he hit her. She gasped in shock and heard Elgar shout, but Tommy was hitting her again. She staggered, tripping on the long skirt of her costume. Out of the corner of her eye, she sensed the camera moving in on them as she tried to ward off his blows.

An instant later, they had pulled him off her, and he was standing near the camera, calm, smirking, not even looking at her.

"Jesus, Tommy," Elgar was yelling. "What the fuck do you think you're doing? This is a goddamn movie. You are supposed to be *acting,* for Chrissake."

"Hey, man, I'm sorry. I was just so into it. It was just like you said. I was very pissed off."

Melinda touched the corner of her mouth and felt the blood that trickled from her broken lip. Tears sprang to her eyes, not from the pain, which was considerable, but from the effort to keep herself from jumping up and attacking Tommy Kray with any lethal weapon she could find. People were crowding around her, murmuring their concern, trying to help her. She pushed them all away.

"You bastard," was all she could say.

"Hey, baby. I was just trying to give you something to react to. It's what you wanted, isn't it?"

"If you ever," she choked, "so much as lay a hand on me again, I'll kill you."

"Oh, yeah. I'd better watch myself. I forgot you do that kind of thing. But now that your faggot friend is in jail, who's going to do your dirty work?"

"Shut up, Tommy," Elgar said before Melinda could answer. Melinda's scandal from a few years back was common knowledge, but everyone had the grace never to mention it. She had been falsely accused of murdering a producer who had been trying to blackmail her. The real killer had been her best friend, a matinee idol named David Burns, who had hidden his homosexuality for years.

Melinda felt herself flushing. A day didn't go by when she didn't think about Dave and remember what he had done for her, but she had hoped her work of the past few years would have made other people forget. Obviously, Tommy hadn't forgotten.

"Fuck you, Tommy," she said. And for the first time in her life, she stormed off the set.

Elgar started after her.

"Hey, Elgar," Tommy called out, suddenly excessively cooperative, "don't you want to do close-ups or reverse angles?"

Elgar was apoplectic. "You have just given my leading lady a fat lip that I can't shoot around. We'll be lucky if she doesn't sue the whole damn outfit, which she'd have every right to do. So, no, right now, I think I'll pass on your close-up."

"Suit yourself," said Tommy, insisting on the last word as he sauntered off. "But it's a damn shame that the whole crew gets held up because she's so unprofessional!"

Elgar caught up with Melinda. "I'm sorry, Melinda. I swear I had no idea he was going to do that."

She didn't slow down. "He's a fucking maniac."

"I know it. I'm sorry. I thought I could control him," he added by way of explanation.

"I can't work with him."

"I know, Melinda. I don't blame you. But he's been really good up to now. Except for you, he's made friends on the set. And his performance has been outstanding."

Melinda heard the panic in Elgar's voice. They'd already shot half the movie. If she dropped out now or insisted that he drop Tommy, they'd be way over budget and the movie would get closed down. Elgar would lose his chance at the big time. She was mad, but she knew he was right. Tommy's acting had never been better. And even though she hated him for what he had done to her today, she knew it had made for an exceptional scene.

"Okay, okay," she reluctantly reassured him. "I'm

not walking. But you'd better do something to make sure he never does that to me again. I mean it."

"I will. I swear it." Elgar was relieved. "Come on, I'll drive you back to the hotel. We'll wrap for the day."

"No, it's all right. I know you'd rather use the rest of the day for pickup shots or extras or something. I'll be okay. I just need to walk it off a little."

"Sure?" he asked, solicitously, but he was already edging back to the set.

She nodded and smiled at him to let him know he was safe. It wasn't his fault that Tommy Kray was an asshole. And if he was an asshole who won an Academy Award or, better yet, made them look good enough to win, then he'd have to be tolerated.

She stepped into the trailer that had been provided for her to rest and change wardrobe on location. The wardrobe mistress jumped to her assistance, smiling and chatty, totally unaware of what had just transpired on the set. Melinda balanced impatiently on one foot and then the other while she was unhooked, unpinned, and undressed. It was a wonder to her that turn-of-the-century women had managed to do anything at all, confined as they were by their corsets and laces and billowing clothes, not to mention domineering husbands. Freed from the tethers of her costume and all it represented, she couldn't even bear the thought of wearing a bra and slipped into her own sundress, pleased to feel her arms and legs bare and the cool air circulating around her skin.

As Melinda stepped out of her trailer, her driver, a young San Domenican named Pedro who spoke perfect English and took her to and from the set each day, ran up to her.

"Done already? Want me to take you back to the hotel?"

"I am done. But I'm not ready to go back yet."

"Want me to take you somewhere else? To the president's palace?"

She looked at him sharply. He smiled sheepishly and shrugged as if to say, It's a small island; everyone knows everything.

"Not today," she said, deciding any other comment would be imprudent.

"For a drink? To a club?"

"No, really, I'm fine. I think I just want to take a little walk." He seemed ready to go with her as if his assignment as her travel captain required him to move when she moved. "By myself," she added, not unkindly but firmly.

"It's not so good to walk alone," Pedro said.

She smiled. He was trying so hard. It had not escaped her that Pedro appeared to have a crush on her and would try to remain in her company whenever possible. The thought of having to make small talk now was unbearable.

"I'll be fine," she said in a way that made it clear there was no point in arguing. "You can wait for me here. I'll be back in a little while, and you can drive me to the hotel."

That seemed to satisfy Pedro, and he climbed back on the hood of the car, leaned against the windshield, and tilted his hat against the sun, his favorite position for most of the day while he waited for his half hour of duty at dawn and dusk.

Melinda walked past the cane fields on either side of her. She knew some of the local crew walked to work from a village only a few kilometers away, although she'd never been there. Taking the turn off the main road she had often seen them make as she passed them in her car, she decided to go exploring. Maybe she'd even find some small gift she could give Jorge. He'd been so kind to her, and she'd never been able to reciprocate.

For half an hour she walked, lost in thought. She was almost at the village before she realized the scenery around her had changed. The road had become a dirt path and the open fields had been replaced by dense underbrush that looked prickly if not altogether forbidding. In the distance, she could see houses, but not the colonial structures that Jorge had brought her to visit. There were row on row of shacks with tin roofs that glinted orange in the afternoon sun. She considered turning back, but she was tired and thirsty and thought perhaps she'd find a cafe or bar, get a drink, and call Pedro to come and pick her up instead of walking back.

As she drew nearer, her sense of foreboding increased, but so did her weariness. The houses that had seemed poor but picturesque from a distance now looked only dilapidated and dingy, and she saw there were people sitting on the stoops and peering out the broken windows. They were looking in her direction, and she turned to see if perhaps there was something behind her that attracted their attention. But she was alone on the dirt road. Again, she thought about turning back, but now she knew they were watching her, and it occurred to her that it might not be wise to show fear—or to appear rude. She forced herself to stop thinking that way, reminding herself that everyone she had met on the island had been unfailingly friendly, even as she realized that everyone she had met had been selected for her. Again, she pushed the thought out of her mind. Instead, she forced herself to smile and walked directly toward the nearest house, where a man and a woman sat side by side, their dark eyes examining her, making no effort to disguise their interest. She would ask for a drink and to use the phone. It occurred to her they might not have a phone. Maybe she would just ask where the nearest cafe was and use the phone there. Her resolve faltered as she realized she didn't have her purse, would not be able to pay for a drink. But she could call Pedro, and he would come and bring money, pay for whatever she bought, and get her out of there. She pushed her smile back up on her face and told herself to stop being silly. Everything was fine.

Pointedly ignoring the squalor, she stepped onto the first porch and approached the couple. She felt their eyes assessing her and composed her face into an expression of friendly neutrality, aware that it was taking all her skill as an actress to mask her fear.

"Excuse me," she said, smiling. "I'm working on that movie down the road and I'm afraid . . ."

It was apparent they were not listening to her or didn't understand. They were murmuring to each other, staring at her. The woman reached out and touched the hem of her skirt. The man stood and placed himself squarely in front of her, scrutinizing the soft white skin of her face, her arms, her chest. No matter how tired she was, it would be better to walk back, she decided.

"Never mind." She smiled. "Thank you, it's fine, I'll just go now . . ."

But as she turned, she saw that a crowd had begun to gather at the foot of the steps. They were coming from the surrounding shacks and from the town behind them. She shuddered. These were not the open, friendly faces of the San Domenicans she had met so far. She didn't expect them to have the elegance of the friends that Jorge had introduced her to or even the rough-hewn but amiable professionalism of the locals they had hired to work on the film. But what she saw was an ugly hostility born of deprivation, and it shocked and frightened her.

They were talking to each other now, making no attempt to communicate with her, and pressing in on her. She tried to remain in control, speaking slowly and calmly but firmly, assuming they might not understand the words, but if she sounded strong enough, they would discern the intent and back off.

"Please. I have to go now. They are waiting for me on the set. If you'll just move away . . ."

She tried to walk forward, expecting the sea of faces to part for her or at least recede. Instead, a hand reached out and caressed her skin. She screamed.

She knew instantly she had made a mistake. The first touch had been more curious than provocative, but now, they were pushing each other to get to her and pushing her in the process. She wanted to scream again but found her voice had left her. She fell, and her dress caught on a post and ripped. It had not been done on purpose, but it did not matter. The sight of her breast inflamed them and now they were screaming, too.

A shot rang out, and for a moment Melinda was almost relieved. It would be better to be killed first than to be ripped apart alive. It took two more shots and then a third before she realized they were not directed at her. Someone was shooting into the air.

The mass of bodies closing in on her started to pull back. She felt the air move around her again, and she could see the shadows the sun made on the ground beside her. She lay where she had fallen and listened to shouting and then grumbling and then more shouting. She saw a hand coming toward her and cringed.

"Miss Myles, it's me, Pedro. Take my hand; you are safe."

She uncovered her eyes and saw him standing over her, reaching for her, and had never been so relieved in all her life. She grabbed his hand and hoisted herself up, holding the fragments of her dress around her. The people were still watching her, but they had moved back, leaving a semicircle of space around them.

"I was . . . they were . . ." She was shaking.

"They said they didn't want to hurt you, just to touch you. But you screamed and it made them angry. They said you looked at them like they were wild dogs, not people."

Melinda was startled. She *had* thought of them as wild dogs. She'd been practicing all the things she'd been told about encountering barking dogs. Don't let them smell your fear. Talk with authority. For a moment, she let herself look into the eyes of one of the women standing on the edge of the group. This time, she did not see hostility, only desperation. Suddenly, they no longer looked like a belligerent mob; they just looked poor and dirty—and hungry.

She barely heard Pedro's admonishments as he pushed her into the car. "I told you it's not good to walk alone. It's a good thing I decided it was a bad idea and came after you. If anything had happened to you, ay-ay-ay, my job would be over. No, my life would be over. Don't do this to me again, okay? Okay?"

"Okay," she agreed, but her mind was somewhere else. "Pedro, are there more villages like that one on the island?"

"Are you kidding?"

"Well, I've never seen anything like it before, and I've been all over."

He snorted. "All over with *el presidente.* That's not all over."

"So there are?"

He shrugged. "Every place has slums. Don't you have slums where you come from?"

"Not like that."

"Well, this is not Hollywood, California."

Elgar was waiting for her in the lobby of the hotel.

"Jesus, what happened to you?"

"Elgar, I think this may have been the worst day of my life, and I'd like it to be over. So if you don't mind, I'm going to go to my room, take a long, hot bath, and go to sleep."

But when she lay back in the tub and closed her eyes, luxuriating in the silky bubbles of her bath, she saw the faces of the villagers. And when she went to bed, the last thing she remembered before she slipped into a dead sleep was the haunted look of their hungry eyes.

"She eats whenever she wants to, but that's usually about eleven-thirty for lunch. Then she'll need a snack in the afternoon. She loves bananas, and if you cut up an apple, she'll eat that. But don't give her any grapes.

I don't know if you know that, but babies can choke on grapes . . ."

"Don't worry, Mrs. Symington. I've been around babies all my life and taking care of them since I was ten years old. Moira will be okay."

Sam looked at Natalie. She was a pretty girl, with dark brown hair and liquid brown eyes ringed with dark lashes. She had the pink cheeks of a country girl and a quick smile. Moira had taken to her right away, and Sam had heard the baby laughing with her new au pair while she got dressed. Still, as highly recommended as she was, Natalie was virtually a stranger to them, and she'd never before left Moira with anyone other than family or the staff at Belvedere whom Drew had known all his life.

Natalie saw her hesitation. "Really, Mrs. Symington. I already spotted a little playground in the park where we can go. And I brought some toys with me."

"You did?"

"Well, Uncle Amos said you'd just moved in, so I thought just in case your things hadn't arrived or you hadn't unpacked. You know, just to be safe. It's no big deal. Just blocks and some books that my kid sisters used to like."

Sam felt the weight move off her heart. "That was so thoughtful, Natalie. And you're absolutely right. The stuff's all here, but I couldn't tell you which box it's in. I'm very grateful."

"Oh gosh, no. I'm the one who's grateful. I was starting to get in the way at Uncle Amos's. But I really love Washington, and I want to stay. This is just perfect for me. And I love my room. I don't know how to thank you, Mrs. Symington."

"You can start by calling me Sam like everybody else. And just take good care of my baby here and love her like I do," said Sam, smothering the child in her arms with kisses and then handing her over to Natalie.

"How can anyone help it," laughed Natalie as Moira happily reached out her arms and put them around Natalie's neck. "Wave bye-bye to Mama. She's going to work."

Sam looked at the two of them from the driveway, smiling and waving.

"Let's get dressed and go to the park," she heard Natalie say.

"Pock," repeated Moira. "Pock, pock."

Sam got into her car. They were going to be just fine.

She called Drew from the car. "Where are you?" she asked him.

"I'm looking at a former factory in Virginia," he said, speaking into the cellular phone they had both agreed to carry, since for the time being, neither of them knew how else to be reached. "I think it'll work out fine. But it's going to need about six months for renovation."

"That's not bad," Sam boosted.

"No. It just means six months of cooling my heels until it's done. I've been thinking of just working out of the house until it's finished and I can put an office right in the plant."

"That's a great idea, honey," Sam enthused. "I'm sure Natalie will be fine with Moira, but I have to admit, I love the idea of one of us being around all the time."

"Well, I don't expect it to be all the time."

"I know. I didn't mean that. But you'll at least be in

and out a lot for the first few months. In case something comes up."

"Like what?"

"Like I don't know. I'm a nervous mother, do you mind?"

He laughed. "Where are you?"

"Funny you should ask," she said. "I don't exactly know."

"Where are you going?"

"I'm on my way to Senator Kilmont's office. Just to see what he's offering."

"Good idea. Anyway, that should be easy to find. The Capitol is that big white building on top of the hill."

"Very funny. As a matter of fact, I have to go to the Russell Senate Office Building where his office is. It's on Constitution Avenue and I've already figured out how to get there."

"Then what's the problem?"

"There's a monumental traffic jam for no apparent reason, and I can't seem to get anywhere close. The cops keep diverting me. I think I'm going to have to learn how to use the Metrorail."

"My, my. Samantha Myles without wheels. That will be quite a sight."

"I'm hanging up now. What time will you be home?"

"Sixish. How about you?"

"The same, I guess. I have no idea what Kilmont expects me to do. I'll call you later."

As it turned out, finding the Capitol wasn't difficult at all. Finding a parking place was another matter entirely. By the time Sam stood in front of Senator

Kilmont's receptionist, in his office facing Constitution Avenue, she was over an hour late and more than a little frazzled.

"I'm Samantha Sym—" she began, but she wasn't given a chance to finish.

"Sam!" burst out the perky gray-haired woman who sat at the desk in front of her. "I hope you don't mind if I call you that. He's been out here so many times asking if you arrived that I already feel like I know you. But of course, you don't know me." She stood up and came around the desk with her hand outstretched. "I'm Dotty. That's not my condition, that's my name."

She laughed so heartily at her own joke, that she knocked over a Lucite organizer on her desk, spilling pencils, scissors, and paper clips in all directions.

"Oh, my goodness," she exclaimed. "The senator won't like this. Though he should be used to it by now," she added with a sigh. "I'm a little clumsy," she continued apologetically to Sam.

Sam stooped to help her gather the fallen paraphernalia, but Dotty suddenly remembered why she was there and, jumping up, insisted they leave the mess and go on into the senator's office.

"He doesn't like to be kept waiting," she explained, conveying a sense of nervousness that made Sam uncomfortable.

She led Sam to the door at the back of the room, tapped lightly, and opened it wide enough for the senator to see Sam from his desk. Sam was dressed in a soft suit in tones of beige, the skirt hovering just above her knee. And even though the effect was meant to be relatively conservative, there was no hiding the fact that her shapely legs went on much farther and that beneath the folds of fabric lay delicious curves, covered but not concealed. He was on his feet in a fraction of a second.

"Sorry, I'm late. The traffic—" she began.

He didn't even let her finish. "You don't need to explain. Someone should have warned you. I'm so glad to see you. It is so good of you to do this."

"Well, Senator," she said with a smile, "you almost had me convinced that if I didn't, I could be held in the same regard as Tokyo Rose or Hanoi Hannah."

He laughed. "Okay, I know how to put the pressure on. And even though it's strictly selfish, because I know you're going to make me look good, I also think you're going to find it interesting and exciting."

"It's already exciting just being here. I've never been in Washington before. And I know it sounds corny, but seeing the Capitol right there and then walking down the hall to your office, it almost felt like walking on hallowed ground."

"Ah," he said, "a genuine patriot."

She thought she detected a note of cynicism. "Aren't you?"

"I'm afraid I've been here a little too long. I'm not sure if the place is blessed or cursed or sometimes both. Certainly, when it works right, it is awesome. And, there's enough of the optimist in me to think that we can still get it to work right. That's why I want you here, Sam."

"Well, Senator, if you show me how you think I can help, I'll be happy to try."

He put an arm around her. "I'm going to call you Sam, and you have to call me Amos. We're on the same team now. Besides, it would probably make

Drew feel awkward to hear you call me Senator when he still thinks of me as Pickles."

"As what?"

"Don't ask," he said, laughing, encouraging her to ask. "It was a long time ago after way too many beers. Let me just emphasize all participants were consenting adults."

"I think maybe you're right." She laughed with him, deciding not to pick up on the implied invitation. "I'm not going to ask. Show me what your committee is working on and what you think I can do."

He led her to a comfortable sofa, in front of which were piled binders, folders, and miscellaneous papers. He sat close beside her, and zeroing in on one file after another, a particular page, a specific paragraph, he laid out a proposal for a comprehensive program to increase aid to areas where emission control and pollution standards were being met while punishing those areas that refused to meet the challenge for cleaner air. Several hours went by, but Sam didn't notice and Amos didn't seem to mind. She was fascinated and impressed. Once, Dotty came in to ask if they wanted to order lunch. Sam was too excited to eat, and the senator just waved Dotty away in a manner that told her he'd call her if he wanted anything. She tripped on his kilim rug on the way out.

"I don't know, Amos." Sam smiled. "Dotty is not exactly what I had envisioned for your front office."

"Tell me about it," he sighed, exasperated. "But what can I do? If I didn't keep her, where would she go?"

"I have to say," Sam said when the senator took off his glasses and suggested they close the books for a while, "I'm mightily impressed. You really are one of the good guys. You're trying to do something here that really matters, and that everyone—government and industry—has been sweeping under the carpet for an awfully long time."

He beamed. "I'm glad you see it that way. I was hoping you would."

"But I see what you mean when you say you need help. These are magnificent proposals. But the way you've laid it out, it would cost the entire gross national product to implement. You've got to approach this from a more practical standpoint."

Amos grabbed her hand and put it to his lips. "I knew," he said fervently, "that you would understand. You are what I need."

She was touched by the sincerity of his convictions and his faith in her. Still, she could see that involving herself in the political machinations of the legislature was going to take far more work than even she anticipated. And she wasn't sure that she was up to it.

"I don't know . . . ," she began.

But Amos cut her off. "I know," he said with such conviction that she felt she'd be a fool to argue.

"Okay," she said. "I'll try."

He grabbed her in a bear hug and kissed her again, knocking the breath out of her.

She laughed, extricating herself. "Does this mean I can get lunch?"

He looked at his watch. "Oh my God, it's after three. You must be starved."

"Aren't you?"

"Famished."

"Can we get Dotty to order us some sandwiches or something?"

"Are you kidding? After what you've been through?" He pushed down on the intercom. "Dotty, call the Jockey Club and tell them I'm on the way. And get us my car, please."

"I like it here," Sam said when they'd been installed in a red-leather banquette after some initial confusion. Apparently, Dotty had gotten the time of their reservation wrong.

"Me, too," said Amos. "It's one of the few places around here that's cheerful instead of pretentious."

Sam looked around and saw that he was right. Each table was covered with a red-and-white tattersall check tablecloth and held a single red rose. The floors were bare wood planks, and instead of a chandelier, a lantern was suspended from the low-beamed ceiling. It was warm and publike, and Sam immediately felt at home. At Amos's suggestion, she ordered the restaurant's signature crab cakes meuniere and was not disappointed. Amos ordered a bottle of wine, insisting that they deserved it after all the hard work they'd done. Sam did notice that her glass somehow never appeared empty, but she wasn't really aware of when the first bottle had gone and the second bottle had appeared. By the time the waiter came to ask if they'd like dessert, the late lunch crowd had melded into the pretheater diners, and it was getting dark outside.

Sam had ordered an espresso to try to clear the fuzz from her head, but even sipping the rich, dark liquid didn't make the ringing go away.

"Is that you?" Amos asked.

"Yes, of course it's me," answered Sam. "Who else would it be?"

"I mean the ringing," said Amos.

"You hear it, too?" They must have both had too much to drink.

"I think it's coming from your purse," he pointed out gently.

"Oh . . . right . . . ," Sam acknowledged sheepishly as she dug into her purse to try to find her errant phone.

"Where are you?" Drew asked when she finally put it to her ear.

"I'm at the Jockey Club with Amos."

"I thought you were coming home for dinner."

"I am. We're having lunch."

"At seven-thirty?"

"Really? It's seven-thirty? I mean, we came late, but I had no idea. Why didn't you call me earlier?"

"I don't know. I figured if you were available, you'd call me to tell me you were going to be late. I didn't want to take the chance of having your phone go off in the middle of an important cabinet meeting or something."

Amos caught her eye. "Drew?" he mouthed. She nodded. He took the phone from her hand.

"Drew, I never gave you enough credit."

"What's that supposed to mean?" asked Drew good-naturedly.

"Well, in college, you were just a rich kid whose dad paid his way into Harvard. I mean, you did your work, you got by, but it didn't matter because you knew you were going to get to run a company some day anyway. So I never figured you to have much critical judgment. Now I see I was wrong."

"And what brought you to that conclusion?"

"You married Sam. I got to tell you, pal, it makes

82

you look good. And from the work she did with me this afternoon, I have a feeling she's going to make me look good, too."

Sam felt herself flush, if from the wine or the compliments, she wasn't sure. She took the phone back.

"I'm on my way, honey," she said. "How's Moira? Did she and Natalie get along okay?"

"She's fine," Drew said. He was surprised it had taken her so long to ask. "Uh, Sam?"

"What?"

"Are you driving?"

"Well, yeah. Except I parked the car back at the Capitol. So I guess I'll have to go back there first."

Amos took the phone from her again. He was already shaking his head no. "Don't worry, Drew. She can leave her car there overnight. I'll have my driver drop her off."

"Okay, thanks. Hey, Amos?"

"What?"

"Is this going to be a regular practice?"

"What?"

"Taking my wife out for lunch and getting her drunk?"

"Are you kidding, pal? Now that she's working for me, this is probably the last time she'll get out for lunch at all."

Drew hung up the phone.

"Is she okay?" Natalie asked anxiously. She had seen Drew pacing nervously for the past hour. He'd only broken his stride for fifteen minutes at seven to sit with Moira while she fell asleep. He'd insisted that Sam was perfectly capable of taking care of herself, and if she didn't call to say she was going to be late, then he was sure she was involved in something that couldn't be interrupted.

"She's fine. She was having lunch with your uncle."

"You're kidding?" Natalie was indignant. "Why didn't she at least call to—" She broke off, realizing maybe it would seem impertinent for the au pair to criticize the woman who had just hired her that morning.

Drew saw her stricken look and smiled kindly. "It's okay. First day on the job, I guess. You forget things."

Natalie smiled back at Drew. With his black hair and sky blue eyes, she was sure he was the most handsome man she'd ever seen. It would take more than a job to make her forget anything like him.

"I've kept the food hot."

"I have a feeling Sam's not going to want to eat. In fact, I wouldn't be surprised if she rolled into the house and right into bed."

Wanting to make a good impression on her first day of work, Natalie had used the two hours of Moira's afternoon nap to prepare dinner. Since she didn't know her employer's plans, she'd made sure it was something that would keep—beef bourguignonne and a simple salad—but she knew it was good. The year of her eighteenth birthday, she'd asked for and received a summer cooking course at the Cordon Bleu in Paris. Sam had told her that she wasn't expected to do household chores, but she'd tidied the place up and set the table for two, even buying candles for the pewter candlesticks she'd found in one of the unpacked boxes in the kitchen. She hated to see all that effort go to waste.

"You have to eat, don't you?" she asked quietly.

Waiting for Sam to come and share the end of their

first working day in Washington, Drew had felt his appetite ebb. But he heard the disappointment in Natalie's voice and saw her eyes stray to the table she'd so carefully laid out. She was sweet, and she was trying so hard.

"What about you?" he asked. "Have you had dinner yet?"

"No, but I was just going to grab something in the kitchen after I'd served the two of you."

"Don't be silly. Come and sit down and have dinner with me, since Sam's not going to."

"Really?" she asked in such an incredulous voice that Drew had to laugh.

"Of course. You're not the kitchen maid. You're allowed to eat with us. In fact, I'm sure Sam would insist on it."

"Well, if you're sure then." He pulled out a chair for her to sit down, and she blushed at being treated with such elegance. Then he sat down opposite her, and she laughed, embarrassed, realizing she had to get up again to serve the food. To her amazement, he stood as she stood, and she understood that he was not treating her in any special way. He was just doing what he always did, and it charmed her even more to know that his refinement was natural to him.

He lavished praise on her food and wanted to know where she learned to cook like that. She told him the story of her eighteenth summer, trying to make it sound like an adventure, which it had been, but which grew more enticing with every encouraging nod of Drew's head. With so many children in her house, it had always been an effort to be heard. Sitting across the table from Drew, she felt she was the center of a deep, abiding attention, and it fed her soul.

Natalie had just made coffee and was getting ready to serve dessert when they heard the car pull up. She tried not to let her disappointment show as Drew leaped from his chair and opened the door to find Sam fumbling for her keys. She gave him a slightly lopsided smile and entered the house, forgetting that there was a small step at the threshold. She tripped and would have gone sprawling to the floor had Drew not caught her in his arms. Natalie was disgusted. Natalie wondered what kind of woman would get drunk with her boss the first day on her job and leave her husband waiting at home. But Drew seemed more amused than riled as he steadied his giggling wife.

"Tough day at the office, honey?" he joked.

"Believe it or not, we did a lot of work. Amos's committee has some great plans for the future, but they have no idea how to get there from here. We didn't stop for lunch until after three. And then, I don't know, Amos ordered some wine and then you called and it was late."

"Did you eat between the ordering of the wine and my phone call?"

"I guess I must have."

"You definitely drank."

"Definitely."

"Are you hungry? Natalie cooked a great dinner for us."

"She did? Oh, Natalie." Sam turned her attention to her new sitter. Amos had been right about that, too. What a gem she was turning out to be. "That is so wonderful. Your uncle was right. You're wonderful."

Natalie hoped she looked properly deferential. It wouldn't serve her well to let Drew's wife know how she really felt about her. "Well, I had some time when Moira took her nap. We had a really great day."

"That's wonderful," said Sam, knowing she was repeating herself, but it required too much effort to think of alternative words.

"Would you like me to heat some up for you?"

"Oh, no, thank you. I'm not hungry. I think I'm going to just go right up to bed."

Drew looked at Natalie over Sam's head and winked at her, reminding her it was just what he'd predicted. Natalie wanted to laugh out loud, but she settled for a smug little smile, knowing it was a secret they shared. They could talk about it after Sam had gone to bed. She'd congratulate him on his foresight or compliment him on his knowledge of women, something to show she appreciated him. Sam was already moving toward the stairs. In a few moments, she'd have Drew back to herself again.

Natalie pretended to busy herself clearing off the table, but her eyes were still on her employers when Sam reached out from the second step and grabbed Drew's necktie, pulling him toward her.

"I thought you said you wanted to go to bed," Drew said quietly.

"I did," answered Sam, her condition making her unaware that she was speaking louder than she intended. "But I didn't say I wanted to go to sleep. And I didn't say I wanted to go alone."

Natalie felt her spine prickle. How could a man with Drew's sensitivity be expected to find a sloppy drunk desirable. To her amazement, instead of pushing Sam away, Drew seemed to be following.

"Drew, are you ready for dessert?" she called out cheerily.

"Uh . . . you know, Natalie, I'm really full. It was really great, but I don't think I've got room for dessert," Drew said, reaching for Sam with both arms.

"It's apple cobbler. It's really light. It's got to be hot." She hoped there was no hint of desperation in her voice.

"Apple cobbler, eh? I love apple cobbler . . ."

Natalie tried not to see that Sam was nuzzling his neck.

". . . But I like it cold, too. I'll have it for breakfast."

"If you don't feel like cleaning up"—Sam smiled over Drew's shoulder—"you can leave it until morning. I'm not one of those people who can't sleep if they know there's a dish in the sink."

"No, that's all right," said Natalie between clenched teeth. But Drew and Sam were already at the top of the stairs, laughing as they tripped over each other to the bedroom.

Carrying the dishes to the kitchen, Natalie had to resist an urge to crash them one by one against the wall. "Watch out," she said to herself as she loaded the dishwasher. "The baby's good, my room is nice, it's a decent job. Don't mess it up." But watching the cobbler steam up the cellophane wrap as she put it in the refrigerator, she couldn't help wondering, "I wonder if he knows she's not good enough for him."

Upstairs, leaning against the closed bedroom door, Sam pulled Drew to her, kissing him hungrily.

He laughed at her tenderly, "If this is what you're like when you come home, maybe I should get Amos to take you to lunch more often."

∾5∾

Melinda was pleased. Two more days of shooting and her work on the film would be over. As much as she was enjoying the attentions of Jorge Alvarro, as beautiful as the island was, she felt as though she was ready to go home. Her work with Tommy Kray had been grueling, but in fact, she had to admit that his hostile attitude had served her well. She had never had to try so hard to stay in character, and the benefits of her effort showed on screen. She had heard murmurings from cast and crew betting on another Academy Award nomination for her. She downplayed it as much as she could, but even though she had one Oscar already, it was still a thrill to think that she could be recognized again.

She was a little sorry to realize that, out of his hatred for her, Tommy had developed his best role in years and would probably be up for an Oscar himself.

"It isn't Amos," she said, devouring his lip. "And it isn't lunch. It's just you. I always want you."

He felt his desire meet hers as he pressed into her, where they stood, without even taking off their clothes, gently first, then harder as the need grew stronger. She closed her eyes and felt herself lifting and floating. She knew it was partly the result of too much to drink, but it didn't matter. Joined with her husband, she was in safe haven. She could go anywhere, do anything—or nothing. Sooner or later, she would end up in paradise. And in a matter of moments, she did.

By the time they'd undressed and gotten into bed, Sam's head had cleared a little.

"So what do you think of Natalie?" Sam wanted to know, propping her head on Drew's shoulder. "You saw more of her today than I did."

"What can I tell you. Moira loves her. When I came home, they were rolling on the floor together, which I took to be a pretty good sign. We gave her a bath together, and she seemed to know what she was doing. Then, it turns out she trained at the Cordon Bleu and made dinner without even being asked. You missed a great meal."

"She seems almost too good to be true."

"Oh, I'm sure some of her fervor will die down once she's sure we're going to keep her."

"I hope not. Because from the looks of it, pretty soon we won't be able to live without her. I'd hate for her to lose her zeal. So just be extra nice to her."

"Hey, I'm always nice to my employees. Look what I did for you," Drew teased.

"You don't have to be that nice," Sam laughed.

"But she's new in Washington. I don't think she knows anybody except her uncle. And if you're working out of the house, you'll be around more than me. So talk to her."

"You want me to baby-sit the baby-sitter? Somewhere in there I'm supposed to be fulfilling a government contract, remember?"

"I know. I just mean you should make her feel like she's part of the family and not just Moira's baby-sitter. You know what I mean."

"Okay, okay. Meanwhile, what did you think of her uncle after one day on the job? Amos is one of the good guys, isn't he?"

"That's just what I said. I like him. He's very sincere about what he's doing, really concerned."

"Since you had a four-and-a-half-hour lunch, I guess the two of you got along all right."

"I think it would be hard not to. He's a very warm person. He likes to . . ." She hesitated.

"What?"

"Show his appreciation," she finished. She had been going to say he likes to touch but was afraid it would sound funny. She was sure Amos Kilmont's hugs and kisses were just a product of his natural exuberance. There had been a moment, sitting in the backseat of the car beside him, when she thought his hand had brushed against her breast. But they had been going around a curve, and she had drunk more than her usual quota, and truth be told, she couldn't have said exactly what had happened. It was safest to assume that any inappropriate contact had been completely inadvertent. In fact, she was sure of it. Amos Kilmont was her husband's friend and college roommate. He was a senator in the United States Congress.

He had presented her with an opportunity not only to occupy herself in Washington but to do something interesting and meaningful.

"Don't look a gift horse in the mouth," she told herself, forgetting, for the moment, that the cliché was derived from the fact that the first gift horse had hidden an enemy that had ultimately destroyed its recipient.

But then, that meant in all likelihood, Elgar, too, would be in the running, and she certainly wished him success. Young and inexperienced as he was, he knew his craft. The film was his vision, and he was bringing it brilliantly to life. And, true to his word, Elgar had somehow managed to keep Tommy not necessarily civil but definitely under control. There had been no repeat performances of his violent tendencies since that first outburst on the set four weeks ago. Tommy's trailer had been placed as far away as possible from Melinda's, so that once their scenes together were over, they were nowhere in proximity of each other. As the weeks of shooting stretched on, members of Tommy's L.A. entourage had drifted into San Domenico, men with long greasy hair who wore motorcycle jackets even in the tropical heat. So, in essence, the set had divided into two camps, and except when the director called action, there was little communication between them.

Once shooting had wrapped for the day, Tommy left Melinda alone and turned his attention to the San Domenican beauties who had become part of his following. Melinda would see one of them on occasion slipping silently from Tommy's room as the actors gathered for their calls early each morning. Never showing any sign of affection, Tommy would leave her in the hall, and the woman, eyes downcast to avoid looking at any of the other cast or crew members, would scurry out. As far as she could tell, it was never the same one twice, and Melinda could only hope that they wouldn't judge the character of her country by the singular lack of grace of one of its citizens.

To offset her grueling days portraying Tommy Kray's rebellious wife, Melinda had her jasmine-scented evenings. The hours she spent at the presidential palace would be one of the main things she would miss about the island. Jorge had continued to play the gentleman, always captivating, never pressing. She knew he desired her, and he knew she found him attractive, but he recognized her discomfort with the situation and respected it. Still, Melinda was grateful that the punishing schedule had called for her to be up before six each day. It was a lot easier to resist temptation when your nights had to end at ten.

"Melinda, you're needed in five," Audrey, her wardrobe assistant, called, coming through her trailer door, breaking into her reverie. "We're into the home stretch."

"I know it," Melinda said congenially. After so many weeks away from home, they'd developed the team mentality of a bunch of kids away at camp. "Can't wait."

"Me, too," said Audrey, helping the star into her bustle and stays. "Although I never thought I'd hear myself say I'd be glad to leave paradise."

"I know what you mean." Melinda took a deep breath so that Audrey could pull the laces tight. It was a routine they'd been through several times a day, six days a week for five weeks, and working together, they were able to get Melinda in and out of her cumbersome costume in three minutes flat. "It's paradise. But it's not *our* paradise."

"I guess," said Audrey with one last pull that made Melinda gasp. "Can't live without that smog."

Melinda laughed. "And don't forget the floods and the earthquakes. Wouldn't want to take a chance on missing one of those."

"All set," said Audrey, gathering up Melinda's

skirts for the short walk to the area where the camera had been set up. It was to be one of the final scenes, where Melinda joins her lover and her husband tries to shoot them as they run off together.

"You've checked the gun, right?" Melinda asked Elgar nervously as he approached to block her action.

"Melinda, I swear to you. There's nothing in the gun. Not even blanks. No sound will come out."

"Okay. But just to be sure, look at it again before the scene, will you? He's crazy."

Elgar gave her a little hug. "I know. But he's doing a hell of a job."

"Elgar, I will not die for your film."

"Sweetie, I wouldn't let you. I need you for the next one. Don't worry, Melinda. I promise. I promise. The gun is in props. Tommy doesn't have it. I'll check it out personally before I hand it to him. I'll make sure it's the same one he uses in the scene. I promise. Nothing is going to happen."

"Okay. If you promise."

He left her on her mark and went to work with Tommy. They spoke quietly, intensely, for a few moments. She saw the prop man give Elgar the gun. She saw Elgar open the chambers and nod, indicating they were empty. Just to be sure, he aimed it away from everyone and pulled the trigger. Melinda thought she heard a small click. There was no bang. She was reassured until she looked at Tommy and saw the clouds gathering in his eyes as he got himself into his part. Now, she felt like his wife. Now, she was frightened.

Elgar moved away from them both and took his place behind the camera.

"Action," he said quietly, and Melinda went to

work. She saw her lover emerge from the woods. She moved toward him, smiling, arms outstretched. His face was suffused with love. Suddenly, it registered fear. She followed his eyes and turned to see her husband standing behind them. He raised his gun. She grabbed her lover, trying to run with him, cursing the huge skirts that slowed her pace. A shot rang out. And then another. *Bang. Bang.*

Melinda screamed and hit the ground with the terrifying realization that no promise could stop a madman.

The shooting didn't stop. Now, there was a lot of screaming. People were running for cover. Elgar had disappeared behind the camera. Melinda was confused. She looked at Tommy. He, too, was lying face-down on the ground, the gun at his side. Between blasts of gunfire, she thought she could hear him whimpering.

Terrified, Melinda kept her head down. She heard vehicles approach and screech to a halt, then the sound of pounding feet. There was more gunfire, followed by shouting in Spanish. She had no idea what was being said, only that each sentence seemed to be punctuated by another hail of bullets. Finally, after one particularly vicious barrage, there was the sound of pounding feet again, and then, at last, silence, broken by the muffled sobs of people in terror.

"Amigos, you can get up now. You are safe."

She lay still for a moment, not sure whether to trust what she heard. She felt a hand touch her head and she screamed, wrenching herself away, until Elgar's voice penetrated her fog of fear.

"Melinda, it's okay. It's okay."

She threw herself into his arms and let him hold her, feeling his heart beating as quickly as her own. She didn't trust herself to speak.

"Is everyone okay?" Elgar was shouting. "Mike," he called to the assistant director, who was peeking out from behind some equipment boxes, "go and check. Make sure no one is hurt."

The man who had announced they were safe approached them. Melinda saw he was in a military uniform.

"I'm very sorry, señor," he said deferentially to Elgar. "We did not expect this."

"You're damn right, we didn't." Melinda could hear the anger rising in Elgar's voice. Now that it seemed no one had been hurt he was allowing himself the luxury of losing control. "What the hell is going on here?"

"A local matter. Not for you to be concerned."

"What? You let some goddamn *banditos* come in here and shoot at my people and then tell me not to be concerned. Well, I am concerned. I'm very concerned. How the hell are we supposed to finish our movie with stuff like this happening?"

"I'm sorry, señor," the officer said. "Your movie is finished."

"Don't give me that shit," said Elgar, rolling now. "We've got another day and a half of shooting to go, and I damn well expect the government to provide us with adequate protection. I want a guarantee that this kind of thing won't happen again."

"I'm sorry, señor, I can give you no guarantee."

"Why the hell not? Get your goddamn police force out here. Get your goddamn army for all I care. *El presidente* seems to have a pretty big force of his own. Let's get some of them out here to keep the goddamn *banditos* away."

Melinda touched Elgar's arm to calm him. She knew he was upset because he had been frightened, as much for the people in his care as for himself, but righteous indignation directed against the president of their host country was not going to accomplish much.

"The army is not available, señor," the officer was saying, stiffening but with continued politeness. "Those were not *banditos* shooting. They were rebels. We are having a civil war."

"Oh, jeez," Elgar exclaimed, all the fury draining out of him.

Melinda felt a wave of shock. She had talked to Jorge about his country many times. Her solitary encounter with the hungry villagers had led her to ask him to tell her about the people and the political situation in San Domenico. She had admired him for acknowledging their problems and the difficulty in solving them. But he had been so genuinely concerned over the plight of the poor, so earnest in his desire to find a solution. He had been the first to admit that the privilege of the presidential palace was perceived by many as an abuse. But she had understood that the trappings of the presidency were to form the basis of a tourist attraction that would turn the economy around. Obviously, some of his own people had understood it less well.

Tommy was on his feet now, screaming, "Get us out of here. I am not going to get fucking killed in some banana republic's fucking revolution."

"Take it easy, Tommy," Elgar said, and Melinda

saw him trying not to look at the wet spot that had appeared between Tommy's legs on his turn-of-the-century breeches.

"Don't tell me to take it easy, you fucker. You brought us here. You get us out."

"I'm sorry, señor," the military officer continued to address Elgar. "That would be impossible right now. The airport is closed. It is in the hands of the rebels. As soon as we retrieve it—"

"That could take years!" Tommy shouted. "We're not going to fucking sit here and—"

"Tommy," Elgar interrupted forcefully, "why don't you go see Audrey about a change of pants."

Tommy looked down at himself and then at the people who had slowly gathered around when the immediate danger had dissipated. For the cast and crew, the director was their leader. It didn't matter that Elgar was younger than most of them. He was rising to the occasion.

Melinda stifled a laugh, but some of the others were not so polite. They enjoyed seeing that the great symbol of machismo, Tommy Kray, had wet his pants in fear.

"Fuck you!" bellowed Tommy as he stomped off toward his trailer. But he was stopped in midstride by another man in uniform. He started to curse, but then he saw the soldier's gun, and he meekly backed off, looking to Elgar for further instruction.

"*El presidente* invites you and your people to come and stay at the palace until this is settled," the officer addressed Elgar courteously. "We expect it will not be long. Until we have fully regained control, you will be safe in the palace."

"Okay, people, let's pack it up," Elgar said quietly,

knowing Mike would relay the word to everyone else at the top of his lungs. "We're moving into the palace for the duration."

There was a buzz of excitement as Mike started barking his orders. Suddenly, the danger seemed distant, and the air crackled with adventure. Melinda smiled. She should have known they could trust Jorge. She wasn't afraid anymore.

They left for the palace in a convoy of trailers protected by armed soldiers. Driving over the roads of San Domenico, they could occasionally spot bands of people huddled together. They looked more like frightened villagers than marauding rebels, but the soldiers would shoot at them anyway, and the cluster would break up as the people scurried for cover. Once, coming into a town, they saw people running toward them, and shots were fired at their vehicles. But their guards answered with a volley of machine-gun fire, and they were disturbed no more. They were all relieved when their convoy pulled into the palace grounds and the heavy gates were barricaded behind them.

Melinda had never seen so many soldiers outside of a military parade. But these men were not on display. They were posted at every vantage point on the fortress walls and under orders to shoot at any suspicious movement. Sensing that any immediate danger had passed, some of the crew members began to make jokes as they were assigned quarters in one of the guest wings of the palace. But Melinda began to feel uneasy. They would be safe here, and that was important. But she wondered at what cost? To the American filmmakers, this revolution was turning into an escapade that would keep many a Hollywood dinner party going in the months to come. They were ignoring the fact that to the people of San Domenico, on both sides of whatever issue they were fighting about, it was a matter of life and death.

Mornings had evolved into a happy ritual that Sam cherished. Their alarm clock was Moira, who toddled into Sam and Drew's bedroom around seven each morning. With blue eyes sparkling and red curls framing her cherubic face like a halo, she'd hold out her chubby arms and wait to be lifted to the enchantment of her parents' bed. They'd play with her together for a while, then Drew would shower and dress and head out to the factory site to get the foreman started off for the day. Sam would linger for a while with the baby, then go downstairs where Natalie would have prepared breakfast for both of them. The newspaper was always waiting by the coffee, but Sam gladly relinquished it to Natalie, preferring to enjoy every exuberant moment with her daughter in the morning that she could—because she knew, more often than not, it might be all she got.

Working for Amos Kilmont on the Industrial Economic Committee had turned out to be far more demanding than Sam had expected, and office hours sometimes stretched into the evenings. The committee was preparing a report for Congress, and it was crucial that all details, all facts, all figures, be exact and irrefutable. Having undertaken the task, Sam was obliged to see it through to perfection; she could work no other way. Amos knew it and took advantage of it, pointing out that without their evenings together, there would be no way to complete the report and be assured of its accuracy in the time left before its presentation. He certainly tried to ease her suffering, taking her to Washington's most elegant restaurants for working dinners or sometimes bringing her to work in his elegant Connecticut Avenue pied-à-terre when his wife was back home in the family manse. And though he still bussed her hello and good-bye and frequently came in for a hug when things were going well—or badly—the easy informality with which he ran his office made it all seem innocuous enough to dispel any suspicions that something improper was going on.

After the first few weeks, Drew had become accustomed to his wife's frequent absence. He didn't like it, but involved as he was with his own government project, he knew it would be unreasonable to object to her doing a job to the fullest extent of her abilities. Still, Sam felt guilty.

"It's not forever," she said by way of excuse on the fourth consecutive night of the third consecutive week she called to say she wouldn't be home for dinner. "Amos has promised that once the committee has made its report, the workload will downsize."

"Moira misses her mommy," was all he said, knowing it was all he needed to say.

"That was mean," she answered, stung. "Do you think I should quit?"

"What do you think?"

"I think I'm doing something important here. I think it could make a difference in the way this country deals with the environment and consequently in the way the world conducts itself. I think that should count for something."

"I'll tell your daughter that."

"Why are you doing this to me?" The pain in her voice made him stop.

"I'm sorry. I know I'm not being fair. But I miss you. We used to be together all the time. Now you spend more time with Amos than with me. Even in college he was always after my girls. I should never have introduced you."

She knew he was more kidding than not, but she felt more uncomfortable than she should have. "I want to make a difference, Drew. It's a good feeling."

"You make a difference in my life. In Moira's."

"And you make a difference in mine. Does that mean you shouldn't do anything else?"

"I didn't say that. I never tried to stop you from working."

"No. Not as long as it didn't interfere with what you thought I should be doing. Oh, it was okay to doodle engines on graph paper and then turn them over to someone else to build. As long as I didn't test them myself."

"Because it was dangerous."

"No, you only thought it was. But that's okay. I gave it up to come with you to Washington. So now, I've found something here that gives me a sense of accomplishment. It's not dangerous. What's your objection?"

"It's leaving you no time for your family. But, hey, if that's not a problem for you—"

"Of course it is, Drew. But it's not forever," she repeated and then asked if they could continue the conversation later because the senator was calling her.

Drew hung up, knowing they wouldn't be talking again tonight. It was just as well. He knew she was right. If he were the one who could never make it home for dinner because of work, he'd expect her to understand.

"I'm being an idiot, aren't I?" he said to Natalie when he saw her watching him and realized she'd heard his end of the conversation.

"Not at all," Natalie responded with vehemence. "I don't know how she can bear to leave you . . . and Moira," she added quickly so as not to be too transparent.

Drew felt the need to defend his wife, but he was flattered enough by Natalie's implications to return the compliment. "It's not exactly as though she's abandoned us. After all, she's left us with you."

Natalie beamed. Drew's commendations were always offhand, but, for her, they resonated with meaning. She knew he could not say what was in his heart. He was too good, too moral, to ever denigrate his wife. But from the first day when he had invited her to share his table, she had known that he could see it, too. They suited each other the way he and Sam never could. For Natalie, there would never be anything more important than Drew. It was what he deserved.

She lit the candles as she did every night before they had dinner. She still laid the table for two, but waiting for Sam was only a pretense. The flowers she bought were for them, the food she cooked was for them. Drew understood that as well as she did. Even Sam had guessed, although Drew, of course, denied it. The first time Sam actually had appeared in time for dinner, Natalie had served them and heard them talking.

"You eat like this every night?" Sam had asked, more bemused than dismayed.

"She keeps thinking you'll be home."

"I doubt it. Wouldn't you be more comfortable eating off a tray in front of the TV or something when you're alone?"

"I don't eat alone. Natalie eats with me."

"Really?"

"Well, I'm not going to make her serve me and then go back into the kitchen. This isn't exactly Belvedere."

"I think, my dear, that Natalie does this not because she thinks I'm coming home, but because she's counting on the fact that I'm not."

"Shhh, she'll hear you. Don't be silly."

"Don't be naive."

"What are you saying?"

"I think she's got a crush on you."

"Oh, come on. She's all alone in Washington. She's got no one to talk to but Moira. She appreciates a little attention in the evening, that's all."

Sam laughed, "I'm sure she does."

"Stop," Drew said, but he was laughing with her.

After that, Natalie had excused herself by pleading sick on the rare occasions that Sam was home for the evening. There was no way she could stop Sam from eating her food, but she certainly wasn't going to serve it to her. It didn't bother her that Sam saw through her attempts to conceal her feelings for Drew through domestic routine. It was the fact that Sam didn't take her seriously and pushed Drew to share her sentiments. But Drew never laughed at her when they were alone.

She had just served the salad when they heard Moira calling.

"Nah-wee. Nah-wee," she gurgled in the closest

approximation she could come to Natalie's name. Natalie sighed.

"I'll get her," Drew offered.

"No way. You eat the salad. I got those mesculin greens you said you liked. They're too bitter for me. You have to eat it."

She leaped out of her chair and was up the stairs before Drew could object. Maybe if she changed her and stuck a bottle in her mouth, the little brat would go back to sleep and leave them in peace. But as she peeked into the nursery and saw Moira standing on her little legs bouncing up and down as she held on to the crib railing with her chubby hands, she knew it was not to be. The kid was wide awake. There was no point in leaving her there. She'd only start calling for Daddy, and then Drew would be lost to her for the rest of the night.

"I was afraid of this," Natalie announced as a surprised Drew greeted his smiling daughter with outstretched arms. "She didn't take a nap this afternoon, and she fell asleep at five. I was kind of hoping she might make it through the night. Guess not."

"Why aren't you asleep like all good little children?" Drew asked Moira, tickling her. It was clear he was not in the least distressed, and Moira responded with delighted laughter.

"She's definitely wide awake," said Natalie, resigned.

"What's that smell?" Drew asked suddenly, interrupting his play.

"Smew," repeated Moira, as it took a moment for Natalie to register.

"Oh my God," she screamed. "The salmon!" She

ran to the kitchen, and Drew followed with Moira in his arms.

There were little puffs of smoke rising from blackened mounds on the gourmet grill. Natalie looked ready to weep.

"I've got it," said Drew with a flourish toward the child in his arms and the young woman in front of him. "I'm going to take you ladies for a cruise."

"What?" Natalie tried not to let her heart fly out of her mouth.

"Why not? Moira's awake. Dinner's irredeemable. I bet you've never sailed up the Potomac."

"You're right." Natalie's tears were forgotten.

"Well neither have I. So tonight's the night. If we hurry, we can still make the dinner cruise on the *Spirit of Washington.*"

"We can?" Natalie was laughing now. "How do you know?"

"Actually, I checked it out when we first got here. It's really touristy—"

"I love touristy things," Natalie said hastily lest he change his mind.

"Well, good for you. Get a sweater for yourself and for Moira. Maybe the fresh air will put her to sleep. Then we can eat. They've got a show and dancing. We'll have fun."

Natalie didn't have to be told twice. Drew was taking her dancing under the stars. Even with the baby along, it was what she had dreamed of night after night.

In the main reading room of the Jefferson Building of the Library of Congress, Sam tried not to dream as she scanned the Congressional Records of the past five years looking for hearings on environmental issues.

She was only up to 1992 and it was already nine o'clock. She only had half an hour before the library closed. She rubbed her eyes and looked up at the one hundred sixty-foot-high ceiling, embellished with griffins and garlands. The man in the seat beside her rose and nodded to her.

"Do you want my paper?" he asked. "It's tomorrow's *Post.*"

"No thanks," she said, smiling politely. "Too much work."

He nodded again and headed out, dropping the paper in the wastebasket a few feet away. She hadn't intended to read it, but something in the headline struck her. Feeling a little foolish, she got up and retrieved the paper from the garbage.

The headline read, "Civil War Breaks Out in San Domenico." Sam felt her heart start to beat and she became conscious of holding her breath while she skimmed the article. According to the *Washington Post,* rebels had commandeered the airport and radio stations. There were pockets of fighting throughout the island. Access to information was limited.

"I don't believe this," she gasped. She raced to the bank of telephones she had noticed when she arrived, ignoring the dirty looks of the librarians who coughed meaningfully and turned away. Her hands were already in her Gucci knapsack, rummaging for her computer phone file. Still empty-handed when she reached the phones, she dumped the entire bag on the floor at her feet, picking up the wayward file as it clunked on the floor. Nervously, she pecked out the name m-e-l-i-n-d-a, then hit search. Breathlessly repeating the number to herself, she dialed, listened for the beep that signaled her to enter her credit card, punched in that number, too, and waited.

"We're sorry. Due to the political situation in the country you are calling, your call cannot be completed as dialed," came the recorded response.

Sam felt the desperation rise. "Oh God, what do I do now?" Sam stared blankly at the phone, as if waiting for an answer, then dropped it as reality registered. "Amos! Of course."

The night had been balmy, and she had strolled down First Street to the Library of Congress. Now, she ran all the way back to the Russell Building and straight into Amos Kilmont's office.

"He's got someone with him, Mrs. Sym—" Dotty started to say, but Sam had already raced past her and thrown open the door.

"Amos, I'm sorry. Please excuse me," she said to the startled gentleman who had been in animated conversation with the senator. "This is an emergency. My sister is in San Domenico. I can't get hold of her. Please, Amos, you have to help me."

"Of course," Amos said quietly and immediately won her heart. She stopped listening while he gently but rapidly ushered his guest out, trying to focus her mind on thinking positive thoughts. He was back at her side in minutes, taking her hand, telling her not to worry. No one on the Hill was taking this revolution seriously.

"I am," she said. "My sister is there. If anything happened . . ."

He tried to make her see logic. "Nothing is going to happen to her. She's an American movie star. All revolutions are a battle for hearts and minds. You don't get a lot of points for hurting someone everybody loves."

"Aren't Americans always the scapegoats whenever there's internal turmoil in any country?"

"Not always. Okay, sometimes they storm the embassy. But San Domenico doesn't have an American embassy, so that's not a problem."

"Can you help me find her?"

"Of course I can."

He spoke with such assurance that for the first time since she'd seen the newspaper, her heart slowed to its normal pace. She let the relief flood her as she watched him take control.

"Dotty," he said over the intercom, "get me Colin Powell."

Sam was confused. "I thought he was retired."

"He is," said Amos. "That's why he can talk to me. He knows everything that goes on of a military nature anywhere in the world. And he's not sworn to secrecy like the people who are still involved. And he's a friend. He'll tell us what's going on."

His intercom buzzed and he broke off abruptly, picking up the phone. "Colin, thank you for getting on the horn with me right away . . . Fine . . . Golf was great . . . But, listen, I've got a situation here. There's a lady in my office . . ." He stopped and laughed, then went on, "No, no. Not that kind of situation . . . I need to know about San Domenico." Then he just listened.

Seven minutes later, clocked by Sam on her watch, he hung up. She searched his face, trying to ascertain if the news was good or bad. He saw her fear and went to her, folding her in his arms, holding her close as if to comfort her. But Sam wasn't ready to be comforted and pulled away.

"What?" she asked. "Did you find out anything?"

"There's a revolution going on down there."

"I know that already," she said, ready to explode.

"No one on the Hill is taking it seriously as yet. But that's not to say the situation might not escalate at any time. Things can get volatile very quickly down there. We've got to get your sister out."

"Can you do that for me?"

"I'm damn well going to try."

She would have kissed him for that, and he must have sensed it. Not waiting, he stepped toward her, arms open. Taken aback, she side-stepped him, and they bumped awkwardly. But in the next instant he was back at his desk, all business, making more calls, motioning her to sit on the couch while he did what had to be done. He put someone on hold and commanded Dotty to bring her tea. He hung up one call and made another, then another. He spoke in Spanish, then English, then Spanish again. Until, finally, he reached the telephone out to her. She looked at him questioning, but he only answered with a smile and placed the receiver in her hand.

"H . . . hello? Who is this?" she could barely get the words out.

"Hello? Sam? Is that you?"

"Oh my God, my God. Melinda. I don't believe it." She was gasping for breath. "Where are you? Are you okay?"

"Sam. I'm okay. It's weird here. We're in the presidential palace. The whole cast and crew."

"I tried to call you at the hotel. But of course I couldn't get through."

"I know. We were told all the lines were off. How did you get to me?"

"I didn't. Amos Kilmont did."

"Who?"

"He's a senator. It's a long story. Not for now. Listen, Melinda. He's going to help me get you out of there. Okay?"

"That would be great. But there are about twenty of us."

Sam looked at Amos. "Look, I don't know about the others. He's doing me a tremendous favor . . ."

"I can't go and leave the others behind, Sam. It wouldn't be right. Anyway, it might not even be necessary. Jorge says they've got things under control."

"Who?"

"Jorge Alvarro."

"The president?"

"Yeah. It's a long story. Not for now. Anyway, he says its not a real revolution. It's just a bunch of insurgents who don't like the drastic measures he's had to take to try to turn his country around. The army is taking care of it."

"Are you okay?"

"Absolutely. I'm being treated like royalty. If there weren't a whole lot of shooting going on outside the palace walls, I'd tell you to come down here and meet me. It's a fabulous place."

"Maybe some other time," Sam said sardonically. "I still think it would be a good idea for you to leave. Amos is working on it. Something about getting some journalists in who will be able to get you out."

"Thank you."

"You're welcome."

"Sam?" Melinda's voice sounded small, and Sam thought she detected a quiver.

"What, honey?"

"Myles Militia forever."

"You better believe it, babe." Sam heard a popping sound in the background. "What's that? Is that shooting?" The phone went dead.

"Melinda? Melinda?" she tried again, jiggling the phone as if she could shake her sister back. But there was only the hum of an empty line. She looked at the phone in her hand, tears springing to her eyes. Gently, Amos reached out and prodded her fingers from the receiver, placing it back on the hook. He came around to her side of the desk, and again he put his arms around her. This time, unable to control the fear and the emotion, she let herself sink against his shoulder and cry.

"Shh . . . shh . . . ," he soothed. "Your sister is going to be all right. I'm going to get her out of there if I have to commandeer *Air Force One* and fly it down there myself."

Gratitude welled inside her. She knew it was no idle promise. She'd seen Senator Kilmont at work, watched him lobby his friends in the House and the Senate for things he wanted. He was rarely refused.

"Oh, Amos," she choked. "You're really going to do this for me, aren't you?"

"You bet I am."

"I don't know how I'm going to be able to repay you."

"I do," he said softly. And then he kissed her hard on the mouth.

It took a second to register what he was doing, and then she pulled away fast. "Don't do that," she said and felt as though shards of steel were coming out of her throat. "Not again. Not ever."

He held his hands open to her in a display of innocence.

"Sam," he said softly, and it sounded almost accusing, as if she had wronged him. "I just want to help you."

There was no guile in his face or his voice, but somehow it sounded vaguely threatening. "I'm going home," she said, suddenly weary. "I'm going to spend whatever is left of this evening with my husband . . . your friend," she added pointedly.

"Good idea," Amos said. "Give Drew my best. And don't you worry. I've got a handle on the situation with your sister. Let's see if I can make things happen there."

She looked at him sharply. She wasn't sure if he was making a threat or a promise. He smiled, giving no clue.

She wouldn't let herself think about it on the way home. She would talk to Drew, get his perspective on it, find out more about Amos. She would lie in his arms and feel safe, and he would tell her what to do. Coming up the driveway, she was a little taken aback to see the house so dark. She glanced at her watch. It was still only ten-thirty. Perhaps everyone had gone to bed early. That was all right. She would slip into bed beside Drew, wake him up. He wouldn't mind.

She tiptoed up the stairs and peeked into Moira's room. The sight of her sleeping child never failed to soothe her. But the crib was empty. Assuming the baby had climbed out of bed and gone to her daddy, she moved to the bedroom. But it only took a second of adjusting to the dark to see that the bed had not been slept in. She switched on the light and started calling, "Drew? Moira?" Confused, she ran downstairs. She knocked on Natalie's door and opened it a crack when there was no answer—empty as well. She took a deep breath and went to the kitchen, holding down the tiny knot of fear that had lodged itself at the bottom of her chest in preparation. Then she saw the note laid prominently on the counter. "Dear Sam, We'll probably be home before you, but just in case. Moira couldn't sleep. We took her for a cruise. Be home soon."

Sam felt the tears spring to her eyes. They had talked about sailing up the Potomac on the *Spirit of Washington* together. She was hurt that they'd gone without her. "This is silly," she said out loud to herself. "I wasn't here. It's no big deal. I'm tired. And upset. I should just go to sleep."

She dragged herself back up the stairs and, not even bothering to wash her face, stripped off her clothes and climbed into bed. She didn't hear the key turn in the lock a half hour later. She didn't hear the giggles as Drew held the sleeping baby, and they stumbled in the dark. She didn't hear Natalie whisper to Drew that this had been the nicest night of her life or see Drew kiss the top of Natalie's head as she floated away.

Drew put the baby in her crib and tiptoed into the bedroom, where his wife slept. He kept the light off so as not to disturb her. He undressed quickly and eased himself onto the far side of the bed. He lay on his side and looked at his wife, bathed in moonlight, her copper curls spread around her. She was remarkably beautiful. He ran his hand along her cheek, into the pillow, and was surprised to feel that it was damp. He realized she had been crying, and he

was tempted to wake her to resolve whatever it was
that was upsetting them both. But he remembered the
morning's argument and wasn't sure how she'd react.
The evening had been pleasant, and he wasn't up to
another confrontation. Finally, he turned away, facing
the wall, and let himself drift into sleep, feeling as
alone as he ever had in all the years they'd been
married.

～❦ 6 ❦～

A week after they had closed down the airport, the rebels opened one runway to allow a planeload of foreign press to arrive. Mostly the journalists were billeted in the hotel rooms that the film crew had vacated, but they were permitted an hour in the presidential palace each day for briefing. All of them were aware that the real story may have been about the military controlling the uprising, but the *good* story was about the American film crew that got stuck in the presidential palace.

"What are we doing here?" Melinda whispered over her shoulder to Elgar as they filed into the ballroom, which had been set up with folding chairs to accommodate the members of the press.

"El presidente asked us to be at today's press conference. We're his guests. We do what he says."

The photographers were shouting her name as if it

was opening night at the Cannes Film Festival, trying to get her to look in their direction.

"Miss Myles, this way."

"Melinda, Melinda. Over here, please."

"Hey, guys," Melinda said, raising her voice just enough to be heard. "Calm down. This is a revolution, not a photo opportunity." There was laughter and more flashbulbs. Melinda noticed a few people scribbling.

"Can we have a shot with you and Tommy?" someone shouted. Tommy, garnering his share of media attention on the other side of Elgar, pretended he hadn't heard, and Melinda followed suit.

There was a staccato of static and then a disembodied voice announced, *"El presidente de* San Domenico, Jorge Alvarro." It took a moment for Melinda's eyes to adjust as instantaneously, the bright white eye of the cameras stopped beaming on her and began to wink in the direction of the president. Melinda felt herself gently prodded to the dais, where seats had been set up for them behind the podium. She moved to take a seat on the end, but again, she was distinctly nudged to the chair directly to the right of the podium, closest to the post that the president himself was about to assume. As the president began his prepared statement, which he had read to her the night before, Melinda studied the press corps. There were people she recognized: Peter Jennings from ABC and Jeff Greenfield from CBS. She even thought she caught a glimpse of Connie Chung. Then there were others that were vaguely familiar, faces she had seen while channel surfing through the local news back home.

She was almost surprised. Walking in the grounds of

the palace, having festive dinners with cast and crew and assorted palace insiders, spending quiet evenings alone in the garden with Jorge, the revolution had seemed far away. There had been the occasional horror story that Jorge felt compelled to share with her, usually centered around some atrocity perpetrated by Diego Roca, the acknowledged rebel leader. But it was always as though she were a child being told a cautionary fable rather than an irrefutable reality. She had never expected any of it to be newsworthy outside of San Domenico. Apparently, she had been wrong.

Jorge barely had time to finish before the hands were raised and the voices began calling to be recognized: "Mr. President! Mr. President! Señor Alvarro! Please, sir!"

He pointed to Jeff Greenfield.

"Jeff Greenfield, CBS," he identified himself. Melinda listened carefully. Of all the news commentators, she had found him to be among the more astute. "You say that the revolution will fail because it is not a popularly supported movement. Yet isn't it true that the government has failed to regain any territory, specifically in the northern part of the island, because the inhabitants refuse to cooperate and are joining forces with Roca and his followers?"

"You are misinformed, Mr. Greenfield." Melinda could hear the edge in Jorge's voice. "Diego Roca is a bandit, not a revolutionary. His followers, as you put it, are a handful of misfits and criminals. They have temporarily gained control of certain territory, the way, let's say, in your country, the inmates of Attica have, on occasion, taken over the prison. Normal people, right-thinking people, do not support this.

And, of course, an uprising such as this cannot succeed. The outlaws will be brought to justice."

"But Mr. President . . . ," Greenfield had begun again and Melinda had listened, hoping to learn more than Jorge had revealed to her. But the president was already entertaining his next question. Melinda had been right. Connie Chung was there.

"Thank you, Mr. President," Connie began. "Of course I recognize the members of the American film community on your dais. And I know that they were here making a movie and got caught in the crossfire when the revolution began. But do you think that rumors that you are behind these palace walls cavorting with an American movie star, Melinda Myles, while people are fighting in the streets could be contributing to the difficulty of your political situation right now?"

Melinda gasped and felt her face flush. To her shock, Jorge laughed and motioned to her to join him at the podium. She wanted to run away or, at the very least, sink into the floor. Elgar nudged her and hissed, "Go on. He's the president. It wouldn't be good to make a scene."

She tried to play it like a part as she approached the front of the dais, but her legs felt wooden and her motivation was all wrong. Something had gone seriously awry with the script. It made no sense at all for her to be here. The flashbulbs had begun popping again, and Jorge put his arm around her and smiled, urging her to do the same, feeding the frenzy as cameras zoomed in to devour them.

"Miss Myles," Jorge said evenly when they'd taken all the pictures they could possibly use, "and her friends and fellow workers are invited guests in my country. Their presence was of great importance, adding to our economic development and touristic image. I have offered them my protection and am grateful that they have accepted. It would shame us all if any harm were to come to them when their only fault was in appreciating the beauty and opportunity of San Domenico."

Connie Chung was on her now. "Miss Myles, is there something more personal between you and *el presidente?*"

But *el presidente* had not finished. "What the press and outside nations have not appreciated yet is that the timing of this so-called revolution was specifically arranged to coincide with the Hollywood presence here. A few bandits shooting in the streets of a small island does not get worldwide coverage. But movie stars being forced to take cover in the presidential palace—and even better, some indecency with the president himself—this makes news. Diego Roca does not know what the people of San Domenico want. But he knows what the news media wants. You are here, are you not, Ms. Chung?"

There was an uncomfortable shuffling for the space of a breath, and then the shouting began again: "Mr. President . . . Miss Myles . . ." But the president waved a hand and indicated the press conference was over. He took Melinda's arm, then turned to Elgar and Tommy, indicating that they should join them as they made their way off the dais together.

This time, Melinda needed no prodding. She let one hand rest on the arm of Jorge Alvarro and clasped Elgar's with the other. She should have trusted Jorge.

He understood what needed to be said and how to say it. There was nothing to hide or be ashamed of. If what Jorge said was true, and she had no reason to doubt him, they had been thrust into this situation by outlaws trying to exploit some high-profile Hollywood figures for their own fifteen minutes of fame. And if Jorge wanted to share the spotlight with her, so be it. Obviously, the man knew what he was doing.

"Did you see that horseshit?" Lucia Alvarro said to General Raul Guzman as she clicked off the monitor and turned to view herself in the mirror. They had been watching the press conference in her private apartment in the palace, an overdone suite of rooms with heavy, dark wooden furniture and hung with scarlet damask drapes that gave it an almost medieval aura. Like most of the educated upper class in San Domenico, they spoke English. The habit had begun as a way to keep the servants from eavesdropping on conversations and evolved into a status symbol.

"As though Diego Roca could give a rat's ass about some Hollywood whore," she went on, repositioning her breasts in her décolletage in order to maximize her cleavage. "Jorge wants to fuck her, that's all."

"Maybe. But he didn't arrange for a revolution just to get her into the palace. It's real, what's going on out there."

Lucia gave him a withering look before returning to her personal scrutiny. "Thank you, Raul, for that lesson in civics."

"Did you call me here just to berate me, Lucia?" He sounded almost hopeful, and Lucia sneered at him.

"You are incorrigible. You spend your days committing cruelty, then you come to me for penance."

He smiled wickedly. "And why not? Don't you think it's justice?"

"I think it's perverted."

He laughed. "You enjoy it as much as I do."

He watched himself in the mirror as he reached in front of her to stroke the ample expanse of bosom emerging from her black leather corset. Black net stockings and high-heeled shoes completed her outfit. Cliché that it was, her ensemble was still highly effective. She smiled and leaned over as if to afford him more access. He did not notice that she had removed her shoe until she had driven the stiletto heel into the back of his hand.

He writhed in pain and felt the pleasure penetrate his hardened desire. Only Lucia understood how important this was to him. Only Lucia knew that the joy he experienced at her playful punishment made it possible for him to continue to savor the brutal persecution of his enemies.

She unlocked the bottom drawer of her vanity and pulled out the instruments of their special relationship: clamps, handcuffs, and a whip. He shivered with delight as he quickly removed his uniform, careful to fold the creases correctly. Lucia was in a commanding mood. He would be satisfied tonight.

"And what of my satisfaction?" she asked when, under her skilled ministrations, his agony had erupted in ecstasy.

"Don't worry," he said. "A very handsome young soldier. Just recruited. He thinks he's coming on guard duty here at ten."

"Did I make you happy tonight, Raul?"

"Ah, Lucia. It was exquisite."

"Good. I want a favor. A small thing."

"Name it."

"When I'm done, I don't want this soldier taken care of in the usual fashion."

"Not paid off?"

"No. I want him dressed in peasant clothes and sent out front. I want Jorge's men to see him."

"He's a new recruit. They don't know him. If he's caught without his uniform, they'll think he's an infiltrator. He'll be killed."

"Yes," she said pensively. "It's a small thing."

Jorge Alvarro watched a videotape of his press conference and smiled grimly. It was Diego Roca who had invited the press into San Domenico, hoping for sympathy for the rebel cause. But Alvarro was confident that by using Roca's own choice of weapons, he had scored a few points of his own. He had no doubt that Roca would inundate them with propaganda of his own, and the press could be malleable. But there was nothing the press hated more than feeling manipulated, and Alvarro had already planted that seed. Whatever Roca said, they would be afraid to accept it at face value.

Alvarro was also aware that he had impressed Melinda Myles with his handling of the press conference. His intention at having her and her colleagues there had been more to create the proper atmosphere for the government: civilized, sympathetic to American concerns, and just a little glamorous. But the way she had looked at him after he'd squelched that pushy newswoman had been the bonus. He had been moving toward just such an acknowledgment in her eyes in the weeks he'd been courting her. But it had been slow in coming, and he knew women too well to risk making an approach before that look had lighted his way. But this afternoon, he'd seen it in the way she met his gaze, and standing in front of her door with a bottle of champagne and two glasses, he knew he would not be refused.

He knocked gently, and she opened the door without asking who it was. He smiled. He had been expected. Her hair was still wet from the shower, and her silk robe clung to spots on her skin that the towel had missed. Unadorned, all artifice removed, she was more delectable than ever.

"I've just about finished packing," she said quietly as she led him to the sofa. She'd been provided with one of the grander suites, an elegant sitting room adjacent to a plush bedroom, of which the central feature was a large canopied bed. Aside from being close to his own rooms, it was also very romantic, with a small balcony over the courtyard, through which the intoxicating scent of jasmine floated. The doors to the balcony were open, letting in a floral air of moonlight, and he was pleased to note the atmosphere was never more effective than it was tonight.

"Of course. You are leaving on the journalists' plane tomorrow."

"Yes. My sister is working for a senator. Apparently, he was able to get them to send down a plane big enough to take us all back."

"I wish I could say I was happy for you," he said wistfully as he popped the cork.

She took the glass he held out to her. "Jorge, I'm very grateful."

"For what? For getting you caught in a messy political situation you have no business being in?"

"No. For opening my eyes to the beauty of your

country. The rest is not your fault. I know you didn't arrange for this to happen."

"No, but I didn't stop it either. But I will. I promise you that. And then, you must come back."

"I can promise that," she said, "with no problem at all."

He refilled his glass and her own and waited for her to drink before taking it out of her hand and placing it on the table.

"You have shown me beauty also, Melinda. Inside." He pointed to his head, to his heart.

She had been anticipating this with both dread and desire. Jorge Alvarro was handsome, charming, erudite. He was interesting to listen to and interested in listening to her. He was gentle and unfailingly polite. He was also married and the president of a small country in the throes of civil unrest. A casual affair would be inappropriate. Anything else would be impossible. She took a deep breath, hoping to clear her head, but the air was redolent with flowers and, mixed with the champagne, made her feel like she was floating.

"Jorge . . . ," she began, not certain if she meant to plead with him to stop or to go on. But he didn't wait for her to choose. Gently, he pressed his lips against hers, testing, not demanding. She made no move to embrace him, but she did not move away either. It was all the encouragement he needed. He kissed her again.

"Jorge, I can't. The situation . . . your wife . . . I'm going tomorrow . . ." She couldn't seem to say it coherently, but she knew he understood.

"Life is complicated," he said diffidently. "Love is not. My country is in turmoil. Lucia is more an alliance than a wife. When you go, I will be alone. Let me share my heart with you. I have nothing else to give you, and there is nothing else I want."

He ran his fingers down her cheek. She sighed, and he knew that he had won. This time, when he kissed her, it was not gentle. There was passion in his caress, and he felt her blood stirring beneath his touch. Slowly, so she hardly knew it was happening, he untwisted the ties of her robe and caught his breath as it fell open, revealing the beauty of dark secrets on ivory skin.

"What am I doing?" Melinda wondered to herself. "This is crazy." But by then, his hand had moved to her breast, and she realized it was too late for questions.

Suddenly, there was shouting, followed by gunshots. They had become accustomed to the sound of automatic fire but always at a distance, like a percussive backdrop too faint to interfere with the melody of daily life. But this sounded close, as though it was coming from beneath the window. Jorge let her go and ran to the balcony. Frightened and self-conscious, Melinda pulled her robe around herself and followed.

At first she could only see a group of palace guards in a huddle, and for one absurd moment, she thought they were playing a game, circling the quarterback for their next move. Then she realized that in the center of the huddle was a man, lying on the ground, and the surrounding players were beating and kicking him.

"My God, Jorge. They are going to kill him."

"He must be an intruder."

"How do you know? How can they know? Whatever he is, he doesn't deserve to be beaten to death. Don't you have a justice system in San Domenico?"

El presidente frowned. He had looked at the man.

He did not know him. Whoever he was, he had no business being on the palace grounds. He was especially annoyed that the intruder had interrupted what was about to become a most successful evening. And for that alone, Jorge believed the man deserved whatever he got. He would have liked to pick up where they had left off, but he could see that in Melinda's agitated state, there would be no possibility of that unless he made it appear that he would handle the matter and, at the very least, remove the entire scene from her line of vision.

He shot his pistol in the air, making Melinda jump and let out an involuntary scream. The men in the huddle rose, without letting their quarry do the same, and looked in the direction of the shot.

"Do not harm him," Jorge shouted when he had their attention. "I am coming to investigate and to see that laws of justice are obeyed."

The men stopped laughing. They were confused. *El presidente* must be joking, they assumed. They were meting out justice the way they usually did—not only with *el presidente*'s approval, but with his encouragement.

"Thank you," Melinda whispered.

"I will come back to you," Jorge promised, silently reminding himself to bring another bottle of champagne, as he would, in all likelihood, need to start over from the beginning.

Across the courtyard, Lucia watched her husband comfort the woman he intended to make his lover. She saw him take his leave and appear, moments later, in the courtyard below. She could see he was annoyed, and it made her smile to think of what the little commotion had interrupted.

"Now, Raul," she said to the general waiting inside her room, out of sight. "She is alone. Do it now."

Moments later there was a knock on Melinda's door. For a moment, she was confused. Standing on the balcony, she had just seen Jorge striding over to his men, already issuing orders. How could he have returned so quickly?

"Miss Myles, it is General Guzman. *El presidente* has sent me to fetch you."

She opened the door. She'd met Guzman frequently at palace dinners, but they'd rarely exchanged more than a few pleasantries. There was something about the smugness of his smile that had always put her off.

"I don't understand. I thought he was coming back here," she said, instantly regretting her words. Dressed as she was in her robe, she seemed so transparent and indiscreet. But the general appeared not to notice.

"The situation is graver than he thought. The rebels have infiltrated the palace. You are in danger. You must come with me."

Melinda felt her heart quicken. "What about Elgar and Tommy and the others?"

"Don't worry. They will be protected also. It is just safer if we move each of you separately. We do not wish to attract the attention of the guerrillas."

That made sense. "Okay. Let me just get dressed and finish packing."

"There is no time. We must go now. While they are still distracted in the courtyard."

"But . . ."

"Please, Miss Myles. Is your life worth a bag full of clothes? We must go now or it will be too late."

The general took her arm firmly and guided her out.

He was moving quickly and she had to run to keep up. She didn't have time to think. He led her through back corridors that she hadn't seen before, and out a side entrance where a car with blackened windows waited. He opened the back door and urged her in. She looked around, hoping for a sign of the others. She would have even been happy to see Tommy at that moment. But there was no one. She was alone with the general.

"Go," he said and pushed her into the car.

She wanted to protest but held her tongue, assuming that his rough treatment arose out of concern for her safety. The night was balmy, but she pulled her robe tighter around her, shivering a little, more with fear than cold. She hoped someone on the plane had an extra pair of sweats or something she could borrow. She didn't relish landing in the United States to a hail of press photographers in her robe and slippers. She stopped herself. Had she become so much a movie star that she was more concerned with how she looked than getting out alive?

The drive took longer than she expected, the roads were bumpier. She peered out of the darkened windows and noticed they were no longer in view of the villages and open fields she remembered from her previous drives. Palm fronds brushed against the windows and huge rubber plants hung like arches over the top of the car as they bounced along a dirt road. They seemed to be driving through a jungle and, ahead, lay more of the same.

"We are going to the airport, aren't we?" she asked nervously, suddenly realizing the general had only said he was taking her to safety but had never mentioned where exactly that was.

"Of course," he answered. "A plane is waiting for you there. But we have to use back roads so no one will spot us."

"And the others?"

"They will be at the airport, coming by different routes."

She stopped asking questions then but couldn't subdue the thread of suspicion that began to snake its way from her stomach to her throat. When the shots came and the car screeched to a halt, terror gripped her. But she was not surprised.

She screamed when the butt of a rifle smashed through her window and a hand reached in to unlock the door. Through her thin silk robe, she felt the cold steel of the gun's barrel as it prodded her side, indicating that it was time to get out of the car. She trembled as she emerged from the car and saw that they were surrounded by men wearing camouflage, their faces covered with bandannas or ski masks that left only their eyes visible. The men were shouting at the general, who stood with his hands raised in surrender. She could not understand what they said. But there was no mistaking the meaning of the guns that faced her from all directions or the eyes of her assailants, black and hard and devoid of pity.

Suddenly, the general seemed to lose control. Shouting back at their captors, he swung around blindly than raced back to the car. Melinda cringed, closing her eyes, waiting for the rat-a-tat of machine-gun fire she was certain would follow. A second later, hearing only the sound of the car starting, she opened them again. She watched in horror as the car careened back down the road they had come. She looked around her. Guns were trained on her from all directions. And then she realized what had happened, and she began to scream. She kept screaming until someone shook her hard and said in English, "Stop. It will do you no good. You are a hostage of the San Domenican Liberation Front."

By the time Jorge Alvarro reached the courtyard, the intruder had been beaten senseless. He made a vague attempt to find out what had happened, but in fact, his heart and mind were still with the beautiful woman he had left upstairs, and he had little interest in the fate of a stranger, who was, in all probability, an infiltrator. His guards were adept at handling situations like this, and he would not even have graced the scene with his presence had not Melinda insisted. He stayed only long enough to make it appear that he was taking humane action, conspicuously calling for them to cease their beating of the hapless victim. He saw her watching briefly from the balcony, but when she disappeared, he quickly told the captain of the guard to get rid of the man, dispose of the body, and do it all out of sight of the palace. Then, he hurried back to his waiting movie star, his blood quickening with the thought of what they had begun and what he would, at last, be able to finish.

The door ajar did not alert him. She was as anxious as he to return to what they had been doing, he assumed. She was anticipating his arrival. The empty room did not alarm him. Everything was just as it had been when he left not ten minutes ago. Perhaps she was in the bathroom. He envisioned her standing naked at her mirror, his hands familiarizing themselves with her body. Slowly, he pushed open the door, softly breathing her name. It only took a moment for him to realize that she was not there and that he was alone. Then, he knew there was something to fear.

He forced himself to calm down and think. He was a man whose powers of logic kicked in at moments of panic. If Melinda was gone, it could only be because someone had made her go, if not by force, then by reason. There was only one person who could possibly care if he spent a night with the American movie star. Only one person who would enjoy depriving him of the pleasure.

"Lucia!" he roared as he stormed down the hall. "Lucia!" He threw open her door, not bothering to knock, and found his wife not a moment too soon, climbing over her balcony.

"What the hell are you doing?" he shouted at her, grabbing her, pulling her back. She screamed back at him to let her go, and he noticed that she fought him off with only one hand. The other clutched a small case to her bosom so tightly that her knuckles were white. He looked below. A ladder leaned against the palace wall. A car was waiting.

"Is she in there?" he asked, indicating the car.

Lucia laughed, a bitter, scornful sound. "What would I want with your whore? She is gone."

"Where?" She tried to pull her arm away from him, but he held tight. "Where?" he demanded again.

"To the rebels," she spat out. "Her life for mine. We are finished here. The revolution spreads slowly, but they will win. Diego Roca is not stupid. He knows it will take time, and he will need money, protection.

Hostages. I would be of no use. Who would ransom me? But the movie star—no American bombs will drop on her. And she could fetch a tidy sum."

Alvarro looked at his wife with both new horror and new respect. "You traded your life for hers?"

"Why not? Wouldn't you have done the same?"

"Where are you going?"

"They have guaranteed me free passage to the port. A ship is waiting. Cuba. Haiti. I don't know. From there, perhaps to the south of France. They are kind to former dictators there."

"Former dictators who can pay," he amended and noticed her shift the small satchel surreptitiously, trying to maneuver it out of sight. He grabbed it.

"Give that to me," she shouted. "It's mine."

He opened it quickly. The contents glittered, capturing moonbeams in its folds. He saw diamonds, emeralds, rubies, gold, platinum; a treasure of necklaces, bracelets, rings, and tiaras that had been gifts to her, as wife of the head of state, over the years. He knew the value to be tens of millions of dollars.

"Yours?" he questioned sardonically.

"Give it back." She grabbed for it, but he pulled his hand away. She knew there was no hope of his giving it to her, no hope of her surviving without it. "Come with me," she said.

She saw the flicker in his eyes, knew he was as afraid as she was. If the rebels reached the presidential palace, as they surely would one day in the not too distant future, *el presidente* would not be treated kindly. In spite of the benevolent image he liked to portray for his guests, his pride in insisting he was democratically elected, it had been a long time since democracy ruled in San Domenico. His people knew him as a cruel pretender who robbed the coffers of the country while proclaiming his concern for its poverty-stricken inhabitants. And those who were not on his payroll, not his sycophants, detested him.

They stared at each other for a minute, their hatred for each other naked and palpable. There was a soft honk from the car below.

He gave her his hand, "Let's go."

She let him guide her over the rail of the balcony and onto the ladder. He followed, the satchel of jewels safely stashed in his inside pocket. By the time General Raul Guzman returned to the presidential palace, Jorge and Lucia Alvarro were gone. It took Guzman thirty minutes to consolidate his power and proclaim an emergency military rule in San Domenico, with himself the de facto leader.

By morning, even the Americans, gathering in the courtyard, had heard that a military junta had occurred. More anxious than ever to get out of the country before whatever powers that be changed their minds and refused to let them go, they paced in front of the minibus waiting to take them to the airport.

"Where the fuck is she?" asked Tommy for the tenth time. "She's the only one not here. She's probably holed up with *el presidente* somewhere. Let's just go."

"We're not leaving without Melinda," Elgar was adamant. But he could see that Tommy wasn't the only one who was impatient. He didn't understand it. It was not like Melinda to keep people waiting, especially in such a critical situation. "I'll go to her room and see what's happening."

Elgar headed back into the palace. He was as nervous as the rest of them, but he was still trying to maintain some directorial dignity. But his resolve failed almost immediately when a soldier with a gun blocked the entrance and told him he could not enter. Somehow, with Alvarro gone, even though none of them had been overtly threatened, there was an air of menace that had not been there before.

Elgar hoped his trembling didn't show as he explained, "I'm just going to get Miss Myles. She must have overslept or something, and we're kind of late—"

"No," the soldier cut him off abruptly. "No entry."

It was clear there would be no point in arguing with this man. He wasn't even sure the guy could understand English. Hoping to convey his urgency with his tone of voice if not his language, Elgar got louder. "I need to get Miss Myles. Now."

"No entry," was the only response.

Elgar turned around and saw the crew loading into the bus. He wasn't going to be able to keep them here much longer, but he wasn't going to let them leave without Melinda either.

He started to shout, "Melinda! Can you hear me? Melinda? Are you up there?"

The soldier brandished his gun and tried to shout over him, but Elgar refused to give up. "I am not leaving," he screamed at the soldier, "until Miss Myles comes down here."

In an instant, General Guzman himself appeared at the end of the corridor, striding purposefully toward Elgar.

Elgar felt himself shake. "Act calm," he told himself. "Don't let him see he scares you."

But the general was as affable as he had been at the

various dinners they'd shared as guests of the man he'd deposed. "Mr. Franz, what seems to be the problem?"

"Oh . . . uh . . . hi, General," said Elgar, opting for a show of casual ignorance. "I was just going to get Melinda. We're supposed to be on that journalist plane and she's kind of late."

"But Mr. Franz, didn't anyone tell you?"

"Tell me what?"

"Miss Myles has already gone. When the unfortunate political situation forced President Alvarro and his wife to leave hastily last night, Miss Myles decided to go with them."

"What?!"

"She didn't inform you?"

"She didn't even leave a note. This is unbelievable."

"I'm afraid it's true. Perhaps, in all the haste, she forgot. You know, things can get quite hectic when . . ." He shrugged, leaving Elgar to imagine the rest. "In fact, I think it would be a good idea for you and your friends to hurry a little yourselves. There is only one plane leaving San Domenico, and if you are not on it, well, shall we say, things might get hectic again."

Elgar was reeling. It seemed incredible that Melinda would just take off and not say anything to him. On the other hand, although they'd never talked about it, everyone on the film suspected that Melinda and Jorge Alvarro were having an affair. He supposed it must be true.

"Actors!" he sighed with disgust as he ran toward the bus, which was already revving its engines. He expected he'd be reading about her in *People* magazine in a week or two, talking about her dramatic escape and her fabulous new life somewhere on the Riviera.

The phone was ringing. Gradually, it penetrated Sam's deep, dreamless sleep and floated her back to the surface of consciousness. She sat up and saw that Drew was still asleep beside her. The clock on her bedside said eight. They must have all slept in. She picked up the phone and forced some cheer into her voice to try to camouflage the fact that she'd just been awakened. She did not succeed.

"Did I wake you?" Amos Kilmont asked after all she'd said was hello.

"Amos . . . oh . . . no . . . it's fine . . . I mean . . ." She couldn't pull her thoughts together. She had a vivid memory of his body pressing against her and an urge to slam down the phone. But he'd never called her at home before. She wondered if he were going to apologize.

"It doesn't matter. I've got news worth waking up for. Your sister's on her way home."

"What?!" Suddenly, her mind was completely clear. "Melinda's coming home?"

"Yup. There's been a coup. Don't say anything because it's not even in the news yet, but the president has fled the country and a military junta has taken over."

"Oh my God."

"But don't worry. I called my connection down in San Domenico. I made sure all our people got out of there—the journalists and the film group. The plane got off this morning. They should be landing in L.A. in a few hours."

"Oh, Amos. Thank you. I was afraid after last night . . . But you still did this for me."

"Hey, forget about it. You take things too seriously, Sam. I like to kid around, that's all. Glad I was able to make everything work out okay for you. Say hi to your husband. And get into the office, will you? We've still got a report to finish."

"Okay," she laughed. "Thanks Amos. I really owe you."

"Forget about it," he said again and hung up.

"What was that all about?" Drew asked groggily, looking at Sam's shining face,

Sam didn't know where to begin. She felt like years had gone by since they last spoke, but it had been only a day. There was too much to say and she was too tired to say it all, so she opted for the abbreviated version.

"Melinda was caught in the revolution in San Domenico."

Drew was shocked. "What? I didn't hear anything about that. How do you know?"

"It was in last night's edition of today's paper. You'll see it in the paper this morning."

"Why didn't you tell me, for God's sake?"

"You weren't here. Remember?" she said quietly, trying not to sound accusatory.

He felt guilty. That's why she had cried herself to sleep, and he'd been too much of a coward to wake her and find out what was wrong because he'd assumed it was about them. "That's why you were upset."

"Among other things," she said, deciding in that instant that there was no point in dwelling on what had happened with Amos. He had gotten her message,

139

and he had still come through for her. There was
nothing to be gained by making an issue out of it.
"Anyway, it doesn't matter. Amos just told me she's
on a plane on her way back to Los Angeles."

"So everything's all right?" he asked, and she heard
in his voice that he wasn't just talking about Melinda.
She looked at him. His eyelids were still at a sleepy
half-mast, their black lashes framing brilliant blue
eyes that managed to look clear even without enough
sleep. A lock of his black hair had fallen over his face,
and she couldn't resist the temptation to brush it off
his forehead.

"You need a haircut," she said.

"I need you," he answered and pulled her to him.

They kissed, tasting sweet to each other even in the
morning, and would have done more, had not Moira
toddled in.

"Mommy pway," she said, smiling brightly.

And Sam and Drew parted, making room for their
laughing daughter to climb between them. Reminding
themselves without a word not to let their priorities
get confused.

From the doorway, Natalie watched them and remembered her own priorities. Drew had danced with
her last night, held her in his arms as the baby slept.
She knew he felt what she felt. She watched the little
family playing in their big bed and knew it was just a
matter of time before she was in that bed with him.
And until then, the less time he spent there with
anybody else, the happier she'd be.

She pasted a bright smile on her face and strode into
the room. "Okay, everybody," she announced affably.
"Time to get up. Breakfast is ready."

Welcoming her as part of the family, Sam and Drew

laughed and did as they were told, pulling on their robes and marching behind her as she carried the baby down the stairs. Natalie heard them laugh and turned around. Her heart beat happily as she was certain she saw Drew wink at her. She didn't notice he was patting his wife's behind at the same time.

7

By midmorning the revolution in San Domenico had been thoroughly covered by the media. Because the newspapers only had access to the previous day's information, their pages were filled with analysis of the causes of the revolution and profiles of its leader, Diego Roca. The government's side was also explored, with an examination of Jorge Alvarro's tenure as president, which unavoidably touched on his excesses. It was left to the morning news shows to announce last night's coup and discuss its effect on the current political situation. There was speculation about the possible fate of Jorge Alvarro and his wife, who had still not turned up as guests in any friendly nations.

And, just as the rebels had guessed, what made the situation all so newsworthy was the added gloss of a group of American movie stars caught in the internal politics of a tropical paradise. With clips by satellite from President Jorge Alvarro's precoup press conference, prominently featuring Melinda Myles, it was a ratings bonanza for the news departments of all three networks.

"She seems so uncomfortable." Sam was watching a monitor in Amos Kilmont's office and talking on the phone to her mother in Oakdale.

"At least she looks okay. She didn't get hurt or anything," Diane Myles responded, peering at her own television set. "You should have heard your father cursing when that lady asked those rude questions about Mindy. He called Jack right away. Wanted to know if we could sue."

"Connie Chung? She was just doing her job, Mom. Don't sweat it. What did Jack say?" Sam was glad that even though Jack and Melinda weren't together anymore, he was still connected to the family.

"He said she was just doing her job."

Sam laughed. "Anyway, none of it matters. Melinda is on her way home."

"Do you think someone will get in touch with us to let us know when she gets there?"

"I don't think they'll have to, Mom," said Sam. "I have a feeling you'll be able to see for yourself on TV."

At three-thirty eastern standard time, all three networks interrupted regular programming to televise the landing of the plane from San Domenico at Los Angeles International Airport. Sam watched excitedly as the journalists disembarked first, waving and smiling at their colleagues, taken aback but not displeased to be making news instead of reporting it for a change. Then the Hollywood contingent began to emerge, first the crew and lesser actors, then Elgar Franz, who pressed forward through the thickening corridor of photographers, and finally Tommy Kray, sunglasses in place, dramatically shaking off the press without actually avoiding them.

Sam smiled to herself. She would not have expected Melinda to want to make a grand entrance, but she guessed movie stardom brought about changes in even the most earthbound personalities. Amos came in to watch with her, and she hugged him without thinking, forgetting for the moment that there had been anything awkward in their physical contact, thinking only that Melinda was about to get off a plane, safe and sound, because Amos had arranged it.

The cameras seemed to anticipate Melinda's appearance as well, as they lingered for a moment on the empty frame, waiting for it to fill with her magical presence. Then, as if confused, the picture swayed as the camera moved away.

"Whoa," said Sam, "get a grip there." She switched the channels, hoping to get a better picture with another team. But even CNN had nothing to offer for a moment. Suddenly, they were back in focus, as lenses zoomed in on Connie Chung.

Sam turned up the sound to hear Connie say, "Rumor has it that Academy Award-winning actress Melinda Myles has joined President Jorge Alvarro of San Domenico in exile. There is no indication of how the president's wife, Lucia, feels about the situation, and we have had no statements from any of the parties. According to reliable sources, the information came from General Raul Guzman, the acting leader of San Domenico. But all we know for fact is that Melinda Myles was not on the plane with the rest of the film crew when it departed San Domenico."

"What the hell?" Amos was addressing the television as much as Sam. But she was already switching channels. On CNN, someone had pushed a microphone in Elgar's face.

"I don't know," was all he said. "She didn't tell me anything. I have no further statement to make." He pushed his way past the reporters who were still firing questions at him.

The instant analysis was beginning as newscasters were ready with a cache of earlier rumors linking the president and the movie star. Sam, astute enough to realize they had no further hard information, turned off the sound. The desperation on her face was plain as she looked at Amos.

"I thought she was on there," he was as baffled as she. "Nobody told me any different."

"Something's happened to her," said Sam. Her voice icily calm. This was not conjecture; she knew she was speaking the truth.

"We don't know that. Maybe she did just go off with old Jorge. He's supposed to be a pretty suave fellow. She could turn up in a day or two in some villa somewhere."

"No. You don't know Melinda. I do. Something has happened to her. She wouldn't just take off without telling anybody."

"Hey, there was a revolution going on down there. It probably wasn't such a great time to reach out and touch someone."

"No." Sam was even more vehement. "She isn't like that."

Dotty knocked lightly and opened the door. "Sam, it's your mother on line one."

Sam picked up the phone. "Are you watching it, Mom?"

"Sam, what's happened? I don't understand. Where's Melinda?" Diane asked plaintively.

On the extension, Harvey didn't wait for her to finish before he chimed in, "What's this garbage about her going off with the president? Isn't he a married man? Ain't she learned her lesson?"

Sam felt her anger rising, but she tried to control it. Getting into an argument with her father now wouldn't help anything.

"Dad, I don't believe it and neither should you. Something's happened to her."

"What? What's happened to her?" Diane was alarmed.

Shit, thought Sam, *now I've scared them.* That's not what she had meant to do.

"Sam, is that you?"

Sam recognized Jack Bader's voice. "Jack. Thank goodness you're there with them. Can you calm them down?"

"I'll try. Do you know anything?"

"No. But I'm going to find out."

"I don't give a shit what some military dictator says, Melinda did not run off with Alvarro."

"Not to mention his wife," Sam added, calm again now that she had an ally in her thinking.

"I'll get in touch with Elgar Franz. He looked like he might know more than he's saying."

"Okay. I'm working in Senator Amos Kilmont's office now. He's been great so far. Maybe he can help us figure it out. I don't want to lose my sister."

"Me neither," said Jack, sounding more fervent than he realized. "Me neither."

By the time Sam had hung up with Jack, Drew was already on hold on another line. It was only when she heard his voice that she began to cry. "Drew, I'm really scared."

"I know you are, honey," he said. "But my guess is she did get out of San Domenico some other way, even if it wasn't with Alvarro. She'll probably just show up in a day or two."

"That's what Amos said. But, Drew, what if she doesn't?"

"Then we'll do whatever we have to to find her."

They made her walk. At first, frightened, Melinda had obeyed. But with only her silk robe to cover her and a pair of ballet slippers on her feet, it became clear to all of them that the jungle made no allowances for stardom. Then she grew angry. She stopped, ignoring the prodding of the rifle in her back.

"I am an American citizen. You have no right to do this."

They looked at her as though she were crazy.

"I demand that you take me to the American consulate." She had no idea if there even was an American consulate, but it was an initial demand. She would entertain alternatives if they offered one.

"Paso," was the only response.

She pretended not to understand. "I insist that you return me to the presidential palace. I am an American. America does not look kindly on abuse of their citizens." She realized her vocabulary was probably too technical, but she thought, somehow, if she just kept repeating *American,* they would get the message.

"Move," someone translated, pushing her so firmly with the rifle that she involuntarily took a step forward. She saw then that they understood her but were not prepared to listen.

There were half a dozen of them surrounding her: two in front, navigating the terrain; one on each side, grabbing her on occasion to steady her balance; and two behind, propelling her forward. The men ahead pushed aside the wild growth with their weapons only to let it swing back and smack her in the face as they moved on. Vines grabbed at her ankles, tripping her, cutting into her skin. She walked for what seemed like hours, cursing herself for leaving her wristwatch on the edge of the sink at the palace. She knew it made no sense, but she could not help thinking that if only she knew what time it was, how much time had passed, she'd be able to calculate when help would arrive. She refused to allow herself to wonder *if* help would arrive.

At first, she had shivered in the cool night air of the jungle. But the brisk pace set by her captors had kept her heart beating and her blood moving, and by the time the sun began to beat through the veil of palm fronds, sweat dripped from her forehead, and her robe clung in dark wet circles to her body. The stinging jungle floor had already pricked its way through her slippers, and she could feel the blisters swelling with each step she took. Thorns dug into her arms and legs, leaving tracks of blood that dried into a crisscross map of wounds.

At last, they stopped, and she saw that they had come to a camp so completely hidden that until they were in the middle of it, she hadn't even suspected its existence. There were about a dozen more rebel soldiers moving in and out of tents, laughing and calling out to each other, secure that here, they were beyond the reach of their enemies. Melinda's arrival brought the camp to a standstill as they gathered around her, quickly covering their faces with the scarves that hung ready around their necks, so only their eyes showed. Most of them were dressed not in camouflage but in the simple, rough pants and shirts of workers. Strangely, they looked familiar to Melinda, and then she realized, she had seen them before. Not these people in this place but people just like this. When she had ventured alone into the village, they had gathered around her, reaching out to touch her as they did now. In the camp, they covered their faces, but she knew them from their eyes— haunted and hungry for something she could not begin to understand.

She tried not to let her fear show. "Who is your leader?"

"We have no leader. Here, we are equal." Melinda looked at the person who spoke. With a body covered in thick olive drab pants and shirt, a face hidden by a ski mask, only the voice gave a single clue to identity. This rebel was a woman.

"Look," she addressed herself to the one who had spoken. "I don't know who you are or what you want from me, but I really have no part in this. I'm an American—"

"You are Alvarro's whore."

Anger replaced fear. "And you're a goddamn out-law!" She knew it was not a diplomatic thing to say, but she was too tired and sore to care. "You have absolutely no right—"

"I am a soldier in the San Domenican Liberation Front. I can and will do whatever is necessary to gain freedom for my country."

149

They threw her in an underground cell, reached only through a storm cellar door that was covered with a net of dirt and branches to keep it hidden from sight. There was a small air vent that allowed only a narrow shaft of light to break the claustrophobic darkness. They brought her food, which she took to the light to eat. But she saw things moving on the plate and screamed for them to take it away. After that, they brought her nothing. She lay on the ground and wept, fell asleep, woke, and wept again. She watched as the light grew even more narrow and finally disappeared and knew that it was night. But she no longer knew how many days she had been beneath the ground.

Melinda was dreaming. Motes of dust danced in the hazy rays of light that pierced the darkness of her tomb. A black shadow descended through the light, blocking the sun, until it hovered over her. She looked up at the shadow and saw two eyes of such unsurpassed kindness that for the first time since she had been taken into captivity, she let someone see her cry. The arms of the shadow reached out to her, and she let herself be clasped. *I am dying,* she thought. *Death has come to take me, and I am happy.* She prepared to float.

But instead of wafting skyward, she felt herself being laid back down on the ground.

"I'm ready," she wanted to shout. "Don't leave me here." But she knew that the only sound she made was a low moan.

"Agua!" the shadow demanded, and the door was pulled back all the way, so that his order could be carried out. For the first time in days, she felt the full force of the sun. She blinked rapidly, and water flowed from her eyes, partly tears and partly irritation at the sudden brilliance.

The shadow held a cup of water to her lips and with his gentle eyes urged her to drink. She sipped slowly, and as her eyes became used to the glare, her vision cleared. She was not dreaming. The shadow was not death. He was a man dressed like the others in dark rough clothing, his face covered to avoid recognition. But his eyes did not devour her like the others, and she knew without question that she had not seen him before.

He took something from his pocket, and in the sun, she saw a glint of steel and knew it was a knife. In someone else's hand, it would have made her flinch, but there was no menace in his action. She watched curiously as he reached into his pocket for something else, and she caught a glimpse of coral before he cradled it in the palm of his hand. He stabbed at it expertly and, seconds later, handed her the smooth, fleshy half of a ripe persimmon. Ravenous, she let her teeth sink into the succulent fruit and was rewarded with a burst of sweetness so pure that it instantly dismissed the dust that had gathered in her mouth and throat. Juice dripped down her arm, and she caught it with her tongue before she bit into the springy flesh again, savoring each morsel before she allowed herself to swallow. He handed her the second half before she asked and watched, his eyes smiling, as she greedily consumed it.

"They tell me you would not eat," he said in almost unaccented English as he gave her another.

She ate more slowly but with no less enjoyment. "They gave me food with bugs."

"They gave you what they eat themselves. But, of course, you are used to better things. They are not."

There was no reproach in his voice, but for the first

time, she felt contrite. Perhaps they had not intended to be so cruel. He climbed up the ladder and out into the open air, then reached down his hand for her to follow. She grabbed his hand, expecting the rough touch of a laborer and was surprised to find it surprisingly soft, like the hand of an artist or a scholar. She let him guide her up the ladder and onto the ground. Her legs were shaky and it hurt all over to stand up, but she raised her face to the sun and absorbed its heat like a dry sponge drinks water. A short gasp of air escaped his lips, and she opened her eyes and saw that her silk robe hung on her in filthy tatters, and she stood virtually naked before him. She felt exposed and humiliated until she saw that he was not looking at her body, and his gasp had risen involuntarily from horror, not delight. He was staring at her feet, which were covered with a scabrous network of dried blood and open blisters. She swayed, feeling suddenly faint at the sight of her own distress. He quickly caught her up in his arms and carried her into a tent, out of the sun and away from the eyes of the others.

There was a plank floor in the tent and room to stand. The furnishings consisted of a desk covered with a pile of papers and maps, a folding chair, and a pallet on the floor, where he carefully placed Melinda. In the corner was a basin and a ten-gallon tank of water. He poured some water into the basin and brought it to her. He made her sit in the chair, then took one foot at a time and put it in the basin. The water was cool, and she sighed as the initial sting gave way to a soothing liquid caress. Then, this gentle man took the bandanna from around his face, dipped it into the basin, and gingerly bathed each individual wound on her feet, until the dirt dissolved and the crusted scabs had fallen away.

"Not so bad as it looked," he announced looking up at her from his position at her feet.

For the first time, she saw his face and saw that his eyes, as wonderful as they were, were not his only good feature. The sun had darkened his skin to a deep gold, and the sunlight appeared as yellow flecks in his luminous brown eyes. His hair was black and lustrous, and his chin was strong and shaded with dark stubble under high cheekbones that spoke of some exotic ancestry. But it was his smile that transformed him, changing a visage that would have done justice to a Mayan prince into benign and beautiful humanity.

"Thank you," she said, feeling rescued, though she did not even know her rescuer.

He saw her looking at him and stopped smiling, as if parting his lips revealed more than removing his mask.

"Can you stand?" he asked.

She did, carefully sidestepping the basin, now filled with a swirl of brown water. The remnants of her robe slipped open, and she saw his eyes brush over her and quickly turn away.

"They should have given you clothes. I'm sorry."

His apology seemed sincere, and he rummaged through a rucksack behind the desk and pulled out another camouflage shirt and pants and held it out to her. "It's all we have."

"It's fine," she said hastily, taking them. A faint smell of lye hit her nose, and she knew, at least, that they were clean, which was more than she could say about herself. "I'm so . . . Could I . . ." She looked around the tent. Clearly, there was no shower. She doubted that there was running water anywhere in the camp. A sudden desperation overwhelmed her. In spite of having survived a barefoot trek through the jungle, days without food in a dungeon, she felt if she could not wash, she could not go on.

He seemed to read her thoughts. "Of course, you must wash. Fresh water is trucked in, but there is a stream not far from the camp." He saw her look of panic at the thought of walking another gauntlet in her rags. "Or," he went on almost without pause, "if you stand in the corner, I could pour water over you, give you soap to wash, then rinse you off."

"Oh, please, could we do that. I can't . . ."

"I understand."

He held her hand as she gingerly made her way on her bruised and torn feet over the splintering planks to the far corner of the tent. He seemed to cringe each time she winced in pain. He fetched the basin and emptied it under the flap of the tent. Then he filled it with fresh water and handed her the bar of castile soap that sat in an empty coconut shell by the water tank.

He lifted the basin above her head, then turned away discreetly and said, "Tell me when you are ready."

She dropped her robe and kicked it away. "Now."

She gasped as the cool water coursed down her body, then maneuvered her head so that a stream fell into her matted hair and over her dusty face. It stopped much sooner than she would have wished and he heard her sigh of disappointment.

"Wait, I'll give you more," he said, and she heard the laughter in his voice. This time, he poured it over her in a rush and she laughed and rubbed the soap through her hair, over her face, along her arms and legs and neck, working it into a lather over her entire body.

"You'd better rinse me off," she said finally when she was certain she'd covered every inch of herself with soap.

He poured basin after basin over her, and she watched with satisfaction as the cloak of bubbles flowed off her body in rivulets, revealing the fresh, dewy white of her skin. He tried to concentrate only on directing the stream of water, but her beauty caught him by surprise, and he could not keep his eyes from wanting to verify what his heart had told him he had seen. Of course, he had seen pictures of her, and even in the darkness of her underground cell, covered as she was with dirt, he was not unaware of her beauty. But the sight of her standing in his tent, dripping wet, washed clean of everything but her bruises, touched him in a way he had not expected. He had anticipated the glamour, the artful splendor of overripe, surgically enhanced bodies with which he identified Hollywood. But this woman was vulnerable and achingly real, and it made him want nothing more than to fold her in his arms and abandon the revolution.

He was glad when she shook the excess water from her hair and stepping out of the pools of soapy water that had gathered at her feet, slipped into the clothes he had given her. Only then, did he allow himself to look at her fully, and it made him smile.

"They're a little large, but you wear them well. I will get you boots also. I'm afraid mine won't do."

She smiled back at him, feeling that through the ritual of her cleansing they had formed a bond. She could see he was not like the rest, blind misguided followers of the revolution waiting for orders from their criminal leader.

"I don't know what I'm doing here," she began and struggled to keep the tears from choking off her words.

"Let's not talk about that now," he said. "You need to eat. I cooked something for you myself."

"You did?" she said with such shock that it made him laugh.

"Why not? I'm a very good cook. I come from a large family. We didn't cook, we didn't eat. Do you like snake?"

She gulped. "To eat?"

He shrugged. "We don't have much by way of meat in the jungle. I was lucky to catch one. I think you need the protein. And I can promise you: no bugs."

He was being so kind, she agreed to try, and indeed, it was quite good. She hadn't realized how hungry she was, and she ate with gusto while he watched indulgently, offering her more whenever her plate was empty. When she had eaten as much as she could, she tried to thank him but yawned instead. He took the plate from her hand and gently coaxed her to lie down on his pallet. It was only a mattress of straw covered with coarse cotton, but to her, after days on the hard stony ground, it felt like the softest of featherbeds. In seconds, she was asleep.

She dreamed again of shadows coming to take her away, but this time, when she opened her eyes, it was dark, and he was lying on the pallet beside her. It was a warm night, and he had taken off his shirt and rolled it into a ball that he had placed as a pillow under her head. The heat coming from his body comforted her, and she moved closer to lie within its radius. He opened his eyes and saw her maneuvering herself next to him. She was embarrassed and started to roll away, but he drew her to him gently and closed his arms around her. His arms were strong, his skin taut, and feeling as though she were safely inside a cocoon, she went back to sleep again.

By the time she woke up in the morning, she was alone on the pallet, and she could not be sure if the night before had been a dream. He must have heard her stirring, because moments later, he entered the tent with a steaming mug of coffee. The smell alone made waves of gratitude wash over her, and when she sipped it, she was sure it was the elixir of life.

"Is it because of this mess that I am in or is this the best coffee I have ever tasted?"

He laughed. "One thing everyone has in San Domenico is good coffee. It's as important as bread to us. I see the sleep has done you good," he added in lieu of telling her how radiant she looked, even in oversized camouflage.

"The sleep, the clothes, the food, the coffee—you," she finished a little shyly. Since he was here, he had to be one of the rebels, but everything he did confirmed her belief that he was not like the rest of them. Jorge had told her that the rebel factions were filled with good people who had been forced to fight with the guerrillas for fear of losing what little they had. It was obvious to her that her savior was one of those casualties. She had to make it clear that he would not suffer because of her. She had to explain that if he helped her escape, then she was in a position to reward him beyond his dreams.

She broached this subject of escape when he returned with a second cup of coffee along with a pair of boots that fit her remarkably well. For some reason, it pleased her that he had guessed her shoe size simply by holding her foot. She thanked him, then blurted, "Listen, I know why you're here."

"You do?"

"Yes. I've heard how Diego Roca forces good people into this nasty little war he's waging to try to put himself in power."

He didn't react. "Who told you this?" was all he asked. She understood he needed to know he was safe.

"The president. You know who I am, don't you?"

"I have heard." He remained noncommittal.

"I shouldn't be here. I have no part in this. Get me out of the jungle and I can help you. I can get you out of San Domenico, bring you back to America, set you up there. You'll be able to help your family."

This time, she could see he was taken aback. "Why do you think I would leave San Domenico? This is my home."

"But look at how you're living. You have nothing. I know you can't want to be part of this fight. The rebels will lose because the people don't support this rebellion. They voted for Jorge Alvarro."

"He told you this?"

"Yes. We became quite close. He taught me a lot about your country."

"Then you are worse than his whore. You are his dupe."

His cruel remarks were like a slap in the face. She struggled for words, for breath.

Someone entered the tent. From the voice, Melinda recognized the woman who had confronted her when she first arrived.

"Commandante," the woman said, *"lo fotógrafo . . ."*

"Not yet," he said, summarily dismissing her, not even thinking to switch out of English. But a man with a camera and several lenses around his neck was already in the tent.

"Diego!" he called out merrily, *"Com' esta?"* Then he saw Melinda perched on the pallet. *"Que hermosa es."*

"She's not ready. Come back later," Diego said. He spoke softly, but there was no mistaking his authority.

"Okay, Diego. Whatever the *commandante* wants."

The name seemed to ring through the tent and pierce her soul. He had let her believe that he was an ally, when, in fact, she'd been placing her trust in the devil himself: Diego Roca.

"Commandante?" Melinda said, her voice heavy with sarcasm. "But I was told there are no leaders here. Everyone is equal."

"That is true," he said. "No one," he added with heavy emphasis, "no one is forced to stay with us."

"Except me."

"We will set you free when Juan-Marcos is set free."

"What? You're using me for a prisoner exchange? I've heard of Juan-Marcos. He's a murderer."

"He's a freedom fighter."

"He killed three men in cold blood."

She saw the gold in his eyes turn fiery and knew that she had angered him. "Is that what your lover Jorge told you? My God, you are so naive. Did you think to ask who were the men he killed? Why did he kill them? They were not just men," he spat at her. "They were soldiers. Alvarro's soldiers. And Juan-Marcos killed them because they had come into his village, raped his wife and mother, killed his three children, and set fire to his house. I think, in your country, they call that justifiable homicide."

She was silent. She had no way of knowing if what he said was the truth, although he was right about her naïveté. She had never questioned Jorge, simply accepted his version of events as he imparted it to her.

"Jorge Alvarro was never my lover," she said and was angry at herself for saying it. Her personal relationships were irrelevant to this man who was holding her hostage. She owed him no explanations. And yet, she wanted him to know.

"I wondered," he admitted, and she knew it was more than he wanted to reveal.

"Not that it matters," she said, trying to regain some ground. "He's not the monster you make him out to be."

"And do you think I am the monster he says?"

"I think this is all so stupid. People killing each other and blaming everyone else. For what?"

She saw him tense and knew she'd made him angry again. "For what? I will show you for what. You call the revolution stupid? I will show you what is truly stupid. People starving in a land of plenty. People with nothing forced to toil and die for people with everything. That is stupid."

He grabbed her arm and started to pull her out of the tent. She felt the heat of his outrage in his touch and was afraid he might throw her back into the pit.

"Where are you taking me?" she cried, pulling back. He saw how frightened she was and relaxed his grip enough so as not to hurt her but did not let her go.

"I want to show you something. Come with me, please."

She let him lead her then, and Diego wondered

160

what the hell he was doing. Why should it matter to him that she understand the revolution? What difference did it make if she thought he was a hoodlum? She was simply the pawn he needed to recapture his knight. After that, she would be out of his life. She would go back to Hollywood, and he and his revolution would be just another adventure to tell about on the talk shows. But he had felt an involuntary surge in his heart when she had said that Alvarro was not her lover. And even if he never saw her again, he wanted her to know who he was and what he stood for.

He had commandeered a jeep, and they drove in silence, bumping over rough-cut paths that crossed through the jungle. She held fast to the roll bar, and once or twice he looked over at her to make sure she was all right, but he said nothing. When they emerged from the jungle, they were in a shantytown, much like the one she had stumbled upon on her first solo foray away from the set. Shacks made of corrugated tin drew in the full fire of the noon sun. A few scattered inhabitants dozed on the porches, escaping the ovens of their homes in the shade of the narrow eaves. In the distance, she could hear the intermittent *pop-pop-pop* of sniper fire.

When they spotted the jeep, the villagers seemed to come alive, running out to the street to greet them. "Diego, Diego," they called, running behind the jeep. Melinda could see no one was forcing them to react this way. These people seemed to love the man that she was with. He stopped the car and helped her out. People surrounded them, reaching out, trying to shake Diego's hand. They touched her, too, as though, because she stood beside Diego, she was some sort of talisman. But this time, she wasn't frightened. Their eyes were still haunted, but now, layered over the pain, she saw a thin veneer of triumph and pride. And she understood that things had changed for these people because of Diego Roca.

Diego introduced Melinda to Juan-Marcos's mother, Esmeralda, who insisted they come and sit on her porch while she served them lemonade sweetened with sugar cane. With Diego translating, Melinda learned about the soldiers who had come to collect "taxes" for the president and what they had done when they were told there was no money. Esmeralda said she did not care for her suffering, she was an old woman, but she ached for her daughter-in-law, who lost her virtue, her children, and now her husband. Melinda interrupted to ask where Juan-Marcos's wife was now, and Diego told her she was in another rebel camp in the jungle.

"She only lives," said Esmeralda, "to see Juan-Marcos home and San Domenico free. If not for what Diego has done, she would have died long ago. All of us would have. He has given us back the desire to live. He has shown us a future is possible for those who remain."

There was a chorus of assent from the others who had gathered around the porch to hear the old woman tell her story, even though they knew it well enough to be able to recite it themselves.

"But didn't you vote for Jorge Alvarro?" Melinda asked.

They laughed. "There was an election," Esmeralda said, "but we did not vote. Only his friends were allowed to vote. And you yourself know that he is good to his friends."

Melinda blushed, remembering the lavish dinners at the palace, the guests in designer clothes and jewels. Now she understood why Jorge would never allow her to explore the island alone. He had carefully orchestrated everything she saw, everyone she met. She knew, without a doubt, that Diego was right. She had been duped.

When Esmeralda had finished her story, others came to tell tales of their own. Some spoke in English, others allowed Diego to translate for them. All of them seemed acutely in need of being heard, and Melinda, eager to know the truth, listened thoughtfully. She heard about brothers, husbands, children, who had disappeared; about women who had gone to find their men and had been raped and tortured; about the harsh abuse of life in the shantytowns and the desperation it bred. Every story ended with a paean to Diego Roca for convincing them they were not born to be battered, that life could offer more if they insisted on more. He was leading them into battle, but they preferred to die as human beings than live like animals.

The sun began to set, and though Melinda would have listened to more, Diego gently told her that they had to go. General Guzman's forces roamed at night, and it was too dangerous for her to be here.

As if on cue, a jeep came careening out of the jungle, screeching to a stop in front of them. Melinda's instant reaction was to grab Diego, and she was gratified that he calmed her quietly without making an issue of her fear. "One of ours," he murmured as he went to meet the driver.

The others respectfully kept their distance, and Melinda stayed in her place on the porch as the driver conferred with his *commandante*. Their tones were low, grim, and when Diego returned to the porch, it was obvious it had not been good news.

"Juan-Marcos e muerte," he said simply.

He opened his arms and held Esmeralda, the two of them weeping quietly together. Melinda remembered the safety she had felt in his embrace and fervently wished the old woman would find the same comfort. Her own eyes filled with tears, and she brushed them away, feeling as though her life of privilege gave her no right to intrude on their pain. One by one, the neighbors came to Esmeralda and, taking her from Diego's arms, cradled her themselves, knowing they could not lessen her anguish but wanting to share it. The moon rose while they wept.

"We must go now," Diego said, and after hugging Esmeralda one more time and promising the woman her son would not die in vain, he led Melinda back to the jeep.

They began to drive, not back into the jungle but on a dirt path that skirted it.

"Where are we going?" Melinda asked.

"I am taking you to the church. I do not trust Guzman's soldiers. They might treat you worse than we have. The priest will know who to contact and make sure you are brought to safety."

"I don't understand."

"You are free. We wanted to exchange you for Juan-Marcos. He is dead. There is no reason to keep you. You can go back to Hollywood."

"No," she said quietly. "I can't."

"The priest will help you. He knows—"

"No," she interrupted. "I mean I won't. Please, stop the car."

He slowed to look at her, but he did not stop.

"Please," she asked again, and this time, he came to a halt, turning off the lights as he parked by the side of the road.

The darkness closed in around them, but above, the sky was ablaze with light. A crescent moon, low on the horizon, allowed the stars to beam their brightest and the sky was dusted with the diamond glitter of endless constellations. She knew he was waiting for her to speak, but there was too much going on in her mind and she needed time to sort it out. It was as if a door to an unused closet had been opened, and amid all the rubbish stored without regard was one essential, important thing. If she could just find it.

"Let me stay," she said finally.

"Why? You said yourself this has nothing to do with you."

"It does now. I know too much. I can't just go back to making silly movies and pretend the rest of the world doesn't exist. Maybe I can help you here."

Diego looked at her. He would have liked her to stay with him forever.

"No," he said. "It's impossible. You know nothing about war."

"I know about publicity. I know you've got a message that isn't getting across. People listen to me just because I'm an actress. It's silly, but it's true. I could tell them what's going on here, and they would believe me before they'd believe you."

"Melinda," he spoke her name for the first time and thought his heart would burst. "I can't let you do this. It is dangerous. You could be killed."

"So could you."

"These are my people, not yours."

"They are human beings. That makes them my people, too. I've been very lucky in my life. I've made money. I've been famous. But none of it's important. Not like this. If I never make another movie, what difference will it make? Believe me, there are plenty of starlets just waiting to take my place. But I can make a difference here. If you let me."

Diego knew that she was right, but that was not why he wanted her to stay. It was daunting to think that this woman could change the course of his country's history. It dismayed him even more to admit she could change the course of his life. If he let her. He felt a swell of emotion arcing its way toward her from his heart. Quickly, before she could perceive it, he wrenched it away, forcing it back into the dark recesses of his soul.

His voice was cold when he spoke. "Whatever you may have heard about me, I do not give orders. You can do as you please. But if you stay, you must understand I cannot take responsibility for you. I am not in the business of orchestrating romantic adventures to titillate bored celebrities."

His harsh words took her by surprise, knocking the breath out of her like a sucker punch. She had heard that this man was cold-blooded, but she had seen him with her own eyes as a man of feeling. Now, it appeared, he arbitrarily chose when to reveal his separate sides. She had done nothing to deserve his disdain, and yet she had had done nothing to gain his respect. What she understood was that Diego Roca could not be the reason she stayed in San Domenico. And she had to make that clear to him as well.

"You have a remarkable command of the English

language," was all she said in the same detached voice that he had used with her.

In the darkness, she could not see his smile. But a moment later, he turned the jeep around and headed into the jungle, back to the camp. Looking straight ahead, both purposefully avoiding thoughts of the other, they did not see the sudden burst of fireworks as a meteor shower sent stars falling through the night sky.

8

The picture made both the cover of *Time* and *Newsweek* as well as the front pages of every major newspaper in the United States. According to the story that accompanied it, it had been sent via portable fax machine to Reuters, which would account for its lack of clarity. But even in a grainy photograph, there was no mistaking the likeness of Melinda Myles. She was dressed in camouflage fatigues that seemed a few sizes too big for her. And though she carried no weapon, the people around her, dressed as she was, but with the addition of a variety of face coverings, all did. A letter had followed the photo, also by fax, stating that Melinda Myles had joined the San Domenican Liberation Front because she had come to recognize the suffering of the people in San Domenico. She asserted that though she would not take up arms, she would fight in her own way along-side Diego Roca until the revolution had been won and the people were free from the tyranny of both exploitive dictators and military juntas. She promised to continue to send missives from the front as regular-ly as could be managed under the harsh conditions.

"Damn it." Sam knew she was shouting, but she didn't care. "She looks like Patty Hearst, for God's sake. You can't believe this is for real."

"Sam, honey, I'm on your side," Amos said, putting an arm around her. "I'm just saying that it's going to be tough to find her if she doesn't want to be found."

Sam started to pace around the room, extricating herself from his grasp in the process. She'd become quite adept at limiting her contact with Amos, if not actually avoiding it, these past few weeks. She be-lieved Amos meant her no real harm, but his constant touching disturbed her. Still, in addition to heading the IEC, he was on the Foreign Relations Committee, he had the ear of the secretary of state, he had connections she could only dream of and if she had any hopes of finding her sister, she needed his help. It wouldn't do her any good to make a fuss about something that probably meant nothing. It would only make Drew feel uncomfortable about one of his oldest friends and turn a benefactor into an enemy.

Sam took up a position in the far corner of the room.

"Drew says he'd pay for an investigator to go to San Domenico, but he won't let me charter a plane and go down myself."

"Drew's right. All you can do is get yourself killed. Who are you going to talk to, providing they even let you land? An investigator would be just as useless. You need the kind of clout you get from the State Department. I got you an appointment to talk to the assistant secretary tomorrow."

"Oh, Amos. Thank you."

"Don't I get a kiss for that?"

Sam cringed inwardly but smiled and joked, "Add it to what I owe you. I'm going home."

Since the crisis with Melinda had begun, Sam had been spending even more time in Amos Kilmont's office, and she was looking forward to a quiet evening with her husband. She still spent her mornings with Moira and often came home in time to play with her before putting her to bed. But more often than not, once Moira was asleep, Sam had to head back to the Russell Building to discuss another strategy with Amos and plan the next day's assault. Sam knew Drew missed their time together, as did she, but she also knew he understood she had no choice. There were people who questioned the validity of her search for Melinda, but until Sam had heard directly from her sister that she was remaining in San Domenico of her own free will, she could not accept it. And even then, Sam was going to try her damnedest to talk Melinda out of it.

Coming off Q Street and rounding the corner onto Thirty-first, Sam had already forced herself to stop speculating about Melinda's future and start reflecting about her own present. She had every intention of displacing Natalie at the candlelit table for two and not even feeling guilty about it. In fact, she decided, she would give Natalie the night off and encourage her to go to the movies or something. It had been a long

time since she'd been completely alone wi
husband in their own house, and she could th
many things she'd like to do and many rooms
like to do them in.

But the instant she let herself into the house,
knew that something was wrong. Even though it \
almost dinnertime, the table had not been set. It w
long past Moira's bedtime, but she heard murmurin
upstairs. She took the steps two at a time, her heart i
her throat, afraid to even think what the problem
might be. To her relief, the door to the baby's room
was ajar, and with the light from the hallway, she
could see that Moira lay sleeping peacefully in her
crib. The talking was coming from her own bedroom,
and she went in to find Natalie sitting on a corner of
the bed, while Drew packed a bag.

When they saw her, Natalie got up from the bed
with a guilty start and Drew stopped packing.

"What's going on?" she asked, genuinely confused.

"I just got a call from Belvedere," Drew told her,
coming to take her hand. "My father's had a stroke

"Oh, shit," she said, knowing it was less th
adequate but selfishly wishing the old man had |
better timing.

"Buddy's with him in the hospital. He tried to
hold of my mother, but she's sailing with the Buck
somewhere off the Cap d'Antibes. I've got to
There's a flight at ten."

She looked at her watch. It was already seven.
Drew, I'm sorry. I probably should go with yo
Amos got me an appointment at the State D
ment tomorrow. If I miss it . . ."

"No, I understand. There's no need for both

171

be there. There's nothing we can do anyway. Melinda
should take priority for you. I'm sorry I can't stay and
help you with that."

"Don't worry about that. Amos is really cutting
through the red tape for me. If anyone can help me
find her, it's him."

They went into each other's arms and clung to each
other for a moment, each thinking about the burden
that would have to be faced alone. Natalie coughed
discreetly, and over her shoulder, Sam saw her try to
get Drew's attention.

"What is it, Natalie?" she asked, not bothering to
hide her exasperation as she pulled away from Drew.

"I just . . . I mean . . . I thought . . ."

"Natalie thinks she and Moira should come with
me to Woodland Cliffs," Drew answered for her.

"No, absolutely not," Sam responded, not even
considering the idea. "There's no reason to take
Moira away from home. Forrest wouldn't even recognize her." A look of half dejection, half defiance
appeared on Natalie's face as if to confirm that she
knew Sam would say no.

"Not for my father," Drew said. "For Moira. Think
about it. You're at the Capitol more than you're at
home these days, and it's for a good reason. That's
where you need to be. But I'll be gone, and Natalie
will be on her own mostly with Moira. It's a big
responsibility."

"I'm not saying I can't handle it," Natalie interrupted, not wanting to put herself in too bad a light. "I
just don't think it would be so great for the baby."

Sam didn't like what she was hearing, but she could
no longer dismiss it out of hand.

"There will be a lot of people around. My mother

will be coming back, Sarah and Ian will be there. There are your parents, of course. You know they'd die to have her with them for a while. And there's all that room to run around. It might actually be good for her. But like I told Natalie, it's up to you."

Much as she hated it, Sam knew they weren't wrong. Until she knew what was going on with Melinda, Moira would be better off in Woodland Cliffs. And, even though she didn't want to admit it, it would probably be better for herself as well. It wasn't that she didn't trust Natalie, but it would be a lot more comfortable knowing that a dreamy twenty-year-old from North Dakota with a crush on her husband wouldn't be the sole caregiver for her child.

"Okay," she finally said and could have done without Natalie's jubilant "Yes!"

"I'll go pack for me and Moira," Natalie said as if instant action could keep Sam from changing her mind.

"You do that," said Sam. "And please close the door behind you."

When they were alone, Sam looked at her watch. "We've got two and a half hours before you have to go. How long will it take you to finish packing?"

"Do you have something else in mind?"

"Yes."

"In that case, I'm done now." He slammed the suitcase shut and clicked on the lock.

She went to turn off the lights, but he stopped her hand.

"I want to see you," he said hoarsely. "We might not get to do this again for a while."

She agreed, and they watched each other undress. He was excited before they even touched. They stayed on top of the covers and studied each other's faces, registering the nuance of each movement, each thrust and slide, responding as much to what they saw as what they felt.

"I love you Samantha Myles," he said when he could contain himself no longer and saw a rosy flush tint the ivory of her skin and knew that it was time.

"I love you, too, Andrew Symington," she responded with a smile that came from deep within her soul.

Drew felt himself stirring inside her and would have started again, but the phone rang. They looked at each other and cursed softly, but situations being what they were, there was no possibility of letting it go unanswered. Gingerly removing himself from her, Drew picked up the receiver with a gruff hello, then handed it to her.

"Reuters got another fax," she heard Amos say.

"From Melinda?"

"What do you think?"

"Is it in the papers?"

"Not yet. I've got a contact bringing an advance copy to the office. You might want to come down here and see it."

"I'll be there in half an hour. I'm sorry," she said, turning to Drew as she hung up the phone. "Another communication from Melinda came in. Amos is getting me a copy in his office."

"Okay. Go. I've got to get up and finish packing anyway."

"I thought you were finished already."

"I lied."

Sam laughed and kissed her husband. She would

miss him. But if the fax from Melinda shed some light on her situation, maybe they'd be able to arrange an immediate rescue, and they'd all be free to join him in Belvedere. She took a quick shower and dressed hurriedly.

She went to kiss Moira and saw that Natalie had already dressed her for the trip without waking her.

"She's not even going to know that she's on a plane," laughed Natalie delighted. "She's just going to wake up tomorrow in a new place. Isn't that great?"

Natalie's suitcase and the baby's bag were already waiting by the door when Sam left to go back to Amos Kilmont's office. It wasn't until she was halfway down Constitution Avenue that it struck Sam that, in all the time she had known her, she had never seen Natalie so happy.

There was no routine to their lives. Each day was different with its hazards and its adventures. Like the others, Melinda slept in a tent, bathed in the stream, foraged for food. Her specialty had become the care of the injured. While new recruits learned to load and shoot weapons, Melinda learned to clean and suture wounds. She was taught by an Italian doctor named Vincenzo Fumi, who had worked with the World Health Organization in war-torn countries like Somalia and Rwanda. Like many of the others she met, Vincenzo seemed to be a personal friend of Diego Roca and would lay down his life for him if asked. Vincenzo and Melinda were assigned a vehicle, and when they received word of casualties, the two of them would drive to the site with their limited supplies and equipment in the back of the jeep. It was primitive emergency medical service, but they saved lives where they could and gave comfort where they could not.

The government forces struck frequently and furiously. They went into the villages, ostensibly seeking guerrillas, but finding nothing, branded all citizens rebel sympathizers and blew up their meager houses anyway. When possible, the San Domenican Liberation Front organized resistance, and they were able to fend off Guzman's men. Diego Roca's followers had fewer arms and less ammunition, but they were fighting for their lives and the lives of their children, and they had nothing to lose. Still, victory never came without cost.

In the camp, Melinda shared in the easy camaraderie. After a certain amount of initial mistrust, the rebels had accepted her as one of their own. She, too, they decided, was a personal friend of Diego. Unfortunately, Melinda hardly saw him. He spent the nights on maneuvers and the days in hiding, planning strategy with his advisors.

"Where did you meet Diego?" Melinda asked Vincenzo one day after they had returned from a skirmish in the north of the island.

"Columbia."

"Is he originally from South America?"

"No. Not Colombia the country. Columbia University. He's San Domenican. But he was raised in New York. We studied history together before I went into medicine and he came back here."

"That accounts for his perfect English. I wondered."

"He doesn't like to talk about it."

"Ah, yes. The mystery. I guess in these parts

revolutionaries are like movie stars. They need to maintain their mysteriousness."

"Not at all. He doesn't talk about it because it is painful to him. His father was a journalist, his mother, a poet. They were exiled by the government because they wouldn't promote the sham democracy. Instead, they went to New York and wrote the truth there. They were killed by a letter bomb when Diego was twelve. There was never any question why they were killed, but no one was ever accused. Diego worked in a sweatshop at night so he could go to school during the day. I think he does not have fond memories of New York."

Melinda felt like a fool. She was beginning to realize that Diego Roca was not like any man she had ever known. She could not judge him by her normal standards.

"Is he . . . Has he ever been . . . I mean . . ." She could not resist the question, but she was too embarrassed to get out the words.

Vincenzo understood. "Yes, there were women. When we were younger in New York. Maybe here, too, at one time. He's an attractive man in case you haven't noticed," he added with a twinkle and was rewarded by her blush. "But now, everyone knows the revolution is his mistress."

After that conversation, Melinda had forced herself to stop thinking about Diego. It had not been difficult. The fighting had intensified, and her days were filled with the helpless and the wounded. By the time they returned to the camp at night, she was so exhausted, she would fall into a dead man's sleep for the few hours she could be spared. Even dreaming was a luxury denied to them.

The people in the countryside grew to know and love her. They called her *l'estrella,* the star, and flocked around her when she came to their villages. When she was able, she ministered to the simpler ailments. When Vincenzo's surgical skills were needed, she stood by to offer comfort and hold a hand. The villagers responded to her warmth and genuine concern and to her beauty as well. It was health more than vanity that made her always wear a hat in the tropical sun. But even Melinda herself, who disparaged the importance of outward appearance, had to admit that her paleness seemed to have a palliative effect. They would reach out to touch her, and she would let them, seeing how the softness of her skin made them smile. At first, they questioned her motives; some even suggested she was a spy for Jorge Alvarro, who was simply waiting for his opportunity to sabotage the revolution and return. But soon, stories spread about her goodness and her indefatigable spirit, and they grew not only to accept her but to claim her as one of their own.

True to her word, Melinda continued to send her missives from the front. "My eyes have been opened," she wrote, "to things I have always taken for granted. The freedom to say and do what I want. The ability, even on a modest income, to live in a decent home. The expectation that our leaders, while fallible, are still required to obey the letter of the law, just as we are. All these things, I have learned, were not possible in San Domenico under Jorge Alvarro. As his guest, before the revolution, I experienced the luxury that I had come to expect simply because I had the good luck to be a successful actress. Only now do I see at what expense it was bought. The cost was not worth it.

I sleep better on a pallet in a tent than in a canopied bed with satin sheets because no one suffers for my comfort. I understand now that that is the real luxury."

"Did you see her latest?" Vincenzo asked Diego on one of the rare occasions that the two old friends met. They were in a village in the south where the rebels had repelled a thrust by government forces. But it had been a costly battle and the casualties were high. Melinda had gone into one of the shacks to comfort a pregnant widow when Vincenzo had spotted Diego making the rounds of the wounded.

"I saw it," Diego said tersely.

"What did you think?"

"What could I think? It was beautiful. Brilliant."

"Did you tell her?"

"You tell her for me."

"What's with you, Diego? I see you with the troops, always congratulating them, cheering them on. Melinda, who has no business being here in the first place, has been doing the work of an angel for a month, and you've never even acknowledged her. Don't you know what she's done for you? Not just with the people in San Domenico but with her letters that go out to the world?"

"I know."

"Then why don't you speak to her?"

"I can't."

Vincenzo would have pressed him, but he suddenly noticed a dark stain spreading slowly over Diego's shirt.

"What's that?" he asked, alarmed.

"Nothing," was Diego's brusque reply. "I have to go. The council is waiting for me."

"Hold on. You're not going anywhere until you let me look at that. You're bleeding."

"Not very much. I'm fine. I was grazed, that's all."

"Diego, you are not going to do the revolution any good as a dead man. Stay still."

Seeing he was not going to escape his friend's scrutiny, Diego sighed with exasperation and proffered his shoulder.

"See? Nothing's there. No problem."

"Well, the bullet went right through, I grant you that. But I wouldn't say it's no problem. You're living in the jungle, my friend. It's not exactly antiseptic. I wouldn't go in there with an open wound unless you are determined to be a martyr instead of a hero."

Vincenzo looked up and saw Melinda walking out of the shack. Tears had tracked white lines on her dusty cheeks. She had been crying with the women, and now, she took a moment on the porch to wipe her eyes and compose herself.

"Melinda, come here!" Vincenzo called to her. "I need you to stitch someone up. She quickly blew her nose and headed in his direction.

"No," exclaimed Diego vehemently. "Either fix it yourself or let me go."

"Excuse me," said Vincenzo in his most authoritarian voice. "Melinda is quite capable of handling this. I have more serious injuries to attend to. We are all equal in the revolutionary army. You get the same treatment as others." And then he was gone.

"What's the matter, *Commandante?* Are you afraid to be treated by a bored celebrity?" Melinda asked, ripping open his shirt with perhaps a touch more force than necessary to get at the wound.

"Don't call me that," he responded, embarrassed to

have his deliberately cruel words quoted back to him. "I have never commanded you."

"Sorry," she said as she blithely poured antiseptic on his injury causing him to wince in pain. He was not sure whether her apology was for her choice of words or her brusque efficiency. She began to stitch the open wound together, and trying not to flinch, she forced herself to ignore his sharp intake of breath with each stab of the needle into his skin. Had she not been helping him, he would have been certain she was trying to hurt him. She finished her work in silence, praying he could not see that as much as she had learned about medical trauma, she was fighting an urge to kiss it better.

When she had finished, she poured more antiseptic on her handiwork and told him he could go. He looked and saw that she had done a commendable job and he thanked her quietly.

"See me in a week and I'll take out the stitches. Or if you prefer, Vincenzo will do it," she added, preempting the possibility of a rebuff. She turned to leave.

He took a deep breath. "Melinda," he said, and her name alone caused his heart to beat faster.

She stopped and looked back at him. "Yes, *Com* . . . Yes?"

He wanted her to say his name, but she would not. He did not know what effort it cost her to hold it back.

"I've read your dispatches to the States. They're good. If you want to say, I told you so, go ahead."

She shook her head. "I didn't write them to prove you wrong about me," she said and walked away. She wasn't sure she had spoken the truth, and she would not give him the satisfaction of seeing her disappointment in the meagerness of his praise. He was a hard man. If she wanted to survive his indifference, she would have to be harder.

"You're an idiot," Vincenzo said as he watched Diego watch Melinda walk away.

"Please," said Diego impatiently, knowing full well why Vincenzo had said it, "I don't have time for this. I am leading a revolution here."

"Excuse me," Vincenzo's voice was filled with mock respect. "You're an idiot, *Commandante,* sir."

Melinda did not see Diego after that, whether by circumstance or design, she did not know. The fighting intensified, and though there were numerous triumphs, the casualties increased as well. But with each victory, the people seemed more determined to win their freedom from the grip of the military junta. And every time the government forces were routed, they seemed less inclined to return.

For the revolutionary forces, it was a heady time. But for Melinda, it felt like the end of the world. Arriving at the end of each battle with Vincenzo in their medical jeep, she would be confronted by the bodies in the field. But by now, they were no longer just brave young men and women in a revolutionary struggle for freedom. They were her *compadres,* people she knew by name, and they were dying all around her. When she saw their bloodied bodies and closed their anguished eyes, all the principles they claimed to be fighting for eluded her. She was exhausted in a way she had never experienced—beyond sleep, beyond tears. This, she decided, was the essence of world-weariness, and even in the heat of the jungle, it chilled her soul.

"I don't feel anything anymore," she told Vincenzo.

There had been another victory, another dozen dead, and far too many wounded.

"That happens," he said.

"It's never happened to me."

Vincenzo had been through this before. In Rwanda it had been worse. He looked at her. She'd assisted him in the amputation of a soldier's right arm. The soldier had told Melinda he was seventeen and never been kissed. She had kissed him then, gently but full on the mouth, ignoring the dirt and blood that transferred itself from his face to hers. The boy had smiled all during the operation.

"What you need," Vincenzo said, "is a hot bath, a good meal, and a strong lover. You'll feel plenty after that."

"I agree," she laughed, and he felt inordinately proud of himself for giving her even a moment's lightness.

"Would you settle for a dip in the stream, some snake stew, and me?" He was only half joking.

"I'm too tired to do you justice," she deflected his offer with grace. She rubbed her cheek with her hand and saw the grime. "Maybe I'll just go for the wash."

"Well," he sighed ruefully, "it wouldn't be my first choice, but there's no denying you could use it. You're a mess."

She laughed again and had him drop her off by the stream outside the camp that served as the rebels' de facto bathhouse. One end of the stream had been dammed up to form a shallow lagoon. All day the water absorbed the heat of the sun, so that by night, it was a warm caress. She could hear the others back at the camp, celebrating their victory with singing and laughter. She would have liked some wine, which was always a part of the festivities, but she could not bear the company of others tonight. She looked at her clothes, stiff with dried blood and dirt, and was grateful for the warmth in the air as she stripped. She dropped everything in the shallow part of the stream and swirled the clothes around, watching the sludge ooze from the fabric and get carried away by the gentle current. Then she laid it all on a rock to dry and waded out to the lagoon. In its deepest part, the water was only waist high, but she took a deep breath and submerged completely, longing for salvation by this self-administered baptism. She sat on the soft, sandy bottom and began to count, wondering how long she could stay below the surface. At fifty, she burst out of the water, gulping for air. Diego Roca was standing on the bank in front of her.

He was as shocked as she was. "I didn't know anyone was here," he said, taking a drink from the bottle of wine in his hand while he tried to regain his equilibrium. He was acutely aware of the play of moonlight in her hair, on her skin. The water lapped softly against her belly and she folded her arms across her breasts. She made no other move to cover herself.

"Why aren't you celebrating?" she asked quietly.

"I can't," he said. "People died today. Maybe because of me."

"Maybe their children will live better lives because of you."

He smiled. "You really are *la seniorita bendita.*"

"What?"

"Don't you know that's what they call you?"

"A bandit?"

"No," he laughed. "Not *bandito, bendita.* It means

184

blessed. It loses in translation, but they're calling you the revered maiden."

"Oh, I see," she joked, "I'm the maid of honor of the revolution. Which I guess would make you the bride," and was rewarded with another burst of laughter that seemed to light up the night.

"I should go," he said when he had caught his breath. "You were here first." It took all his willpower to turn away from her. With the moon shimmering in the lagoon around her, she looked like a siren luring him to the watery depths of abandon.

"Diego," she called softly. In that instant, he would have gladly renounced ten years of revolution for ten minutes in her arms. He stopped, but he did not turn. Blindness was his only hope of salvation.

"What?" he said harshly, trying to disguise the knot of emotion in his throat.

"If you're going," she pressed on, refusing to make room for disappointment, "could you at least let me have a drink of that wine?"

He tried to set it on the ground for her to retrieve after he had achieved a safe distance between them, but the bottle refused to remain upright on the craggy slope that led to the stream.

"It's open," he said gruffly. "You'd better come and get it, or it will spill."

"I don't have any clothes on," she reminded him. As if he could have forgotten.

"Where are they? I'll bring them to you."

"In that case," she smiled, "you might as well just bring me the wine."

He could think of no excuse, and he could not tell her the truth: that he was more afraid of her and what she could do to him than a whole squadron of government troops. He stripped off his shirt and stepped out of his boots, but he left his pants on and started wading into the stream toward her. He had a warrior's body, lean and muscular. The tropical sun had made his skin a lustrous bronze, and the moonlight reflected on his torso turned him into a moving sculpture. There was a dark scar below his shoulder where he had been wounded, and she noticed he had not had his stitches removed.

She reached out her hand to take the bottle and, in so doing, uncovered her breast. He was glad that the waist-deep water prevented her from seeing the effect it had on him. He took a deep draft of the wine and handed it to her.

"Make a toast," he said jocularly, trying to defuse the static of emotion that crackled in the air around them. "And you can keep the bottle." He started to wade away, not daring to stay and watch her drink.

"To you," she said without hesitation, surprising him with her solemnity, "for letting me share your dream."

He heard something in her voice and turned and saw that she was crying.

"I'm sorry," she said, taking a drink of the wine and making him ache with the beauty of her. "It's been a long, hard day." She took another drink and smiled, waving him off as if to say, it was okay, he could go. But she could not stop the tears.

Diego was lost. "Melinda," he whispered and, having said it once, found release and could not stop. "Melinda . . . Melinda . . ." He touched her hair, and let his fingers drift to her face, wiping away her tears, then tracing each feature before moving down her neck to her breast. The current seemed to push them together, and they let themselves go and floated into each other. Their bodies pressed together, and he felt the softness of her skin, washed with the warmth of the lagoon. He kissed her gently first, then hungrily, over and over again, like a man who had come to feast after a long famine. The bottle of wine slipped from her hand and drifted away.

"Diego," she said his name, and it was as though it had never been spoken before. The crowds that chanted "Di—e—go" when he drove through the villages might as well have been calling someone else, for he felt that he had been born only here in her arms, when she spoke his name.

"I tried not to love you," he said.

"Why?" It made no sense. She had loved him from the moment she saw him, even if it had taken her a while to realize it.

"Because in all my life I wanted nothing more than freedom for San Domenico. Now, I only want you."

Somehow he stripped out of his clothes and lifted her legs from the bottom of the stream and placed them around his waist. Buoyed by the water, she floated onto him, crying out with pain and pleasure as he pulled her to him, sealing them together. She clung to him as he moved in her, undulating slowly, so close that even the water could not come between them. He pushed her back into the water, so that she lay floating on her back, weightless, anchored only by his ardor. His mouth was on her mouth, her neck, her breast, each kiss burning its mark into her flesh, until her whole body was an inferno of desire. And when he felt her release begin, he clasped her to him, pulling her on top of him as he lay in the water, so that she could move effortlessly, all of her touching all of him, bathed by the warm waves of the lagoon below and the cool light of the moon above. Still not letting them drift apart, he brought her to shallow water and sat her on a rock. He kneeled before her and, pulsing with a prayer of love, attained his own divine grace.

In the camp, the singing had stopped. The moon was already sinking, and the stars had begun to fade by the time they put their damp clothes back on and trudged back to the camp. All was still, except for the quiet footsteps of the two guards posted to keep watch while the others slept. They smiled but didn't speak as Diego and Melinda walked by and entered his tent hand in hand. In the tent, he undressed her and then himself, and she lay beside him on his pallet as she had done once before. His arms folded around her, and she marveled that in the midst of war, she could know such peace.

9

Love teaches you fear. Until she had found Diego, Melinda had managed to ignore the dread that hangs like rain clouds over countries at war, waiting to pour grief on the unlucky inhabitants below. She had ridden in the jeep with Vincenzo to wherever they were charged to go, thinking only of the work that had been done before or needed to be done anew. While she cried with those who had lost friends or family, they were tears of sympathy that she shed, not tears of experience. Those who died were martyrs, those who lived were patients. But none of them belonged to her.

Now, suddenly, everything was different. Her heart stopped at the news of each battle. She could not begin her work until she had combed the field of dead and wounded, searching for that dear face she dreaded to find. Their time together was minimal, an hour or two snatched before dawn and the next foray, but he was

189

on her mind constantly. All at once, the cause she had once found so just didn't seem to matter at all. All she cared about was that Diego stayed alive.

"I am invincible." He tried to tease away her fears when he saw her trembling at his departure.

But she did not believe him. "I wish the revolution were over. One way or another. Just so that I could know you'd be safe."

"The only way for the revolution to be over," he said solemnly, "is for the San Domenican Liberation Front to win. Otherwise, the fighting continues. Even if I die, the people will not give up their arms." He saw her face fall and hastily went on. "But I'm not going to die, and we will win and the revolution will be over. I swear it."

He kissed her, and in his passion, she felt the promise. It soothed her for a time. But an hour later, Vincenzo came to tell her that medical assistance was needed at a skirmish in the east, and the terror grabbed her by the throat again.

"Melinda," Vincenzo said as they bumped along a dirt road that had been cut by hand through the jungle, "my prescription was for a little sex, not this heart-wrenching devotion."

She blushed. "Does everybody know?"

"Why? Just because you devour each other with your eyes when you are within one hundred meters of each other? Or because when you are in the camp together, first one than the other has to immediately go to the stream for a bath? Or because Diego no longer lets anyone into his tent at night and your place in the women's tent remains empty? Why should anybody know?"

"We can't help it."

"I see that. But from the looks of what it does to you, you would have been better off taking my original advice and having a little fun with me. At least you would always know where I am."

She laughed and leaned over to kiss him. "You're very special, Vincenzo. And believe me, any woman would have to be a fool not to want you."

"And you just happen to be that fool, eh?" He smiled ruefully. "Never mind. Unlike me, *el commandante* is a committed man. I flit from war zone to war zone, woman to woman. But Diego, he is loyal. Maybe it's better for you."

"If he lives, it is. I don't know what I'll do if he dies."

When she'd seen that Diego was not among the rebels lying on the ground and they'd done what they could for those who were, she returned to the camp. The portable fax had stopped working, and she knew it would be at least a week before she could get to one of the hotels on the island that might still have working equipment. Nonetheless, there were things she needed to say, and in her quiet moments, waiting for Diego to return, she began another letter home. "Love teaches you fear," she wrote and hoped they would understand.

"You did what?" Sam had heard Amos's words, she just couldn't believe him.

"You heard me. I called Jimmy Carter. I think I can get him to go down to San Domenico, find your sister, and bring her back." He'd called her back to the office from home with the promise of important information. She'd hesitated, and he'd realized that maybe he'd been doing that too much lately. But he was alone at the office, and it just seemed too good an opportunity to squander. But he knew he was going to have to make it good, and he could see from her face that this qualified.

"Are you kidding me?"

"Sam, I don't joke about politics. Carter is very concerned about human rights issues around the world. I told him the situation and said you thought Melinda was being brainwashed or held against her will and that the letters were a hoax."

"I didn't exactly say that."

"I didn't exactly quote you. The point is, I got him interested enough to consider handling this personally."

"Do you really think he can do it? Do you think he *would?*

"Lord knows, he has plenty of experience especially in the past year or two. And yes, I think this is right up his alley. He's going to let me know for sure before the end of the week."

"Oh, Amos. You are wonderful," said Sam, meaning it until she saw him heading toward her, ready for a clinch.

Quickly, she found something that needed immediate attention and barricaded herself behind her desk. It bothered her to have to avoid Amos like this. Under normal conditions, there's nothing that would have seemed more natural than to hug the man who had extended himself so much to help her. But with Amos, she never knew what interpretation might be made of an innocent display of gratitude.

For a moment, he veered away from her so smoothly that she wondered if perhaps she'd been mistaken, and he'd never meant to come toward her at all. She was so on edge from the number of times she'd found herself pinned against the wall while Amos pressed into her that she had lost all judgment as to what was or was not appropriate behavior. But it turned out he'd only made the detour to the filing cabinet to retrieve a bottle of twenty-year-old scotch and two glasses. Sam didn't want to have a drink with him, but she knew that refusing would only make him press harder. She'd be better off just accepting, taking a sip or two, and getting out of there as quickly as she could.

"You owe me one," he said, arching an eyebrow as he set the glasses on the desk and poured them both half full of whiskey.

"You bet I do," she answered cheerily, clinking his glass and taking a small sip of the liquor, trying to diffuse the suggestive remark and keep the talk ordinary and banal. With his predilection for double entendre, even conversation had become a hazardous obstacle course. Yet Amos had helped her so much in her search for Melinda and she felt as if she owed him a huge debt of gratitude. It hurt her not to be able to show him how deeply she appreciated all he had done, but she didn't dare risk encouraging his already out-of-control appetite for fondling her.

He drained his glass and poured himself another drink, which he drained as well.

"Are you driving, Amos?" she asked, keeping her tone lighthearted.

"Are you worried about me, sweetheart?"

"I need you to finish negotiating with Jimmy Carter to get my sister back," she joked.

"That's right, you do," he said, and there was something in his tone that made her look at him sharply. He had come around to her side of the desk and was perched on the edge, his feet against the wall, effectively cutting off her exit route.

Sam sighed. She was backed into a corner again. She knew she ought to sit Amos down and have a heart-to-heart talk about this with him. She knew he'd be offended and insist he was just being warm and friendly, maybe go so far as admit he was harmlessly flirting. It would take a lot to convince him that his actions could be construed as sexual harassment. And the truth was, she didn't want to risk alienating him until Melinda was safely back home.

"You've been great, but I've got to get going, Amos," she said, trying to keep the mood light. She stood up and stopped in front of his legs, waiting for him to put them down so she could pass. He made no move to let her by.

"Why? Your family's away. No one's going to be waiting for you."

She looked at her watch. It was a little past nine. After several days of working late into the night, the rest of the staff had gone home early. Even Dotty, who was usually too nervous to leave before Amos, had excused herself because of a burgeoning flu. Sam was starting to get nervous.

"Amos, please, I'm tired," she said, walking into his legs, hoping he'd be forced to put them down and let her pass. Instead, he stood up and blocked the way even more effectively with his body.

"You said you owed me one. I think now would be a good time to collect."

She tried once more to divert him with a joke. "Hey, you've got to deliver the merchandise first.

Bring me my sister, then we can talk," she said, putting on the voice of a mafia don.

"Uh-uh," he responded, swaying back and forth to keep her from stepping around him. "I require payment in advance. You know, no tickee, no washee."

"No, Amos, I don't know." She was getting really offended now. "What are you trying to tell me with that ugly little racist phrase?"

"Oh, excuse me, Miss Politically Correct. You feminists are all alike. Can't say anything, can't do anything. What you all need is a good screw."

"Okay, that's it. I'm going now, Amos. I'm going to put this conversation down to too much to drink and try to forget about it. I suggest you do the same. Let's start fresh in the morning. We've still got a lot to do." She was very angry, but she was forcing herself to stay in control. Amos had never spoken that way before. She also had to remind herself that he was one of her husband's oldest friends, and no one had done more for her since the crisis with Melinda had begun than he had. And the crisis wasn't over yet.

"We've got a lot to do right now." Instead of moving out of her way, he took a step closer, locking her between her chair and his body.

She tried to push him away. "You don't get it, do you?"

"No," he said, pushing her back, *"you* don't get it. I've put myself out for you. Now I expect you to do the same for me."

"Or what?"

He shrugged. "Jimmy Carter hasn't left for San Domenico yet. He might decide not to go."

"Meaning you would talk him out of it."

"Let's put it this way. I've only pointed out the advantages of this mission. We haven't really gotten into the down side. And there's always a down side if you look hard enough."

There was still a part of Sam that wanted to believe that this was all just Amos's idea of a bad joke. "Let me get this straight. You're telling me if I don't have sex with you, you're not going to help me get my sister out of San Domenico?"

"I'm just saying, you want me on your side. Be on my side."

Sam felt herself going into a state of shock. For a moment, her primary senses stopped functioning, and she felt herself pulled into a whirlpool of memory. She had traded sex for assistance once before with a man who was more discreet and sensitive than Amos could ever be. She had slept with him just once to save her husband's life, and it had almost cost her her marriage. She would not make the same mistake again. A surging anger pushed away thoughts of the past.

"I can't believe this," she spat out. "Amos, you've got a wife and kids. My husband is one of your oldest friends."

"No one has to know. Drew's away. My family hasn't been in Washington all year. Come on, Sam. We've always had a thing for each other, let's admit it."

"What?! I have *never* . . ."

"Are we suddenly playing coy? This isn't the first time I've had my arms around you. Or the first time I've kissed you."

She tried to struggle away, but there was no room to maneuver. He wrapped himself around her and pressed his lips against hers. His arms were like restraints, and she realized that the more she pushed against him, the more excited he became. She tried going limp, hoping her sudden slackness would alert him to the fact that his passion was not reciprocated. Instead, it gave him the opportunity to push her back into the chair without resistance and to straddle her so forcefully that she had no hope of getting out from under him.

"Amos, don't· do this," she cried with one last irrational hope that reason might prevail. But one hand had already found its way beneath her blouse and was kneading her breast, while the other had unceremoniously ripped through her pantyhose and was prying its way between her clenched thighs. His eyes were closed, and he was breathing hard.

Sam was panicked now. She knew if she didn't do something, she was going to be raped. Overpowering him physically was out of the question. If she was going to get out of this, she would have to be clever. She took a deep breath and kissed him, her lips full and pliant, her tongue creeping into his mouth. He moaned, surprised and pleased, and she could feel him relax his grip.

"Let's not do it this way," she whispered. "I want to do it right. I want to take off all my clothes. I want you to see my body. Wouldn't you like that?"

"Oh, baby, you know I would."

"Pour me another drink," she commanded. She felt him hesitate. She kissed him again, grinding her body into him, letting him feel what he would be getting if he only cooperated. "I want this to take all night," she drawled.

He grinned, "I could tell from the beginning we'd make a good team."

"Me, too," she said. "Now pour me that drink and let me get more comfortable."

He got off her then and turned to the desk to pour the drinks. She slipped out from under him and stood in front of him, not putting any distance between them. She saw him tense and abandon the bottle to take up his sentry position again. Slowly, she started to undo her blouse. He wet his lips with his tongue and she could hear him panting softly. She let her blouse fall open, let him catch a tantalizing glimpse of her exposed breast.

"Like what you see?" she asked.

"You bet," he said, reaching out to touch them, but she pulled back just a little.

"Want to see more?" she asked seductively.

"You know I do."

"Then where's my drink?" she asked huskily, giving him a little tap on the knuckles as though he'd been a naughty boy.

He laughed, enjoying the game, and poured her a drink and one for himself.

She held her glass up for a toast, and in the split second when his glass clinked against hers, she made her move, flinging the scotch with an upward thrust into his face.

"You stupid bitch," he screamed and rubbed at the fire in his eyes.

But she had already jumped over his outstretched leg and was running out the door and down the corridor of the Russell Building, her unbuttoned blouse flapping over her heaving chest. She didn't start to cry until she had arrived home and was in the dark and lonely house with the door double locked behind her.

Natalie had already changed into her flannel night-shirt when the phone rang. Assuming it might be Drew calling from the hospital, she ran to the den to get it, but by the time she got there, the answering machine had already picked up. Ready to override the machine, Natalie reached for the receiver but stopped short as she recognized Sam's voice.

"Hello? . . . Is anybody there? . . . Drew? Natalie? It's after ten, shouldn't the baby be in bed? Where are you all?"

It was hard to mistake the distress in Sam's voice. Natalie even thought she heard some sniffling, as though Sam were crying. She listened grimly, making no move to answer.

"Anyway," Sam was saying, "I'm coming home. I can't stay in Washington anymore. I'll explain when I see you, but I'm taking the night flight, which means I've got to go to the airport in about a half hour. So call me if you get home before that. Otherwise, I'll see you in the wee hours."

There was a pause, and Natalie assumed that Sam was putting down the receiver. But a second later, there was another audible sniffle and Sam got back on the line.

"Drew . . . I love you and I really need to see you. Which I guess I'll be doing soon. Okay. Bye."

This time, Natalie heard the distinct click of the phone being hung up. She waited until the answering machine had turned itself off. Then, very carefully, she hit the proper button and watched as the machine erased the message.

She had been disappointed when Drew had had to forego dinner because of a call from Buddy at the hospital, informing him that his father was having trouble breathing. But now, she realized, it could work to her benefit, provided the old fart didn't go and die on them tonight. In fact, Natalie had taken a keen interest in Forrest Symington's health, aware that if he either died or recovered, there would be no need for Drew to remain at Belvedere, and they'd all be carted back to Washington, to the unbearable scrutiny of Drew's unbearable wife. So, each night, Natalie included Forrest in her prayers, wishing for him a purgatory of lingering ill health.

From the moment she had arrived at Belvedere, Natalie had felt the potential of fulfilling all her dreams. It wasn't just the beauty of the estate, which was formidable, but the fact that, here, everything seemed to turn in her favor. There was a staff to cook and clean for them, and she did little except play with Moira and keep Drew company when he was home from the hospital. Drew's mother had still not arrived from France, and his sister and brother-in-law spent most of their time in the east wing, which they had occupied since Drew and Sam had moved to Washington. Often, Sam's mother came to pick up Moira for a day with her grandparents, and on those days, Natalie had Drew to herself. Although Drew spent a good deal of his time at his father's bedside and much of the rest of it on the telephone and computer, dealing with his various business interests in absentia, she could tell that he was not only aware of her presence but appreciated the fact that, unlike his wife, she was always there for him. He'd never told her so in so many words, but she did not need to hear it. She could tell just by the way he looked at her. She always knew it was just a matter of time before everything came together for her, and she knew the time was now.

Expecting he'd come home from the hospital late, she'd had the kitchen prepare a tray for him. Even though she intended to go to bed early, knowing he probably wouldn't be in the mood to talk to anyone anyway, she'd wanted him to know that she was thinking of him. But now, there was a change of plans. She looked at her watch. She still had at least three hours before Sam arrived. If luck was with her, she'd have at least two alone with Drew before then.

Not knowing when he might walk in the door, she moved quickly. She knew exactly what she wanted and where to find it. Sometimes, when no one was around, she would go into his room, look through his things, not to spy, but as a way of getting closer to him. Now, she went straight to the medicine cabinet in his bathroom and pulled it open. Beside the razors and the Band-Aids, the little bottle was still there. She read the label: "Andrew Symington, Take one as needed to sleep." She tapped some pills into the palm of her hand. They looked very small. She put three of them in her pocket.

Hurrying into her own bathroom, she threw off her flannel nightshirt, turned the faucet on full force, and dumped a half a bottle of scented bubble bath into the tub. Letting herself relax for a moment, while the heat and perfume penetrated her body, she imagined what it would be like, having Drew in the tub with her, having his hand instead of her own moving the soap gently over her body. Entranced by the vision, she almost didn't hear the door open, and his footsteps heavily climbing the stairs.

She cursed softly. She hadn't even decided what to wear yet, and he was already there. Then she smiled. In fact, he had made the decision for her, and it was perfect. Climbing out of the tub, she grabbed a towel and wrapped it around herself. It covered her from breast to thigh and left the rest of her damp and delectably exposed.

"Drew, is that you?" she called softly coming out of her room just as he reached the top of the stairs. He gave an involuntary start as he saw her, and she knew she'd had the effect she intended.

"Oh, sorry, Natalie. I didn't mean to disturb you."

She held the towel in front of her, letting it dip just a little to reveal one softly rounded breast. "You didn't. I just didn't expect you back so soon. I had the kitchen make up a tray for you. Let me get it."

"Don't bother," he said quickly. "I'll get it myself. I just want to call Sam before it gets too late."

Natalie glanced surreptitiously at the antique grandfather clock that graced the hallway. It was forty-five minutes since Sam had called. If she was coming, she'd have to be on her way to the airport. "Okay, you make your call and I'll go get your tray. It's no trouble. Really."

She was already moving toward the stairs, and Drew didn't have the energy to dissuade her. No matter how much he insisted that her only job was to take care of Moira, she seemed determined to take care of him as well. Her delight in serving him made him uncomfortable, but it was flattering as well, and if it pleased her, as it seemed to, then why should he argue. She was a sweet young thing and she had a crush on him, and so far, the day hadn't offered him even mild diversion. But, even so, there were limits.

"Natalie," he said, stopping her, "maybe you should put something on."

"Oh." She blushed and lowered her eyes, hoping that he noticed the faint pink tint flow from her face to her breast. "I'm sorry . . . I didn't mean . . . At home . . . ," she stammered.

"It's okay." He smiled, charmed by her apparent oblivion to the impact a young woman's body could generate. "You didn't do anything wrong. But as much as I want you to feel at home, clothes might be a good idea."

"Of course. I was just getting ready for bed. But I'll put something on and bring you your tray."

"Listen, I can—" he began, but she didn't let him finish.

"Please," she said, "I want to." And too tired to argue, he went into his bedroom to call his wife.

Turning her drawer upside down, Natalie found what she was looking for. It was a nightgown that seemed demure and innocent beyond question. The neck was high, the sleeves were long, and the lace edge of the hem hung to her ankles. But Natalie knew that with the light behind her, the fabric became virtually transparent, and she knew just where to stand.

Drew was just hanging up the phone as she came into his bedroom with the tray.

"No answer," he said ruefully.

"Did you try the office?" Natalie asked.

Drew nodded. "Not there either."

"Poor Drew," she sympathized, handing him the tray. "This is such a hard time for you. You really need somebody . . ."

She stood back and let the light from the open bathroom door silhouette her body. From the look on Drew's face as he hastily studied his tray, she knew it was working.

"Well, Sam's got her troubles now, too. I'm sure she'd rather I be with her while she's trying to track down her sister."

"I guess," said Natalie, then added as if in afterthought, "but she was working nights with Uncle Amos even before Melinda disappeared, wasn't she?"

Drew looked at her, but her face was without guile. Through her sheer nightgown, he could see the soft voluptuous roundness of her breast, the gentle curve of her hips leading into the long lean lines of legs that went on forever. He wanted to tell her to go put on a robe but remembered how embarrassed she'd been when he'd noticed her state of undress before. He didn't want to start sounding like a vicar in a Victorian novel. But he didn't need to be reminded that temptation was never far from reach either.

"You know, I'm really more tired than hungry. I think I'm going to just hit the sack."

Natalie started to panic, maybe she had gone too far too fast. She moved out of the light and cloaked herself in modesty.

"Why don't you at least have some wine. It might relax you. I made them open that '86 Lafitte you like so much. In fact, I thought maybe I could have a little, too."

Without waiting for him to reply, rightly certain of his assent, she poured herself a glass from the bottle and handed him the glass that had already been poured for him.

She sipped the wine, tasting it on her lips as though it were an exotic nectar she'd been privileged to drink for the first time. She looked as chaste as a Norman Rockwell painting, and he was abashed by his earlier prurient thoughts. But as innocent as her concern for him might be, he did not think it would be right to encourage it too much. So he could dismiss her, without insulting her, he drained his wineglass and thanked her profusely for her consideration. She beamed with his praise, and before he could deflect her, she threw her arms around him and kissed him.

"Natalie, really, I don't think . . ." He was more tired than he thought. He couldn't seem to stay upright. He felt himself falling against the pillows and wasn't sure if she had pushed him back or he had just collapsed.

"I've got to go to sleep," he said with as much firmness as he could manage.

"Of course, you do," she whispered, and he felt her breath on his face. "Let me help you undress."

She started to unbutton his shirt, and for a moment, it made sense, so certain was he that he would not be capable of such a simple act himself.

"No, it's okay," he mumbled, his eyes already half-closed, as she opened his belt and began to maneuver his pants.

"Just pick yourself up for a minute, I've got it," she said with just enough authority to make him do it.

He tried to open his eyes, but the room seemed to swirl around him. He had drunk the wine too fast on an empty stomach, but he'd never expected such a strong reaction.

He smelled lilac and felt the supple velvet of a

woman's skin against his body. Soft lips touched his and he responded, his body aroused though his mind drifted.

He groaned, feeling desire take control.

She whispered, "I want you to take me."

For a moment, lucidity returned, sharp and cold as an icicle down his back.

"Natalie, stop!" he demanded, trying to remove her hands from him, but the haze began to close in again. "I don't want this."

"Yes, you do," she answered with utter conviction. "I can feel you do."

He cursed his body's betrayal but felt powerless to stop it. His volition seemed already to have abandoned him and he was rapidly losing his ability to think. Something's wrong here, he wanted to say, but speech was out of the question. And then, it didn't matter anymore. Losing the struggle for consciousness, he fell into a deep, drugged sleep.

Natalie felt him go limp beneath her. She wondered if perhaps she should have dissolved just two pills in his wine instead of three. It wasn't exactly as she had envisioned it, but it didn't worry her. She knew that perception in this case was going to be far more important than reality.

She got up and, taking his glass into the bathroom, she carefully washed out any traces of the sleeping pills she'd mashed into the glass. Pouring a drop of wine from the bottle, she swirled it around, so the glass looked used. She put it back on the tray beside her own half-drunk glass. Then she pulled off her nightgown and, leaving it in a heap on the floor, slipped naked into bed beside the sleeping Drew.

It was after two A.M. when Sam finally arrived

home. There had been a delay at the airport, and they had sat on the runway for an hour before taking off. She would have called Drew, but there was no telephone on the small commuter airline that took her to the local airport outside of Woodland Cliffs. The house was dark and quiet, and she tiptoed up the stairs, longing for her own bed and the quiet safety of her husband's arms.

The door to Moira's room was ajar, and she went in, her heart soaring at the sight of her round-faced cherub, pink and warm with sleep, one little fist clenching the square of tattered quilt she called "blankie." She kissed her daughter, not causing even a stir, and went on to her own room.

The room was dark, and she didn't bother to turn on the light. It took her eyes a moment to adjust, and as she moved to the bed, she tripped over something soft on the floor. She picked it up and saw it was a nightgown, not her own. Confused, she looked at Drew asleep in bed and stared hard for what seemed like a long time, wanting to be sure that the form that extended from his was not some trick of the dark. Not yet willing to believe, she turned on the light. Doubt fled and shock flew in to fill the void.

Natalie sat bolt upright in bed, her eyes wide open in fear as she clutched the sheet to cover her naked breast. "Oh my God, Sam. What are you doing here?"

"This is my home," said Sam coldly. "And in case you've forgotten, that's my husband."

It took Drew a moment longer to wake up, and Sam could see him struggling to attain a minimal level of consciousness.

"Sam, honey," he said, "you're home," with such equanimity that Sam was outraged all the more.

"Care to explain?" she asked, her voice filled with indignation.

He looked confused. "What . . . ?" he began, and then Natalie took over, sobbing her apology.

"We didn't mean it to happen. It's just that you're away so much and Drew was so lonely . . ."

Sam felt her mouth drop open. She looked at Drew. "You are blaming me for this."

"No, I didn't say that. I don't even know what this is."

Sam gave a bitter laugh. *"This* is sleeping with the au pair when your wife is away."

"But I didn't . . . ," he started to say and then registered Natalie cowering naked beneath the sheets behind him. His head ached more than it ever had in his entire life. He couldn't think straight, and the truth was, he couldn't remember what had happened. He remembered drinking a glass of wine too quickly, letting Natalie help him undress. He even remembered a kiss. None of which he was proud of. But from the looks of things, it got worse from there, and that part was a complete blank. Still, in the face of Natalie's state of undress and her continued sobs and muffled apologies for what they did, denial seemed not only pointless but ludicrous.

"We didn't plan it, Sam. It just happened," Natalie was saying. "We couldn't help ourselves."

Drew wanted to tell her to shut up. She was irritating him; he could only imagine what she was doing to Sam. But considering his position, he thought it best to be diplomatic.

"Natalie, do you mind? Could you give Sam and me some time alone?"

"Don't bother," raged Sam, sweeping out the door. "I'm going."

Drew tried to go after Sam, but Natalie grabbed his arm.

"Maybe it's best, Drew . . ."

He shook her off, trying to shake off the fog in his head at the same time. He jumped out of bed and was profoundly embarrassed to be naked in front of her. He wondered why he would feel such shame if they had slept together. Nothing was making sense, but he didn't have time to figure it out now. He found his pants on the floor and slipped into them, then ran after Sam. She had Moira in her arms, wrapped in a blanket, and was heading down the stairs.

"Sam!" he called after her.

"Shhh!" she hissed. "Don't make things worse by waking the baby."

He could see she was crying. "Honey, please, listen to me," he pleaded softly. "It's not what it looks like."

She stopped midstep and looked at him incredulous. "Really? Then what is it?"

"I don't know," he said flinching, knowing how lame it sounded even though it was true.

"Spare me," was all she said and kept walking down the stairs.

He ran after her. "You can't go out. It's the middle of the night. Not with the baby. Where are you going?"

"What does it matter to you? I'm away so much anyway. And of course, now you've got Natalie."

"Sam, don't. I don't want Natalie."

"Poor girl. Seduced and abandoned."

"It's not like that."

"What's it like then?"

"I don't . . . ," he started to say, but she finished for him.

"Don't tell me. You don't know. Get yourself a good shrink. Maybe he can help you get some answers. And I'd really appreciate it if you would leave me alone until you do."

The door slammed in his face. He considered trying to follow her, but his head was ringing and he was afraid he'd never make it. Maybe it would be better if he gave her a little space and he could use the time to sort his thoughts out. He started heavily up the steps and saw Natalie, still wrapped in his sheet, quaking at the top of the stairs. If he had taken advantage of her, he supposed he should feel pity for her. Instead, he felt inordinate anger as if he, in some way, had been the victim.

"Natalie," he forced himself to sound calm, even friendly, "tell me what happened."

"Y . . . You know . . . ," she stuttered.

"No," he stayed quiet, though he wanted to shake her. "If I knew, I wouldn't ask you. I must have been very, very drunk, because this has never happened to me before."

"Are you saying you only made love to me because you were drunk?" She was sniffling again.

"I don't want to hurt your feelings, Natalie. But if something hadn't been very wrong with me, this would never have happened. You're very sweet and very pretty. But I love my wife, and I'm not in the habit of fooling around—especially with young girls."

"I wish you had told me that last night . . . before . . ." Tears were rolling down her cheeks now.

Drew had never felt like such a heel. "So do I," he said fervently. "So do I. I feel like I've been drugged."

Natalie smiled inwardly, glad she'd had the foresight to plan ahead. "I drank that wine, too. Nothing happened to me."

He knew she was telling the truth. He actually remembered her pouring the wine, drinking it. He was amazed that he could recollect such little details and yet completely block out the most foolish thing he had ever done in his life.

"Natalie, whatever happened, all I can say is I'm sorry. It shouldn't have happened and it won't happen again."

"Don't say that, Drew. I wanted to make love to you, and you want me, too. It's just the shock of Sam walking in on us. But she's gone now, it's all right."

He looked at her and saw that she really believed what she was saying. He blamed himself. Maybe he hadn't exactly encouraged her little crush, but he should have made it absolutely clear that it was inappropriate. He grabbed his throbbing head. From all indications, he had a lot more to blame himself for than lack of clarity.

"Listen to me, Natalie. I have a very bad headache right now, and I'm not feeling very well. I can't remember what happened, but it doesn't really matter. The one thing I know for sure is that it was a terrible, terrible mistake. In the morning, I'm going to get you a plane ticket either to your uncle's in Washington or back to North Dakota—wherever you want. But you can't stay here."

"Don't do this, Drew. Don't send me away. Let me stay with you. You'll see. It was meant to be."

She had thrown her arms around him and was

holding him, crying, pleading. He pulled her hands off him a little more roughly than he had intended, and she fell against the wall.

"I'm sorry, Natalie. Go to your room. Have your bags packed in the morning."

She began to cry, letting herself slide down to the floor. He knew he should have felt compassion, but all he could think of was maybe, if she left, he could figure out how he'd managed to ruin his life in one awful night.

10

Sam made it a point to be beside Moira's crib when she woke up in the morning. She hadn't slept all night—even on the flight back to Washington, and she didn't want Moira to wake up and be disoriented. It couldn't be good for the child to be continually plucked from one environment and unceremoniously deposited in another with no transition or explanation. But the truth was, she found Moira's room less inhibiting than her own. Here, there was no confusion, no mixed feelings. In this room, at least, there was only love.

As it was, she need not have worried. Moira woke up with her usual sunny disposition and smiled at the sight of her mother. She asked once for "Nah-wee" but seemed to accept that Natalie had gone bye-bye without a problem. Reaching out her chubby arms, she laughed with glee as Sam lifted her out of her crib and tossed her into the air. It was amazing, Sam thought, that no matter how your heart was breaking, a baby could make you smile.

Breakfast was a festive affair, and when Moira had eaten her fill, she happily began to fish out Cheerios from her bowl and arrange them in a soggy pattern on her high-chair table.

The doorbell rang and Sam's heart skipped a beat before it was drowned by a wave of anger. She had expected Drew to come after her but not this quickly. For some reason, she had thought he'd know enough to give her some space, to let them work out their problems with what had happened individually before trying to deal with them together. Apparently, his encounter with Natalie had been a regression in more ways than one. The doorbell rang again, and she wondered why the hell he didn't use his key. It was bad enough his invading her privacy without his insisting she greet him at the door.

By the third ring, when Moira had taken up a chant of ding-dong, it occurred to Sam it might not be Drew. Peering through the window in the foyer, she was even more shocked to see Amos Kilmont standing on her doorstep. He caught her peeking and gave a little wave. He was smiling benignly and seemed to have forgotten all about their encounter the night before. But Sam had not forgotten.

"Go away, Amos," she said through the door. "I'm not working for you anymore."

He grinned as though she were teasing. "Come on, Sammy. Open up. I've got news for you. From your sister."

She didn't know whether to believe him or not.

"Really? How come you didn't wait until the office was deserted to call me and tell me to come and get it."

"Now that's just why I came down here in broad daylight. I was afraid you might have misunderstood about last night."

"Misunderstood? Jesus, Amos, you tried to rape me."

"Hey, let's not exaggerate. But okay, if you want to forget it, you'll probably read about it in the *Post* tomorrow."

He turned to go, and Sam relented. If there was word from Melinda, she didn't want to be the last to know. She opened the door. Amos walked in all business. He didn't even try to kiss her hello. She wondered if his aggressiveness might not be as much an alcohol problem as anything else. In the light of day, he was cordial but nothing more, and she was relieved.

"Do you mind coming into the kitchen? I left the baby alone in her high chair."

He looked at her quizzically. "I thought she was back at the family estate with your husband and my niece."

"She was. She's here now," Sam said offering no information.

"Natalie and Drew here, too?" His curiosity was piqued.

"Not at the moment." She wasn't offering any more. "So what do you have from my sister?"

He looked at her, considering whether to ask more, but she was obviously too impatient for idle conversation. He opened his briefcase and handed her a fax. It was like the ones she had seen before, handwritten in

Melinda's cursive scrawl. She sat down and began to read: "Love teaches you fear . . ."

In the background, the baby sang, "Bye, bye, bwackbood," which Natalie had taught her the week before. Amos hummed along while he watched Sam read.

Anyone who has felt deeply for lover, husband, or children will understand what I mean. No matter how much you tell yourself that love is a gift to be appreciated to its fullest in the moment, it is unacceptable. If you really love, you're on the constant lookout for guarantees: that your choice is worthy, that the heart will remain steadfast, and most of all, that no harm will come to the object of your affection.

Justice teaches you honor. When you know what's right, it seems only natural to want to redress wrong. But when you love, justice and honor seem irrelevant. No fight is worth fighting if it means you might lose the one you love. Every mother in San Domenico knows this. Every wife. And every lover. If you believe in God, you pray and beg him to let your loved one live. If you don't, you simply wait, counting down minutes like rosary beads, until you know if you've been blessed or cursed. In a normal life, these fears are buried. You can't allow terror to take control at every street crossing, every venture into new territory. But in battle, there is no reprieve.

The people of San Domenico believe their cause is just. It is right to fight for freedom. But everyone wants this civil war to be over. Even Diego Roca has admitted he is afraid to lose the one he loves. Maybe, if there is a God, that alone is enough to make Him spare Diego's life.

Sam put down the paper. Her eyes were filled with tears. Reading her sister's words had brought out her own primeval fears. If anything happened to Moira or even Drew in spite of what was happening between them or Melinda herself . . . Life was too precious to be squandered.

"Well," said Amos when he saw that she had finished reading, "sounds like she's boinking Roca, doesn't it?"

"What?!" Sam was stunned. She had been so moved by the emotion of Melinda's words, she hadn't even thought about what had prompted them. Now, she realized that, indelicately as he put it, Amos was right.

"Which means we can forget about Carter going after her. In fact, brainwashed or not, I don't think she's in the rescue category anymore."

Again, Sam knew he was right. There was no point in making an appeal for Melinda's return if she was going to refuse to come back. She wished she could be in touch with her sister directly, to know what was going on with her. But it was becoming clear that Melinda was making her own choices, rational or not, and true to her Myles Militia credo, Sam would simply have to stand by her and support her no matter what.

Sam was more relieved than she let on. She knew she was being hypocritical, but in spite of Amos's unsavory advances, he had, in fact, tried to help her. The gracious thing to do would be to suggest to one of his senior staff members that she get him into a twelve-step program and leave it at that. Her life was in enough of a shambles without Amos Kilmont adding to the complication.

"Well," she said with as much warmth as she could

muster, "I appreciate all your efforts, but I guess there's nothing more you can do for me."

To her shock, Amos disagreed. "I don't think that's true at all."

"Really, Amos." She tried to hide her disdain. "Don't you think you've pushed me enough?"

He laughed as if she'd told a good joke. "I'd have to say not, since I haven't gotten you to do what I want yet. But I don't give up easily."

She couldn't believe her ears. He was trying to make it sound like getting her into bed was the equivalent of passing a difficult piece of legislation.

"I'd like you to get out of my house now," was all she said. She turned her attention to Moira, hoping that he would find his own way to the door. But he wasn't moving.

"Sam, I think you're forgetting that your husband's company holds a very lucrative government contract. I happen to know DMC has already gone to considerable expenditure to fulfil that contract. Now, if for some reason, improprieties were found, and the government were forced to cancel that contract, that would be a substantial hardship even on a family with the Symingtons' wealth."

"Unless you're talking about your own, there are no improprieties, and you know it."

"Don't be naive. This is Washington. There are always improprieties. It's just a matter of who's willing to *bring* them up and who's willing to *cover* them up."

"You would do this to one of your oldest friends?"

"Only if I wanted to fuck his wife," he said with affable good humor.

"Is this a threat? Are you saying that if I don't sleep

with you, you're going to have DMC's contract canceled?"

"I don't threaten, Sam. It's not my style. I'm a senator, not a mafioso. I'm just warning you. Things happen. Oh, come on, Sam," he went on, seeing her face register utter horror. "It's not like I'm Jack the Ripper. I'd make you happy, and you'd make him happy."

She started to laugh and couldn't stop. Moira, always ready to share in her mother's glee, giggled, too, scrunching up her nose and clapping her hands. It was making Amos nervous.

"What's so funny?"

"You're timing. See, the last thing I want to do today is make my husband happy. So, get out."

"Don't make this ugly, Sam." His voice had grown hard and cold.

"You've done that already, Amos."

"Ged out," said Moira, happily seizing on the phrase. "Ged out."

Sam picked up her daughter and held her against her chest like a shield. "You heard the kid," she laughed. She went to the front door and held it open until Amos walked through. "You know, Amos. I think you should consider genetic testing. There's definitely depravity running in your family."

He didn't even bother to question the remark. "You've made a big mistake," he said with such loathing that for a minute, she wondered if he was right.

But the minute she had closed the door behind him, she knew exactly what she had to do. Bouncing Moira on her knee, she picked up the phone and dialed a number in Oakdale.

"Jack Bader's office," a familiar voice said.

"Is that you, Jack?"

"Samantha. Is Melinda okay? Did Kilmont get Carter to agree to go to San Domenico?"

Sam cringed. She'd been so intent on her own mission that she hadn't stopped to think that Jack's first question would be about Melinda. She owed him the truth, but wanting to spare his feelings, she tried to make it sound as innocuous as possible.

"She's okay. But I don't think Carter's going to go."

"Why not? Dammit, she's an American citizen. She's been stuck down there—"

"Jack, stop," Sam interrupted. Jack and Melinda hadn't been together for over two years, and still, she could hear the love in his voice. It made it even harder to say what needed to be said. "Melinda sent another fax. It doesn't sound like she wants to be rescued."

"Oh, please. We don't know what people are making her write."

"I know my sister, Jack. This is Melinda talking."

"Fine, then it's the Stockholm syndrome. That always happens. Hostages identify with their captors."

"It's more than identification now, Jack. It sounds like she's . . . more involved."

There was silence on the line, and she could hear the constriction in his throat when he spoke. "Even so . . ."

"There is no even so, Jack. The government is not going to risk sending someone down there to be refused. I don't think she'd come back now. Not even if I asked her myself."

"I see," he sighed, and Sam's heart went out to him.

"You've got to get on with your life, Jack. You're a wonderful, gorgeous guy. You could find someone else if you wanted to."

He laughed, refusing to accept pity from her or himself. "Is that why you called? To get me a date?"

"No," she said, "I need a lawyer."

"What? You and Drew buying a house out there? I don't do real estate."

"No, Jack. We're not buying a house. I don't know what we're doing. But that's another story completely. I'm asking you as a friend," she said, knowing just how much she was asking, "to drop everything and come to Washington to represent me in a lawsuit."

"That sounds ominous. What kind of lawsuit?"

"I'm going to bring up Senator Amos Kilmont on charges of sexual harassment."

The minute Amos Kilmont walked into his office, Dotty told him his niece was on the phone. She took one look at her boss and knew he was not in good spirits.

"Do you want me to take a number and say you'll call her back?"

"Hell, no. She's exactly the person I want to talk to." He went into his office and closed the door behind him before picking up the phone.

"What the hell's going on, Natalie?"

"Oh, God, she told you already?"

"No, Natalie," Amos said, betraying his impatience. "She did not tell me. That's why I'm asking you. Is there some marital difficulty between Drew and Sam?"

"You could say that." Her voice was quavering.

"Well, what? What kind of difficulty? Spit it out."

"Sam came back to Belvedere last night and found me in bed with Drew."

She heard him let out a low whistle and waited for his next reaction, debating whether to tell him the rest. If she told him nothing really happened, she wouldn't be in as much trouble, but he'd be sure to tell Sam and Drew. And even if things hadn't worked out as she had planned and Drew hadn't vowed eternal love as she had hoped, she wouldn't give his stupid wife the satisfaction of knowing it had all been a hoax. More unbearable than not having Drew would be for them to have each other. She'd be damned if she'd let them kiss and make up and laugh at her. If she was going to suffer alone, then so could the two of them.

"That explains it," was all he said.

"What?" she asked.

"I wish I'd known about this earlier. I would have handled things a lot differently."

"I called you earlier, but they said you were out of the office."

For a long time, he didn't say anything. She wondered if he was fuming.

"Uncle Amos?" She took a chance. "It wasn't really my fault." She figured she was young enough to fob the blame off on someone else. "I was so far from home, and he . . ."

"Cut the shit," her uncle interrupted, "and get back to Washington. There's got to be something I can use in this. I just have to figure out what it is."

Drew awoke to the purple half-light between night and day. He had expected to spend a sleepless night pacing the floor after Sam had left with Moira, but he'd felt so ill and disoriented that he had lain down on the bed just to stop the room from spinning. He looked at the clock. It was after seven. He sat up gingerly and was pleased that it no longer felt like a marching band was drilling in his head. He wanted to be lucid when he spoke to Sam. He had no explanation to offer; there were still gaping holes in his memory. But as soon as Natalie got up, he'd send her packing. And then, at a decent hour, when it had all been set right, he'd call his wife.

He reached for the remote control, figuring he'd scan the morning shows just to keep himself occupied until he could take some action. The logo for the CBS Evening News came on, and he laughed, thinking heads would roll in that control room today. He switched to NBC, and then it struck him. Networks don't make mistakes like that. He tried one more channel just to be sure and confirmed his suspicions. It was not dawn, it was dusk. His clock read seven P.M., not A.M. He had slept for sixteen hours.

Feeling like someone in the twilight zone, he pulled on a robe and went into the hall. The house was quiet. He tapped lightly on Natalie's door. When there was no response, he pushed it gently ajar. No one was there. He walked in and looked around. The closets were empty. Natalie had gone. He felt relief followed quickly by misgiving. Last night, she had been crying and insisting that she wanted to stay. What had prompted her to leave without further argument, without even a note? Where had she gone and who had paid for her to get there? For a moment, he even wondered if she might have been driven to suicide. But the thought left him as quickly as it came. She wouldn't pack to kill herself. If she were really serious about it, she wouldn't need a change of clothing. He considered calling Amos to see if she had turned to her uncle for help. But the thought of having to explain to his old college roommate what had happened if it turned out Natalie wasn't there, was enough to dissuade him.

Guilt was a new emotion for Drew. He was a man who made mistakes, like any other, but his tendency had always been to accept the consequences and get on with his life. But it was hard to move on from an act for which even he saw no justification. What he had done to Natalie was unforgivable, and what he had done to Sam was irrational. How could he explain it to her if he could not even explain it to himself. He became certain of only one thing: nothing would be accomplished over the telephone. His only hope was to face Sam and beg her forgiveness.

He climbed into the shower and let the hot water run over him. He rubbed his face with soap and started to shave, using the little mirror that hung on the shower door. But his thoughts were on Sam and the things he would have to say, and his hand shook. It took him a second to realize he had gashed himself. Cursing softly, he stepped out of the shower and threw open the medicine cabinet, searching for the styptic pencil that he had left three months ago. Blood dripped from his face onto the white tile of the counter, and he grabbed for a tissue to staunch the flow. At the same time, he spotted the pencil behind the razors and Band-Aids and, reaching for it with his other hand, he knocked over a bottle of pills that fell, spilling its contents in the sink and on the floor.

When he'd repaired the damage he'd done to himself, he gathered the little pills that had flown in all directions and put them back in the bottle. He closed the bottle and was about to return it to the shelf when he spotted one last stray pill on the floor. He retrieved it and went to open the bottle to replace it with the others. But the cap was so ingeniously childproof that no matter what he did, he could not get it open. Finally, in utter exasperation, he hurled it to the floor, only to have it bounce right back at him, still intact.

And then it struck him. He had been prescribed these pills years ago after he had returned from a harrowing ordeal in Ireland. Anticipating he would have difficulty in adjusting to normal life, the doctor had taken the precaution of supplying him with a dozen sleeping pills. But Sam had been there to see him through the hard times, and Drew hadn't needed them. Now, he wondered, if it took such skill to get the cap off, how could it have opened so easily when he had dropped it the first time? Unless, the bottle had been opened and the cap not properly replaced. But Drew knew he had never opened the bottle.

Following the instructions carefully, he slowly moved the cap until all the arrows were aligned and pointing in the right direction. With a flick, the cap came off in his hand. He poured the pills into his palm. Counting the one he had not yet replaced there were nine. He searched the floor, the sink, the counter, even the drawers. There were no other pills. The label confirmed his memory. The bottle had contained twelve pills. And in large black letters, it warned not to exceed the prescribed dosage.

"The little bitch," he said out loud as the pieces of the puzzle fell into place.

* * *

The fighting had begun to taper off. There were still skirmishes in the south and east, and Guzman's military forces continued to hold the presidential palace. But in the central part of the island, the revolutionary forces were ensconced. Temporary local governments had been set up to handle the daily rationing of water and rice. A few revolutionary soldiers remained to keep watch or handle any disputes that might arise. But there was little dissent. For the first time in the history of San Domenico, the people felt within reach of power, and it made them jubilant.

Breathing in the night air, heavy with the wild orchid scent of the jungle, Melinda felt she could almost smell the euphoria. Both fighters and supporters sensed the end was near, and Diego spent long hours with his advisors, talking of the political future of his country. But with Melinda, he refused to plan ahead.

"You know what I would like to do when this is over . . . ," she began, whispering in his tent after the meetings had broken up and the others had gone to sleep.

But he interrupted her angrily. "This is an adventure for you. For me, it will never be over."

She hadn't expected his indignation, and she was taken aback. "I only meant the fighting. You have Guzman on the run. He knows the people are with you. Your revolution is going to succeed."

He saw that he had hurt her and was sorry. "Then it only begins. Years of exploitation and revolution have devastated San Domenico. It won't be easy to rebuild. We will have to undergo enormous hardship to make it happen. Now it's exciting. Like Hemingway fighting in the Spanish Civil War. It feeds the creative spirit. But in the end, you'll go home."

She lay on his pallet and looked at him. She could not imagine being more at home anywhere than she was in his arms. "Have you heard the expression Home is where the heart is?"

He wanted to tell her that not only had he heard it, but he would live by it if she would let him lodge inside her soul. But he forced himself to be realistic. "American clichés don't get you far in a third-world country."

"Maybe not. But love works anywhere in the world. Do you love me?" she asked with such directness that his resolve melted.

"Too much," he said and came to her and kissed her.

She laughed. "I love you, too. But there's no such thing as too much."

"It's distracting," he teased. "Tonight, we formulated a plan for taking the presidential palace. I should be studying the maneuvers and instead . . ."

He kissed her again, but this time, her lips were not pliant, and her body was tense. She pulled away before the magic of his touch could dissipate her distress. "*All* of Guzman's men are there now. You've won the countryside, but you don't have so many fighters. It's too dangerous. You shouldn't do it."

"We have no choice. As long as Guzman is in the palace, he is the de facto leader of the country. San Domenico cannot be free until he is removed."

She knew he was right, but she would not speak, would not look at him. As selfish as it was, she saw every battle, no matter how crucial, as a hazard to her love. He did not try to argue her out of it. Instead, he took her face very gently in his hands and forced her to look at him.

"I love you," he said, "and if it's up to me, I will never leave you. But we cannot guess what fate has in store for us. We can only accept the destiny we've been granted."

He kissed her softly, tenderly, then again with more passion. With a will of its own, her body responded, and she moved into his arms. His kisses continued, leaving her face, moving down her neck, over her breast, where he lingered awhile before continuing his pilgrimage to the mecca of his desire. The touch of his lips transported her, and by the time her prayer of love had been fulfilled, all things seemed possible.

Still thrumming with passion, she made him lie back on the pallet and, kneeling over him, bowed her body over his. Moaning with delight, he pushed her back into a sitting position, so he could see her, touch her, watch her, as she moved herself up and down. The gold flecks in his dark eyes seemed to catch fire as she lost herself in the rhythm and carried them both from the halls of the mundane through the corridors of the ethereal until, collapsing on his body, she opened the door to nirvana.

She lay in his arms and slept, dreaming that she was in the house where she had grown up in Oakdale. But instead of her parents' postage stamp backyard, paradise stretched outside her window. Longing for the peace of the garden, she tried to walk outside, but even though the door was open, something unseen barred her way. As she pushed at the invisible barrier, the walls of her house began to rumble and crack. Everything trembled as though in an earthquake. She woke to find Diego shaking her gently.

"Melinda, wake up. Get dressed."

"What? What's the matter?" She was still groggy with sleep and love.

She saw he was already dressed, but that was not unusual. She frequently fell asleep cocooned in his naked body only to wake in the purple light of dawn and find him pulling on his boots. But this time, the black of night still shrouded the camp like velvet and the urgency in his voice told her, even before he did, that something was wrong.

"I don't know. It's a feeling in my gut."

In seconds, she was back in her fatigues, trusting nothing so much as Diego's instinct.

"Stay here," he ordered as he ducked out of the tent.

Suddenly, a deafening blast pierced the air and the orange flare of gunfire lit up the night. Melinda fell to the floor of the tent, terror gripping her by the throat, as another fiery barrage shot through the camp. There were screams of pain and shouts of confusion and more shooting, this time with explosive echoes as the ambushed rebels found their arms and fired back.

Crawling on her belly, Melinda slithered to the door of the tent and peered out. The camp was a light show of horror, with fallen bodies spotlighted in the glow of gunfire.

"Diego!" she screamed but knew that even if he heard her, he would not respond. From the instant of the first assault, he could only answer to the call of the battle. He wasn't her Diego anymore. He was a hero of the revolution. She only prayed he would not become a martyr.

She felt like crying, but fear had drained her eyes of tears, and she lay flat on the floor, her arms folded over her head and waited for the attack to end.

Suddenly, she felt her ankle grabbed from behind, and she screamed again until she realized it was Vincenzo, who had snuck into the tent from the back. She grabbed his hand and pressed it tightly, grateful for another friendly presence.

"Vincenzo, what's happening?" she asked, not bothering to mask her panic.

"It's an ambush by Guzman's goons. I'm afraid they caught us by complete surprise."

"Things were going too well," she lamented.

"They're going well again," he told her. "We're pushing them back."

And, indeed, it seemed to her that the intervals between blasts had grown longer. It was such good news that she kissed him for it.

"Mmmm," he smiled. "I like bearing good tidings."

But a moment later, there was a renewed barrage as fierce as any that had come before.

"I take it back," she said, hiding her head under his arm.

"Just a last volley," he reported with authority. "They are retreating."

A cheer from the camp seemed to prove Vincenzo right. Cautiously they poked their heads outside the tent and were greeted by joyful invitations to come celebrate with their *compadres.* It seemed almost a miracle that no one had been seriously wounded, just a few grazes and abrasions that needed minor attention.

"Can you handle this yourself?" Melinda asked Vincenzo. "I want to find Diego."

He waved her off benignly, and she ran to the center of the camp where the chant was already beginning: "Di—e—go! Di—e—go!" She laughed and joined in, feeling like the cheerleader at a football game where the quarterback has scored the winning touchdown. The exhilaration was infectious, and Melinda's spirits soared as she waited for Diego to appear, looking for the break in the crowd that would indicate his entrance. The refrain grew louder. Still he did not appear. A restless anxiety began to work its way through the crowd, and the chant broke off, replaced with a fearful murmur.

"Where is he?" Melinda asked the people beside her, trying to keep the foreboding out of her voice.

But they were asking the same question, and no one seemed to have the answer.

Vincenzo approached. "What's happening?"

"Diego's not here," she said, her voice trembling.

"Look," Vincenzo pointed.

Relief flooded over her as she saw the crowd separate, making a path that she assumed would momentarily yield the man she loved. She started to run forward, then gasped and stopped dead in her path. It was not Diego. It was a military officer in the full regalia of the official army of San Domenico. In one hand, he carried Diego's rifle, in the other, the bandanna that he wore to cover his face in battle. It was stained with blood.

For a moment, everyone seemed frozen in shock, and then they surged, as if suddenly released, ready to tear the soldier limb from limb. A volley of fire into the air made them pause long enough for the soldier to deliver his communiqué.

"Roca is a prisoner at the presidential palace. Be warned. If I do not return, he dies."

Melinda heard a ringing in her head that drowned out the shouted curses and shrieks of outrage. She felt as though she might faint but forced herself to remain conscious in order to hear the rest.

"You are commanded by General Raul Guzman, acting leader of San Domenico, to lay down your arms. If you accede, you will be treated justly, Roca will be freed, and a peace will be negotiated. If you do not, Roca will be crucified and the military forces will massacre every single participant in this illegal uprising."

A pall fell over the camp, and shrouded in the deathly silence, Guzman's envoy made his exit. No one moved to stop him. By now, the sun was announcing its impending arrival with a message of garish color splashed across the sky. But Melinda only saw black as she felt the earth swallow her dreams.

❦ 11 ❧

Sam had expected Drew's call all day. She even looked forward to hanging up on him. When the call didn't come, she figured either he was giving her time to cool down or he was working on his strategy. Not for a minute did she consider the possibility that he would not attempt a reconciliation, although she still did not know how she would respond when he tried. Nor, for some reason, did she anticipate his arriving unannounced in the house on Thirty-first Street.

Moira was already asleep when she heard his key in the lock, and she planted herself firmly in the foyer, intending to bar his entrance.

"I don't want you here," she said without preamble before he could get out a greeting.

"I know that, honey. But I was afraid if I called, you'd hang up on me. I need you to listen to what I have to say."

There was a buoyancy in his voice that Sam couldn't ignore. He didn't sound like a penitent sinner. It annoyed her but intrigued her as well. "Okay, say what you have to say and get out."

"It was a lie," he blurted out, triumphant.

"What do you mean?"

"A lie. The whole thing was a lie. She drugged me."

"Give me a break, Drew." She couldn't believe he would try such an obvious tactic. If he thought this would get him back into the house or her good graces, he was dead wrong.

"No, no. I mean it. Remember those pills I got from Dr. Saunders when I came back from Ireland?"

"Drew, what is the point of this?" she asked, exasperated at his attempt to stall with irrelevancy.

"The point is, I never used them. Remember?"

"Yes, fine, I remember. You threw them out. Now will you go?"

"No. I didn't throw them out. They were in the medicine cabinet. Do you remember how many he gave me?"

"I don't want to play this stupid game."

"I do. Twelve. I mean, I didn't even have to remember. It says so right on the bottle."

"Is this relevant somehow? Because I'm not getting—"

"It's absolutely relevant. There are only nine left. Did you use any?"

"No, of course not."

"I didn't think so. That's why I couldn't remember what happened, Sam. Nothing happened. She brought me a tray from the kitchen, and when I said I didn't want it, she insisted I drink a glass of wine."

"Oh, please, Drew, just stop."

"No, listen." he insisted. "I didn't think of it before because she had wine too. She poured hers from the bottle. Mine was already in the glass—with three sleeping pills in it."

There was a long silence.

"Samantha? Are you going to say anything?"

"I don't know what to say," her voice sounded small.

"Do you believe me?"

"I guess so." He breathed a huge sigh of relief and took a step toward her, his arms outstretched. She drew away, unwilling to surrender a deeper doubt. She needed to sit down. She moved to the living room and sank into the sofa, shaking her head. He took it as a good sign and followed.

"It's not the only issue, Drew. What was she doing in our bedroom in the first place? Why was she so comfortable there? If even you thought it could have happened, how far away from possibility was it?"

He took a deep breath. He had expected these questions, and she had a right to ask them. "I admit I was way too permissive with her."

Sam gave him a look that told him he wasn't going to get off easy.

"Okay," he amended, "I enjoyed her attention."

"Adulation is more like it."

"Whatever. You saw the warning signs, and I refused to. By ignoring it, I made her think she had a chance. Things had no business going as far as they did. But I never even considered letting it go farther. I swear. That was all in her imagination. Can't we just let it pass and go back to where we were?"

"It's not going to be that simple," Sam said uncomfortably.

He tried to reassure her. "Yes, it is, honey. We've been through much worse. We can't let Natalie—"

"It's not just Natalie," Sam began and then broke off as she noticed Drew staring at the staircase, watching a man's bare feet come down the steps.

"Who . . . ?" he began and stopped as Jack Bader walked into the room, wearing jeans and an open shirt, his hair still wet from a shower.

"Hey, Drew. We didn't expect you here. How's it goin'?" Jack said, reaching out to shake his hand.

Drew hesitated, but his innate breeding forced him to respond. He shook Jack's hand and looked at Sam. "What's . . . uh . . . ?" He didn't know how to formulate the question.

"Jack's staying with me for a while," was all Sam offered.

Drew felt his face get hot and his stomach turn. He suddenly understood viscerally what Sam must have felt when she walked into her own bedroom and found him in bed with someone else.

"Strictly business," said Jack affably, and Drew knew instant relief. He saw Sam smile and knew she was aware of the torture he'd experienced, if only for seconds, and she wasn't sorry. He supposed he deserved it.

Back on solid ground, Drew relaxed. He'd actually always liked Jack Bader. "Are you working on something for Amos Kilmont?" he asked congenially. Sam had often complained about the legal jargon required in compiling a committee report.

"You could say that," said Jack, and he looked pointedly at Sam. She knew it was up to her to fill in the blanks.

"I'm charging Amos Kilmont with sexual harassment, and Jack is going to represent me."

"Is this a joke?" Drew asked, obviously not finding it very funny.

"Far from it," Sam said.

"When did this happen?" he wanted to know.

"It's been going on for a while."

"And you didn't say anything to me?"

"No."

"Why?"

"A lot of reasons."

"Name one."

"I didn't know how serious it was. He's your friend. I thought it might upset you."

"Didn't it upset *you?*"

"Yes, of course it did. What are you suggesting? That I encouraged it? Just because you enjoy inappropriate attention doesn't mean I do."

"Oh, I see. I'm at fault because I don't recognize that a young girl who has never made any kind of sexual advance before is going to go off the deep end. But it's okay for you to let an old college buddy of mine make sexual advances—"

"Unwanted," she interrupted with emphasis.

"Fine, whatever. Unwanted—but over a long period of time you said—and just not bother to mention it to me. Or was it that it took you that long to realize his attention was unwanted?"

Sam was incredulous. "How could you even think that? Amos Kilmont almost raped me. I'm the victim here. Don't make me out to be the seducer."

"Well, that's how I feel about Natalie. Someone drugging you and getting into bed with you is pretty close to rape in my book. So why are you making it out to be my fault?"

They glared at each other accusingly. Jack thought it might be a good time to step in.

"Listen, you two . . ."

They turned in unison and glared at him, but he was unfazed. He was a lawyer. Dirty looks were de rigueur in his business. "I think you both better cool off and think about things before you go for each other's throats."

Sam and Drew spoke at once.

"He said—"

"I'm not—"

Jack cut them off with a wave of his hand. "Here's the point. People make mistakes in judgment that lead to unexpected consequences. You're not the only two people in the world who got stung when something you thought was harmless turned out to be a problem. How the two of you decide to deal with this in your relationship is your business. But what you've got to decide right now for me is if you, Sam, are willing to put yourself up to public scrutiny with a much tougher interrogator than Drew. And Drew, you have to tell her right now if you're going to support her on this. Because you are bringing a United States senator— not just any senator, mind you, but a Democratic presidential contender—up on charges that could ruin his career. And if you guys don't show a united front on this one, then you can kiss it good-bye. You'll lose and be humiliated in the process."

There was dead silence. Jack sank into the cushions of the sofa with a sigh as though his tirade had tired him out. Sam did not dare look at Drew.

"If Amos Kilmont did this to me, I have a feeling

he's done it before. If I let him get away with it, I'm sure he'll do it again. I'm prepared to fight him with everything I've got. But I don't know why Drew should be dragged into it."

Jack shook his head. "Don't be naive, Sam. You told me yourself that Amos threatened to get his government contract canceled if you didn't play ball with him."

"He said that? In so many words?" Drew was outraged. Sam didn't say anything. Her silence told him what he wanted to know. "Then fuck him," Drew continued. "I'll back you up. Put the bastard away."

Sam looked at him. "Are you supporting me because you think I'm right or because your male pride is hurt?"

"Does it matter?" Drew asked, looking at Jack.

"Not to me," Jack said. "As long as you show up at the hearing at your wife's side and corroborate everything she says. It's your only chance," he added to Sam.

She shrugged as if to say whatever was necessary, she'd do.

"Fine," said Drew. "Maybe I should go back to Woodland Cliffs until you need me."

"Hey, I need you now," said Jack, jumping up to block his way. "United front I said, remember? You can't live apart while this is going on. For any reason. Kilmont's going to use whatever dirt he can get on you as it is."

They heard the baby cry. "Mommy . . . Daddy . . . Mommy . . . Daddy," she called, prepared to accept whomever came her way.

"She must have had a bad dream," said Sam, getting up to go to her.

"I'll go," Drew said and was up the stairs before Sam could object. She didn't really want to object anyway. There was no need for Moira to suffer because things were strained between her and Drew.

"This is going to get really ugly, isn't it?" Sam asked Jack after Drew had gone.

"Uglier than you can imagine."

For two days and two nights, Melinda stayed in Diego's tent. She wrapped herself in his clothing and lay on the pallet that they had shared for so many nights. When she counted, she realized that, in fact, it had not been such a long time. No anniversaries had been celebrated, no commitment beyond the moment established. But here in the jungles of San Domenico, hours could add up to a lifetime, and she was bereft. Several times a day, someone would appear at her door with food and drink, which she would ask them to leave but never touch. Vincenzo came and offered a sedative, but that, too, she refused. She wanted to be keenly aware of every moment of her torment. She could not accept comfort while her lover suffered.

On the third day, when she no longer even attempted to move from the pallet, Vincenzo came not with drugs but with news.

"It looks like you're getting your man back."

He said it jokingly, but she could hear the emotion in his voice and knew he had to be telling the truth. In the same amount of time it had taken her to die, she felt herself recover. She sat up. There was a gnawing in her stomach. Life seemed possible again.

"When? How? What happened?" she asked as hungry for information as for food.

Vincenzo sensed the change and handed her a bowl of soup from the tray that waited, as always, at the entrance to the tent. He watched her as she ate greedily, waiting for him to answer her.

"The revolutionary council met. They are going to surrender."

"What?!" She put down the bowl. She was shocked. She didn't know what she had expected but somehow not this.

Seeing her distress, misunderstanding it, he tried to offer reassurances. "Look, no one's saying Guzman is a man of his word. They won't turn in their arms until Diego's release. They'll get guarantees—"

"Stop!" she shouted. "Diego would hate this. You know that, Vincenzo."

"There's no choice, Melinda. These people have no leader. It's over for them."

"How can you say that? You know what Diego fought for—"

"Diego is not here," he reminded her forcefully. Then, seeing her stricken look, he calmed down again. "There is no revolution without Diego. They don't know what to do without him. And maybe it's better. If it can't be won, then maybe it's better to stop the killing now."

"Maybe it can be won."

"How? You know as well as I do that Diego never delegated responsibility. Sure, he had meetings with the council, but he told them what should be done, and they agreed to do it. Without him, they don't know."

"I do."

"What?"

241

LEAH LAIMAN

"I do. I know what Diego intended to do."

Vincenzo was looking at her as though she'd lost her mind. He reached out a hand to touch her forehead and check for fever, but she shook him off.

"I'm not crazy, Vincenzo. That last night, before the attack, he showed me a plan for storming the presidential palace. It's *his* plan. If we follow it, we can win this."

Vincenzo was still looking dubious. "When did it stop being *they* and become *we?* Melinda, you're a good and wonderful person. You're a true humanitarian, and your work here has saved countless lives. But you're a movie star, not a revolutionary. And this is not your battle."

"It is now."

Forgetting her lethargy of moments before, Melinda had already bounded up and was rummaging through the rucksack where Diego kept all his belongings.

"I know I'll recognize it when I see it," she mumbled and then, triumphant, stood and brandished a sheaf of notes, complete with diagrams. "This is it."

As averse as he was to the whole idea, Vincenzo allowed himself to be drawn to the waving papers. Prepared to be disdainful, he took them from her hand and began to peruse them. She saw his face change and knew that the papers were convincing even though he wasn't prepared to concede.

"I'm not a military man," was all he would say.

"But you think it could work, don't you?"

"Even if it could, what business is it of mine? I'm a doctor. My job is to see people stay healthy, not send them to their death."

"They have a right to make their own choices. If they know what Diego wanted to do, then they can

242

decide. Come with me. Translate for me while I talk to them. That's all I ask."

Melinda was an accomplished actress and knew how to command an audience. But she felt that the words that came to her that day were inspired by a spirit not her own. And though many of the *compadres* could not understand her and had to wait patiently for Vincenzo's translation, it was the heat of her emotion that set them on fire. Over the course of the revolution, some had forgotten that they were not only following Diego's charismatic leadership but pursuing their own liberty. Melinda made them remember why they had fought alongside Diego Roca in the first place.

"Winning his freedom at the expense of your liberty would be a hollow victory for Diego," she told them. "You know I love him as you do, but we all know that he would rather die in chains than give up the dream he has dreamed for his country. Because he was here, we share that dream. We cannot give it up because he is gone. His body has been kidnapped, but no one could capture his spirit. That remains with us. If we surrender, his body may go free, but we will have killed his soul. And that, my friends, would be a far greater crime. I would sooner die myself than see that happen. Wouldn't you?"

When she saw she had won them over, she summoned the military strategists whom she had seen in daily discussions with Diego in the tent that they shared. She showed them the blueprints she had found and watched as they noisily discussed the possibilities, shaking their heads, pointing their fingers, and finally, nodding solemnly in unison.

They spoke to Vincenzo, and she turned to him in anticipation. "They say the plan is good," he told her. "They say if *l'estrella americana* is willing to give her life for San Domenico, then how could they not be? Frankly," he added, only half jesting, "I think it would have been enough to send a check or adopt a child, but that's just me."

She laughed and hugged him, then growing serious, she turned to the others and hugged them each as well. A cheer went up from the assembled camp.

They spoke to Vincenzo and looked at her, and she understood that they were now deferring to her as leader and expecting him to be the official translator. Vincenzo understood this as well, and though it didn't please him, he accepted without argument.

"They want to move tonight. Do you agree?"

"Tell them," Melinda said fervently, "that I will be proud to be with them. Will you come with us?"

Vincenzo looked at her, his eyes scolding. He wanted to tell her that this was not a starring part in a Hollywood costume drama. Real bullets would fly, real blood would be shed. No one would call "cut" if she got tired or, even worse, hit. But he saw in the fierce determination of her face, in the deep compassion in her eyes, that this was not a role for her. Working side by side over the past few weeks, they had seen the damage done by civil war. But they had also seen what damage could be done by injustice and oppression. They had often wondered together which was worse. But Melinda, he saw now, had made her decision. She had made a commitment to justice and freedom that was deeper than any she had ever made to any person, Diego included. In Diego's absence, she had ceased to be his consort and become his cohort. She loved the people of San Domenico as much as the man who had introduced her to them. And they loved her for it. Until Diego returned, Melinda would be their leader. And Vincenzo would either have to follow or get out of the way.

❧ 12 ❧

Jack's words proved to be prophetic; charging Senator Amos Kilmont with sexual harassment was far uglier than Sam could have imagined. Once the accusations were made public, the press was relentless. They parked on the lawn of the Georgetown house, waiting for statements and photo opportunities. Since the Symington past was rich with scandal, they had plenty of filler while the real story unfolded. Even Jack got his share of coverage, with a report on his former relationship to the movie star Melinda Myles, sister of Kilmont's accuser and now mistress of the San Domenican rebel leader Diego Roca.

It was heady stuff in an otherwise quiet season, and talk show hosts and columnists took advantage of the tie-in with related topics like: Is scandalous behavior genetically dictated? and Masters of the universe and

246

the women who master them. In Washington, where most people got their jobs by spreading gossip and innuendo about the competition, it was enough to titillate even the most blasé.

In public, Sam and Drew kept up the appearance of being together. But at home, when the curtains had been drawn and they were out of view of the paparazzi, they had little to say to each other. True to his threat, Amos had found a way to question DMC's contract with the government, making sure that it appeared to have no relevance to his case, and they had been forced to suspend operations until the matter was resolved. There was no doubt in any of their minds that if Amos Kilmont retained his power, the matter would never be resolved in DMC's favor. Drew never blamed her, but Sam knew it was adding to the strain between them, if only because they were forced to spend so much time together at a point where they could both have used a little distance between them. At Jack's insistence, they slept in the same room, but every time Sam approached the bed, she still remembered the sight of Natalie's naked body curled against her husband. And Drew, knowing his wife as well as he did, knew what she was thinking and kept his distance.

By the day the Senate Ethics Committee gathered for the actual hearing, a seat in the spectators' gallery was the hottest ticket in town. The press had already commandeered their allotted space, and as Samantha Myles Symington entered the hearing room with her husband, Andrew Symington, on one side and her lawyer, Jack Bader, on the other, the flashbulbs were popping and the TV cameras were whirring. Even wearing a plain dark suit and white blouse, her glorious hair pulled into a severe bun, she still made a striking image. They had managed to avoid the media crush by entering through a back route, made known to Sam, ironically, by Amos Kilmont on one of their inappropriately long evenings together. But it was clear that the last shred of privacy they might have hoped to maintain in their lives was about to be invaded.

"This place looks like a men's club," Sam whispered nervously to Jack, eyeing the walls lined with bookcases and the framed photographs of former committee chairmen.

"Let's face it," Jack whispered back. "It sort of is."

"That's what I'm afraid of," sighed Sam as she watched the committee staffers fill the water glasses and check the microphones at the long judicial bench where committee members were starting to take their places. They sat, Democrats to the left, Republicans to the right, chatting amiably as they waited for their colleagues to gather.

She tensed as she saw Amos Kilmont make his way with his legal staff to a table across the room from hers, cheerily calling out greetings to those he knew— and he seemed to know everyone. His patrician good looks served him well, and the jaunty red tie he sported with his perfectly cut pinstripe suit gave him an insouciant air that said he couldn't take these charges seriously, so why should they. Sam looked at Drew. He would not meet her eyes. Jack noticed.

"Listen, you two. How about holding hands?"

"Please, Jack. Do we have to turn this into a sideshow?" Drew asked, exasperated.

"It *is* a sideshow," Jack pointed out. "We shouldn't be doing it if we're not going to do it right."

Drew reached out to Sam without another word. She could feel his hand lying cold and hard in her own.

"I'm sorry," she told him.

"I said I'd be here for you," he answered, but there was no warmth in his reply, only a kind of noblesse oblige.

Once the hearing had been called to order, it didn't take long to present Sam's case. Sam was the only witness on her side, and in response to the committee's questions, she told her story as unsensationally as possible. She told of the calls at night to come to the office in the Senate building, the unwanted hugs and kisses, the subtle and not so subtle advances. Finally, she spoke of the night Amos had almost raped her and threatened to let her sister languish in San Domenico and ruin her husband's business if she did not cooperate.

When she had finished telling her story, the committee chairman called a short break. Sam looked at Jack.

"That was easy."

"Too easy," said Jack. "Remember Anita Hill? Nobody wants to look like they're grilling you. It's bad for the vote count. They're going to leave it up to Kilmont to skewer you himself."

Drew shifted uncomfortably. "But if Sam is telling the truth, what can he say about her that won't make him look worse?"

Sam eyed her husband. *If* I'm telling the truth? Do you doubt it?"

"I didn't say that. I just meant—"

"Stop it, you two," Jack intervened. "The eyes of C-Span are on you. Smile and look like you love each other. To answer your question, Drew, I have no idea. The problem with these hearings is that unlike a trial, the other side doesn't get to examine your evidence."

They didn't have much time to speculate as the hearing was called back to order. Sam couldn't resist a glance at Amos's table. He was sharing a joke with his staff, who leaned in to listen to him with anticipatory smiles before they all broke into raucous laughter, then hurried back to their positions.

"None of this seems to bother him much, does it?" she asked ruefully.

"He's a politician," Jack answered drily. "To him there's no sin except getting caught or losing. Neither of which has officially happened yet."

The committee chairman was addressing Kilmont directly. His tone of voice was benign and slightly apologetic. "Well, Senator, you've heard the charges against you. We'd like to hear what you have to say in response."

All eyes turned to Kilmont as he leaned toward his microphone and somehow managed to look as though he were relaxing at the same time. Sam was aware that several of the cameras were still trained on her, waiting for her reactions. She forced herself to stare blankly somewhere to the left of Amos's shoulder.

"First of all, Mr. Chairman," Amos began, "I want to thank my esteemed colleagues on the committee for giving me this opportunity to speak to these scurrilous charges. It hurts me to have to take up so much of your valuable time when I know, from personal experience, how busy all of you are trying to perform your senatorial duties . . ."

"Nothing like sucking up and reminding them that he's one of them all at the same time," whispered Sam in Jack's ear.

"Par for the course," he whispered back, then added, "no matter what he says, try not to make comments. It looks disrespectful and inattentive. If you need to tell me something, write it." He pushed a yellow foolscap pad across the table to her. She nodded, reminded again of how much this hearing depended on appearances as well as truth.

Amos was going on. "It also pains me to be put in the ungentlemanly position of disparaging a woman who is married to a dear friend of mine, but my reputation is on the line here, and I just don't see any other way of handling it."

"We understand and appreciate your reluctance, Senator, but we'd like to hear your version of events."

Amos looked at Sam with deep sadness in his eyes. She knew he was trying to make it look like he was the victim and had called this hearing himself. His look said: as loath as he was to do it, he was going to have to expose her. Taking Jack's admonition to heart, she bit her lip and said nothing.

"All right, Mr. Chairman," Amos sighed, all choice eliminated. "I met Samantha Symington several months ago when she and her husband moved to Washington. I've known Drew since we roomed together in college. We haven't been in touch much the last few years, but we've always considered ourselves good friends."

He looked over at Drew, gave him a broad smile.

Sam glanced at Drew. His face remained impassive, but he took her hand and squeezed it. For all their differences, she was grateful for his presence.

"Because of Drew really, I offered her a job assisting me on the Industrial Economics Committee."

"Was this something Mrs. Symington was qualified to do?" the chairman interrupted.

"Well not really, I guess. But I felt sorry for her. I'd heard she'd been involved in cars back where they came from, and here she was coming to Washington with her husband and would probably have a lot of time on her hands. Well, gentlemen, we've all been in that position. We know what it's like when you drag your family here, and your wife doesn't have enough to do. It can get you into a lot of trouble."

There was a laugh of recognition and some nods from the committee. Sam leaned over to say something to Jack, but he gave a minuscule shake of his head and she stayed back in her seat.

He took the pad, wrote on it, and pushed it in front of her again. "We'll have our chance to rebut," it said. She nodded.

"Anyway, she started doing some work for me, and I have to say, she was pretty good. She was working on a report on energy and environmental concerns, and I thought it was going well. The only thing was it took more time than I would have expected, but I put that down to the fact that she wasn't so experienced."

"How do you define more time?" one of the committee members wanted to know.

"Well, she was always coming into the office after hours. A couple of times she even came to my home to go over things. I didn't think anything of it at the time.

You know how it is. You like to encourage an enthusiastic worker whenever you luck onto one."

He paused for more laughter from the committee before going on. "Then, that whole business started with her sister, the film actress Melinda Myles, getting caught up in the revolution in San Domenico. I tried to help her get her sister out of there until I found out that in fact Ms. Myles didn't want to get out because she was . . . uh . . . linked, shall we say, to Diego Roca, the rebel leader. So at that point, I begged off. I mean, I'm not going to get the American government involved in some illicit romance, or whatever it was. And I have to say, I think that's what ticked Mrs. Symington off."

"Are you saying, Senator Kilmont, that Mrs. Symington filed these charges because you refused to help make contact with her sister in San Domenico?"

"Only partially." He hesitated, trying to appear even more reticent than before. There was a hush in the gallery, and Sam could feel everyone inching forward. There was an air of expectancy as reporters poised their pencils, microphones got redirected, and cameras zoomed in. Amos knew if you were going to offer a sound bite, you'd better be sure everyone was prepared to get it.

"I am guilty of wanting what every red-blooded man in this room would want if he got the chance to have it. Look at her. I don't believe I'm making a sexist remark when I say what we all know to be true. That woman is gorgeous. If she offered herself to you, wouldn't you be tempted?"

Even staring at the table in front of her, Sam could feel their eyes on her. She could hear the cameras zooming in for corroboration, and there was nothing she could do to stop the stinging blush from staining her cheeks.

"Are you saying that Mrs. Symington initiated sexual contact, Senator?"

There was an excited buzz in the room. They were getting what they came for in spades.

"Let me say, I am firmly against the kiss and tell syndrome that seems to have infected our society. But, in this case, I feel I have no choice. I have to defend my honor—however little of it remains. Yes, she was the one who proposed a . . ."—he paused, seeking the delicate word, then came up with the demure—". . . liaison. I should have put a stop to it immediately. I am ashamed to say, I did not. My only excuse is that I am human, and all of you can see what I was fighting against."

There were a few appreciative snickers. Sam was writing furiously on the pad while Jack read over her shoulder. "This is all a lie." She triple underlined *lie*.

"I'm afraid I have to ask you, Senator. Do you have any proof of this?"

"Sad to say, I do."

Jack wrote back. "Let's see what he comes up with."

After a whispered conversation with the lawyer at his side, Kilmont went on. "Like many of my esteemed colleagues, I frequently take the liberty of taping the proceedings of the meetings in my office to ensure that all relevant discussions are included in the records that I keep. I make it a point to destroy these tape recordings after my secretaries have transcribed the notes. Had Mrs. Symington not taken offense at my ultimately refusing her advances and filed these charges, I would have destroyed these as well."

Jack was on his feet. "Mr. Chairman, I have to object. We have no knowledge of these tapes. I don't think the senator should have the right to introduce evidence before we've had a chance to examine it."

"Let me point out, Mr. Bader," the chairman was polite but adamant, "this is not a court of law. It is simply a hearing to establish whether a member of the Senate acted inappropriately. One of our colleagues is under fire, and we need to verify whether the charges against him warrant further investigation."

Jack wasn't giving up. "It is still necessary to ascertain that the tape he claims to have of my client is, indeed, my client."

"Well, we'll certainly let Mrs. Symington speak to that. Let's hear the tape."

"But, sir . . . ," Jack persisted, but Sam pulled at his sleeve.

"It's okay," she whispered. "If he's really got a tape of that night, it's going to show I'm telling the truth. And if it's not me, I'll just say so."

"I don't like it," insisted Jack, but a small cassette recorder had already been placed on the committee's table, and a committee staff member was pushing the buttons.

Sam heard her own voice. "Oh, Amos, you are wonderful."

The chairman motioned to the staffer and the tape stopped. "Is that you speaking, Mrs. Symington?" he asked.

She nodded and the tape continued.

"You owe me one," she heard Amos say.

"You bet I do," she answered on the tape, as Sam remembered answering. But then, she heard herself go on. "You've been great, Amos."

Sam was confused. It was still her voice, but she wasn't following the conversation anymore. There was the sound of rustling on the tape, and suddenly, she understood what was happening.

"Oh my God," she whispered to Jack. "He's doctored the tape. He's taken out all the stuff where I was objecting."

Her voice was going on. "Let's do it right. I want to take off all my clothes. I want you to see my body. Wouldn't you like that?"

"Oh, baby, you know I would."

"Pour me another drink," she commanded.

"I want this to take all night," she heard herself drawl.

"You didn't say that stuff, did you?" Jack demanded, incredulous.

"Actually, I did," she whispered back, starting to panic. "I was afraid he was going to rape me. I was just trying to get him to back off."

The senators were mesmerized. Amos was saying, "I could tell from the beginning we'd make a good team."

"Me, too," Sam responded on the tape. "Now pour me that drink and let me get more comfortable."

On the tape, there was the sound of movement. In the Senate Ethics Committee Hearing Room you could hear a pin drop.

"Like what you see?" Sam was asking.

"You bet," was Amos's reply.

"Want to see more?"

"You know I do."

"Then where's my drink?"

There were more sounds, tapping, drinks being poured. Sam looked at Drew. He avoided her eyes.

"It was a ploy," she whispered fiercely. "The next thing that happened was that I threw the drink in his face and ran out of there."

But the next thing on the tape was Amos's voice: "Sam, I think you're forgetting that your husband's company holds a very lucrative government contract. I happen to know DMC has already gone to considerable expenditure to fulfil that contract. Now, if for some reason, improprieties were found, and the government were forced to cancel that contract, that would be a substantial hardship even on a family with the Symingtons' wealth."

Sam heard her own laughter. It took her a moment to place the conversation. "Shit," she whispered to Jack. "This is from the next day after——"

"What's so funny?" Amos asked her on the tape.

"The last thing I want to do today is make my husband happy," Sam responded and then the tape ended.

There was a flurry of activity in the room as some of the press hurried out to file early stories. There was headline material here, more than they had even anticipated. It was a muckraker's dream, and the fact that it was actually hard news made it irresistible.

Jack was on his feet. "Mr. Chairman, while the voice on the tape is my client's, she categorically denies ever making sexual advances toward the senator. Her statements are taken out of context. Those tapes have been doctored to make it seem like she was the aggressor, but she's already told you the circumstances of their last encounter and the fact that she had to make it appear that she was willing in order to escape from Senator Kilmont before he raped her."

The word ignited the room like an incendiary

device. There were shouts from committee members decrying false accusations, slander, character assassination. The members of the press were smiling with collective joy, eager to continue their frenzied attack on the bait that was being fed them.

The chairman pounded his gavel and called the room to order.

"Mr. Chairman, if I could answer to that," Amos was calling over the chaos.

"He's so calm about this. How can he just bold-faced lie and sound so self-assured?" Sam wondered, outraged.

"He's a politician," Jack reminded her. "Why are you so surprised?"

"Go ahead, Senator." The chairman was all deferential respect. "A rather harsh accusation has been made against you, I would assume you'd like to counter it."

"Truth is, I wish I didn't have to. Nothing disturbs me more than telling tales on others. And I have to admit that none of this reflects well on my character either. I should have put a stop to it long before I did, but"—he looked meaningfully at Sam—"you can see why I was flattered by her attention."

The eyes of every man in the room focused on her and clearly stated that they would feel the same way. She was wearing a dark suit with a white shirt buttoned to her neck. Her legs were crossed demurely at the ankle. Still, Sam felt profoundly humiliated, as though she had somehow contrived her natural beauty for the vile purpose of enticing all men.

Jack sensed her discomfort. "Mr. Chairman, it is really inappropriate for the senator to keep referring to my client's physical looks over which she has no

258

control. It is sexist and degrading, and I wish he'd stop doing it."

"I think maybe political correctness is going too far when simply mentioning a woman's appearance in a positive way as a statement of fact is considered degrading," chimed in one of the senators on the committee.

Amos was smiling. "Let me thank my esteemed colleague for coming to my defense, but I'll stand corrected. I am trying to excuse my behavior, which was, in fact, inexcusable. *But,*" he added with heavy emphasis, *"in no way criminal.* All I was trying to say was that I would have liked to think that I was attractive enough to be an object of interest for myself, but I'm afraid that Mrs. Symington had other motives in approaching me."

"What the hell is he going for now?" Jack said barely sotto voce, having long since given up his own dictum not to whisper at the table. In view of the fiasco unfolding around them, it hardly mattered whether they appeared attentive or not.

"Her motivation, I believe, was less my charm than her own revenge."

"Would you care to explain that?" the chairman asked.

"I guess I'm going to have to. I'm sorry to do this, because there's nothing worse than dragging other people's names through the mud, but I don't know how else to defend myself."

"We understand, Senator Kilmont. Again, our only interest here is in finding the truth. We're not in the position to pass judgment."

"Mrs. Symington's husband, Drew, was having an affair with my niece Natalie."

There was a collective gasp from the gallery, shocked by one more juicy revelation, all the more thrilling for being unexpected.

"Oh, shit," said Jack. "I never thought he'd bring her into it."

Sam had turned white. She didn't dare to look at Drew. She could hear his breath coming faster as he pulled his chair closer to hers.

Knowing he had a crowd pleaser, Kilmont continued, not even bothering to feign reluctance anymore. "I'm afraid Sam . . . Mrs. Symington blamed me because I'm the one who recommended Natalie for the job of their au pair. I think she wanted me to go to bed with her because Drew was sleeping with Natalie, and when I wouldn't, she brought the charges against me."

The hum of murmured comments became a buzz and the buzz became a roar. Even in the Senate Ethics Committee Hearing Room, it was hard to stay decorous when offered this kind of titillation. The chairman brought his gavel down again. The roar was reduced to a hum again.

"Do you have evidence of this?" one of the senator's asked, and Sam found herself listening for the answer.

"Unfortunately, I do. My niece has spoken to me about it quite a bit. She was dismissed from the household when Mrs. Symington arrived home unexpectedly and found my niece with her husband in, shall we say, flagrante delicto. She is willing to come and testify to the committee about it. I hoped it might not be necessary. She's still very young and impressionable."

Sam heard Drew's voice in her ear. "It isn't true, Sam. Whatever she says, it isn't true."

Sam couldn't stop the tears from gathering in her eyes. "I guess it doesn't matter anymore, does it? We're both so stuck in this web of lies that we can't make a move without getting in deeper."

"Mr. Chairman, Senator Kilmont has made some outrageous claims and we'd like the opportunity to refute them." Jack was trying to regain control.

"You shall have it, Mr. Bader. But not today. We're already past the hour of our usual adjournment. We'll reconvene tomorrow morning."

Sam had no idea how they made it out of the hearing room. The minute the committee members rose from their seats, their table was bombarded by the press. Somehow, with Jack on one side, shouting occasional responses to reporters' questions and Drew on the other, holding tightly to her arm, they pushed their way outside to a waiting limousine that Jack had had the foresight of keeping on standby.

They drove for a while without saying anything.

"Maybe I made a mistake," Sam broke the silence. "Maybe I should have just kept my mouth shut."

"No," said Drew with finality. "Amos Kilmont is a shit. He deserves what he gets."

Sam gave a derisive laugh. "All he's probably going to get is a little sympathy and a lot of publicity. We're the ones who look bad. It's his word against ours, and he's got this reputation on the Hill as a saint. He won't even fire his inefficient receptionist, for God's sake, because she couldn't get a job anywhere else. And here we are, known adulterers, from out of town no less, calling the blessed Senator Kilmont a liar."

"Stop the car," Jack suddenly shouted.

The driver started to pull over.

"What are you doing Jack?" asked Drew, irritated.

"Did I say something?" asked Sam, confused.

"Listen, guys," Jack was already climbing over them to get to the curbside door. "This could take a while. Don't wait up." He was gone before they could ask any more questions.

"What now?" the driver asked.

They looked at each other. Too many crazy things were happening to them. They had run out of explanations.

"Just take us home," said Drew, and he sounded as tired as Sam felt.

The driver helped them get through the phalanx of reporters still camped on their lawn. Jack had said they would prepare a statement for the press, but Jack was gone. In his absence, they voiced several categorical denials, and Drew went so far as to say outright that his old friend Amos Kilmont had turned out to be an astounding liar.

Once inside, they dismissed the baby-sitter, an older woman named Mrs. Halsey, whom they had hired through an agency based on her assurances that she'd lived in Washington for over twenty years and nothing fazed her. They took turns playing with Moira and put her to bed together. They silently ate some takeout pasta salad that had been left from the day before. They started to watch the late news but turned it off when their own faces appeared, checked their watches, and wondered aloud where Jack was.

"Maybe he's out getting drunk or laid or something," Drew said with a shrug. He'd been cooped up in the house with the silent Symingtons for a week. Who could blame him for wanting to let off steam.

"I doubt it," said Samantha, wondering if Drew

wished that was what he was doing. "I thought maybe he was going to the Library of Congress to do research, but it would be closed by now."

As Jack had commanded them, they went to bed together, aware that the media circus outside could track their movement by the lights that went on and off in the various rooms as they made their way through the house.

They lay beside each other in the darkness, not touching but feeling each other's presence. The invisible wall between them seemed inexplicable and impenetrable at the same time. They had both been wrong and wronged. Explanation seemed superfluous, apology irrelevant, connection impossible. They drifted to sleep, while outside the press corps packed up for the night, all hope of a break in the story extinguished with the last bedside lamp.

In the dead of night, they made their move. Wearing Diego's shirt, carrying his gun, Melinda positioned herself at the head of the column of freedom fighters as they snaked through the jungle. Vincenzo had tried to convince her to remain in the camp, insisting she was not a part of Diego's plan.

"Neither was being captured," Melinda reminded him. "Besides, I'm the one who encouraged them to do this. I'd be a hypocrite if I let them go without me. They need to see me. I represent Diego to them."

The word had gone out quickly to the other camps and the *compadres* had gathered together in the main camp, Diego's camp, throughout the day. They had brought their weapons, such as they were, everything from bowie knives to assault rifles and even one grenade launcher and a heavy antitank gun that took three of them to carry over the jungle paths to the walls of the presidential palace.

Following Diego's blueprint, they surrounded the palace, heavier artillery toward the openings from which Guzman's soldiers would either try to attack or escape. Even the moon seemed to cooperate, remaining behind a thick cloud, offering a heavenly blackout. Vincenzo stayed close to Melinda, and though he said nothing, she could feel that the zeal of their small force had infected him as well.

A quiet signal, the *click-click* of a cricket, indicated they were in position. It was the last clear sound of the night. A moment later, the locked gates of the palace were ripped open by the blast of a grenade. The screams came next, followed by the gunfire. Vincenzo pushed Melinda to the ground. Bits of hot earth flew into her mouth, stung her eyes. She lay still for a moment, as the air pressure changed around her and erupted in more blasts only feet away. She moved and was relieved that she could.

"We have to get Diego," she shouted as she wriggled out from under Vincenzo's protective body and ran toward the gaping hole in the wall that was once the gate.

He chased after her. "Don't be an idiot. The place is crawling with Guzman's goons. We don't stand a chance in there."

"Yes, we do," she said fervently. "They're all too busy fighting. They're not going to pay attention to us as long as we're not shooting at them."

"How do you know that?" Vincenzo wondered, but she was already dashing across the open courtyard and he had no choice but to follow. "This place is huge. How the hell do you expect to find him?" he continued when he'd caught up with her by the side wall where she had paused to wait for an abatement in the crossfire.

"You forget," she said, giving him one of her radiant superstar smiles, "I spent a lot of time here."

She led him through the labyrinth of corridors, sure of her direction. Just as she had anticipated, there were few soldiers in the halls, and those they did encounter were running too fast to notice them as they flattened themselves against the wall and avoided any stance that might be regarded as threatening. She knew where to go. She had taken a wrong turn one evening early in her stay and had found herself in a wing more like prison than palace. She had asked Jorge Alvarro about it. But he had evaded her questions, joking that all old palaces had their dungeons and insisting that it had long since been out of use. She knew now that he had been lying.

Vincenzo took Diego's gun from her hands. She had forgotten that she still carried it. Shouting a warning to get down, he let out a barrage of fire, strafing the locks on the bolted doors. An instant later, Diego emerged.

"Your woman is crazy," Vincenzo told him with affection as the old friends hugged. Happy to be rid of it, he handed Diego his weapon. "This was her idea."

It was then Diego saw her and, face filled with shock and love and utter disbelief, came to her. She didn't even know she was crying until he had swept her in his arms and kissed away her tears.

Then, suddenly, they were falling and Vincenzo was

screaming, "Get down," and pushing her. She heard the blast of gunfire but it was muffled, filtered by the soundproofing of Vincenzo's body, and she felt like they were moving in slow motion, all three of them, sandwiched together, and it seemed forever before they hit the ground. She felt Diego wriggle out from under her, and seconds later, the heat of his bullets, discharging inches from her face, burnt her cheeks.

The silence that followed was more frightening than the hail of bullets that had preceded it. Vincenzo was still on top of her. She could see nothing. She was afraid to call Diego's name. What if he did not respond?

"Vincenzo, get off me," she said. It would be better to see and to know.

He didn't move.

"Vincenzo!" she said again, annoyed, and then felt the warm sticky drip on her hand and knew instantly what it was. She screamed and heard feet run toward her and the weight lifted off her.

"I'm sorry," Diego said. "I had to make sure there was no one else."

He laid Vincenzo on the floor, and she sat over him, looking in panic at the open wound on his chest. "I don't know what to do," she said in desperation. "He always handled major trauma. I just stitched and dressed wounds."

"There's nothing you can do," Diego told her gently, his voice filled with sorrow. "He is dead."

She felt herself choking. "He didn't want to come. I made him come. That would have been me . . ."

"No," Diego said, taking her face in his hands and forcing her to look at him. His grip was hard and it hurt, but it made her pay attention. "All his life, Vincenzo only did what he wanted, which was saving lives. He did that to the end. You know he would not have chosen differently."

He gave her a moment to register what he had said and saw that she knew he was right. Then he took her hand. "We have to go. We will come back for his body. Vincenzo will be buried like the hero of the revolution that he was."

She let him lead her down the corridor, almost tripping over the bodies of the attackers that Diego had shot after they'd killed Vincenzo. She looked down.

"Guzman," she gasped.

"He and his goons were coming after me," Diego said. "You are not the only one Vincenzo saved."

She stopped. "But then . . . if Guzman is dead . . . won't they . . . ?"

"Yes," he answered, and though he felt deeply for the loss of every life, he could not help the smile that transformed his face. "It is over. The San Domenican Liberation Front has won the revolution."

By the time they had made their way to the presidential assembly room on the upper floor of the palace, the shooting had virtually ceased. The rebels swarmed the courtyard, surrounding a regiment of disarmed military captives. When they saw Diego and Melinda step out onto the balcony, they began to cheer.

"*Viva Diego. Viva* Melinda," they chanted over and over again.

Diego took Melinda's hand and held it high above their heads in a salute of victory. There was still an emptiness in her heart left by the death of Vincenzo, but slowly, she began to feel it fill with love for the man beside her and the people below. Vincenzo had died for them, as she would have, if it had worked out that way. As the moon emerged from hiding and beamed its blessing, she understood in a way she never had before the meaning of destiny.

≈ 13 ≈

The telephone was ringing. Sam opened her eyes and blearily gazed at her husband still sleeping beside her. For a moment, forgetting their odd cooperative estrangement, she felt a flood of affection. But the ringing brought her back to the emotional drought of their present state, and she leaned over him impatiently to get to the phone, which was on his side of the bed.

"Are you up?" asked Jack without waiting for a greeting.

"I am now," she said only half accurately. Then suddenly remembering how he had left them unceremoniously the night before, she sat bolt upright and asked, "Where are you?"

"I want you and Drew to get dressed right now and meet me," he said, not even bothering to answer her question.

"Why? What's going on?"

"Just come to the U.S. Senate Restaurant. It's on the main floor of the Capitol, on the Senate side on Constitution Avenue."

"I know where it is. But——"

"Just get here as fast as you can," he interrupted.

"What about the hearing?"

"There may not be one." He hung up, leaving her totally confused.

Drew was sitting up in bed beside her, looking at her questioningly.

"That was Jack," she said, already out of bed. "We've got to meet him right away. Can you call Mrs. Halsey and see if she can come a little early?" she added as they heard the rapid *pat-pat-pat* of little feet, and Moira ran into the room and let herself be scooped onto the bed by her father.

In the shower, she could hear Drew and Moira laughing and singing. She was grateful that the strain between them hadn't seemed to affect the baby at all. Of course, she reasoned, that was because they were both still at home and available to their child at any time. She thought about what Jack had said, about the possibility of there not being a hearing, and realized that much as she hated what was happening, it was the one thing keeping her and Drew together. What would happen when it was over when there was no longer a need to keep up appearances? She turned up the hot water, letting it stream over her and wash away the sudden cold grip of fear.

By the time they had both dressed, Mrs. Halsey had arrived. With lots of cuddles and kisses, they said good-bye to their daughter, pleased to see how easily she responded to the new baby-sitter's warmth. She still occasionally asked about Natalie, but surrounded by love as she was, she didn't seem to suffer the loss too greatly.

Driving over the Roosevelt Memorial Bridge to Constitution Avenue, they had little to say to each other. Sam noticed how silence came as easily to them now as conversation once had. Where they had once shared their thoughts and questions, it now seemed more natural to keep them to themselves. She sighed.

"What?" asked Drew, as keenly aware of the distance between them as she was.

"I didn't say anything," was all she said, knowing there was so much more she could have said.

It was still early enough for traffic to be light, and they made it to the Capitol in fifteen minutes. For a change, even parking was no problem, and in exactly an hour from the time that she had picked up the phone, Sam was leading Drew into the simple public coffee shop loftily known as the U.S. Senate Restaurant.

As he had promised, Jack was waiting for them, but he was not alone. With him was a woman who looked to be in her early forties, reasonably attractive and well kempt, if not outstanding. As Sam and Drew approached the table, and Jack rose to meet them, the woman fidgeted nervously at her place, looking past them as if expecting someone far more frightening to appear fast on their heels.

"This is Tina Mancuso," Jack introduced them.

She shook hands limply with both Sam and Drew, then fidgeted some more. They saw Tina wasn't about to volunteer any information, if, indeed, she had any, and looked to Jack for an explanation.

Jack took a deep breath, and they could see he was

preparing for his recitation. There was an unmistakable air of triumph around him, and he seemed very pleased with himself. Tina seemed in pain and more uncomfortable than ever.

"Tina," Jack began in a low key, anticipating the possibility of a dramatic build, "is Dotty's daughter."

"Really?" said Sam, smiling, but wondering how this could possibly be relevant to the grilling she would undoubtedly be receiving from Dotty's boss in very short order.

"Dotty introduced me." Jack went on, registering Sam's impatience but pausing for effect. "Tina can help us."

Sam raised her eyebrows and looked at Tina. "That would be very nice," she said politely but without much enthusiasm. "How?"

Tina seemed to shrink even more under their scrutiny. Jack touched her arm, gently reassuring. She looked at him as if begging for release, but he just smiled and nodded.

"Tell them," he said softly with such kindness that they all understood immediately why he was such a good lawyer.

There was a pause, and they all waited, expectation hanging in the air. Finally, Tina spoke. "Amos Kilmont did to me what he almost did to you."

Sam gasped. "He raped you?"

Tina nodded.

"There's more," Jack said and deferred to Tina again.

"I . . . I . . . had his baby."

"What?" This time it was Drew who jumped in.

"I'm Catholic. I couldn't have an abortion," she

said as though he had asked her to explain. "But I'm not sorry," she added quickly. "Mikey just turned eight, and he's a great kid."

Sam forced herself to close her mouth. "Excuse me, I know this is rude, but I have to ask. Are you sure that Mikey is Amos Kilmont's child?"

"It's okay," Tina said. "Amos didn't believe it either. So we had a test. But I knew right away because I'd never been with anyone else."

"Amos knows about this?" Drew asked, incredulous.

"He gives me money for Mikey. It was part of the deal."

"What deal?" they blurted in unison, astounded at their windfall of information.

"After . . . it . . . happened, my mom wanted me to press charges. She made me go to the hospital and get examined and all that. Because I was . . . you know . . . a virgin . . . ," she said shyly, "they could tell . . . it wasn't . . . you know . . . consensual."

"And Amos got you to drop the charges in exchange for child support for Mikey?" Sam surmised.

"Well, sort of. He didn't want to give me money directly, you know . . . because he was afraid somebody might find out. They're always looking into senators' finances and stuff. I couldn't work for him anymore . . . I mean, after what happened . . ."

"So he hired your mother," said Sam, putting it all together.

"You're the one who got me on the track, Sam," Jack offered, "when you mentioned that Dotty seemed out of place in the senator's office. Kilmont just didn't strike me as the kind of nice guy who would keep someone he didn't have to. Actually, I think she was relieved when I showed up at her door last night. They'd been following the hearing on C-Span."

"We knew what you were saying about Senator Kilmont was true," said Tina. "And we felt real bad about what he was doing to you. But I was afraid of what would happen to Mikey if I said anything. I still live with my mother. We don't have any other source of income."

"Listen, Tina," Drew responded immediately, "you don't have to worry about that. If you speak up for Sam, we'll take care of you. I promise you that."

"That's what Mr. Bader said."

"I can't believe this," said Sam. "On second thought," she added, "yes, I can. If he did that to me, why wouldn't he have done it to other women? It wasn't about *me*. It was about *him* and his power and what he could get away with. I should have realized right away that this was no isolated incident."

"I want you to know, Mrs. Symington," Tina said diffidently, "I'm really sorry you had to go through all that. If it weren't for Mikey . . ."

"I know," Sam said kindly.

"But I'm glad now that I can help you. That man shouldn't be a senator. He shouldn't even be out on the street."

Senator Amos Kilmont was exchanging a few affable words with members of the press in the corridor outside the Senate Ethics Committee Hearing Room when he saw Tina Mancuso approaching in the company of Samantha and Drew Symington and their lawyer, Jack Bader. He paled visibly enough so that

UPI's Helen Thomas's maternal instinct surpassed even her newshound's nose, and she stopped her pointed question in midsentence to ask if he was feeling all right. Being the consummate politician that he was, he recovered quickly and managed to charm himself away from the press corps and into a private moment with his long-time lawyer, Foster Garvey.

"What the fuck is she doing here, Foster?" Kilmont whispered viciously.

"Damned if I know," said Foster, as worried as the senator.

"What the fuck am I paying you for then?"

"I'll find out," Foster said hurriedly, panicked at the possibility of losing his generous retainer.

Jack was prepared. He had already learned that the Senate Rules Committee was not meeting that day and the room would be empty. Permission had been granted for its use. He suggested all concerned parties gather there for a confidential discussion. Ignoring the shouted questions of the press, he herded them into the room and locked the door.

"Senator," Jack began, preserving the convention of politeness that reigned on Capitol Hill no matter what the circumstances, "I don't think introductions are necessary, are they?"

Kilmont glared at Tina. "If you are trying to blackmail me," he began, and they could see Tina's lip start to quiver.

Serving his clients, Jack interrupted. "Blackmail is not an issue here, Senator. Truth is. We are in possession of all the evidence we need to establish your relationship with Ms. Mancuso. Do I need to lay it out for you?"

Kilmont's face grew red. "Whatever happened in that case, and I acknowledge nothing here, the statute of limitations has run out."

"Maybe so," said Jack, fully prepared. "But she'd make an interesting character witness if Mrs. Symington decided to press criminal charges. Do you happen to know the minimum penalty for attempted rape?"

There was silence in the room. Kilmont looked at each of them in turn, trying to assess his possibilities. Tina looked away but set her eyes on Jack, who smiled and nodded encouragingly. Sam and Drew met Amos's gaze, steady and defiant. He had spent years gauging his opponents. It didn't take him long to know he had lost.

"Really, Mr. Bader. I think we're being a little dramatic here. Wouldn't it behoove us all to negotiate some kind of understanding? After all, there's a small child involved. And even if we, as adults, are willing to bear the consequences of ruined reputations, is it fair to make him live with that kind of stigma? I think Mikey deserves more of a chance than that, don't you?"

It was clear that Sam and Drew were sickened by his cynical turnaround, but Amos was addressing himself to Tina and knew he had chosen his target well.

"He *is* your son," she said in a timid voice, not daring to look at him.

"I know that," he responded sincerely, ignoring everyone but her. "I'd like the rest of the world to know that, too. I've denied him too long. Give me a chance and let me make it up to him."

For the first time, Tina let her eyes meet the senator's before she turned back to the others. She knew what she wanted, but she didn't know how to say it.

"It would be a shame," said Amos, quickly replacing Jack as Tina's spokesman, "if Mikey's one chance at having a real father and an open life was ruined by ugly accusations."

"It's obvious what you're trying to do, Senator," said Jack, not bothering to hide his disdain.

But Sam, who had watched Tina's expression change from one of constant shame to one of unabashed hope, interrupted. "Tina is the one who suffered the most. Tina should decide."

In the end, they came to an agreement. Amos would make a complete confession of his errant ways and resign from his Senate seat. He would publicly apologize to Sam and Drew and acknowledge that he had fathered Tina's son, for whom he now took responsibility. There would be no criminal prosecution. Looking as though he had aged ten years in twenty minutes, Amos Kilmont acknowledged defeat.

"Well, you've won," Jack told them after Amos had gone to prepare his statement and Tina Mancuso had left for home, feeling powerful for the first time in her life.

"Yes, thanks to you," agreed Sam as she hugged Jack. She knew it would sound ungrateful to add what she was thinking: now what?

Sam looked at Drew and saw that he was just as disconcerted as she was. As long as they had been under fire, they had been compelled to be supportive of each other. But now, with the pressure gone, submerged misgivings surfaced into harsh reality. Somehow, they had allowed themselves to reach a point where trust had given way to suspicion. But the wounds they had inflicted on each other were still open and the pain too raw to know if the damage had been permanent.

They were on their way out of the Capitol Building when a committee staffer hurried over to them.

"Mr. Bader?" he asked deferentially, "Senator Roth would like to know if you could come up and see him in his office right away, sir?"

Sam and Drew looked at Jack, but he shrugged, having no more idea than they did why he was being summoned. The senators had all understood that the hearing was being abandoned and that Senator Kilmont was preparing a statement. As far as the Ethics Committee was concerned, their work was done.

"You guys go on ahead," Jack volunteered. "I'll let you know what's going on."

He followed the staffer through the underground passageway into one of the Senate office buildings, although approaching from below, he had no idea which one. He was ushered directly into the senator's office, where he was greeted cordially, and offered a drink, which he declined.

"I've been watching you at work," Senator Roth began when all the pleasantries were over, "and I like what I see."

"Thank you, sir. It's kind of you to say so," Jack responded politely, still curious as to what this was all about.

"You must be curious as to what this is all about," Roth went on, and Jack smiled.

"Actually, those were my thoughts exactly."

"Well, as you may know, while I sit on several

committees, I'm the chairman of the Governmental Affairs Committee, and we've been issued a delicate task. Are you familiar with the country of San Domenico?"

Jack felt his heart jump-start but simply nodded.

"Good, then I don't have to go into history here. It seems that Diego Roca has managed to defeat the military regime with his little band of rebels. We consider this good news."

Jack considered it good news, too. It increased the chances of Melinda coming home safely.

"Roca is an ally. He's calling for democratic elections, and he wants the United States to send down a delegation to help them handle it. Naturally, nothing would please us more."

"I can see why, Senator," Jack added, his enthusiasm apparent.

The senator warmed to Jack's positive attitude. "We need a few good people to make up the delegation, and we thought it would be good to include a lawyer."

"Me?" asked Jack, incredulous.

"Why not?" asked Roth, clearly unaware of Jack's possible connection. "You're familiar with the Constitution, aren't you? You understand due process, I take it?"

"Yes, of course," Jack hastened to confirm his qualifications. "It's just such a surprise. I'm not exactly a Washington insider."

"That's what I like about you," smiled Roth. "We can use more outsiders on the inside. The delegation leaves tomorrow. You can be briefed on the flight down. Will you go?"

"I'd be honored," said Jack, hoping he sounded

appropriately humble and not as overeager as he felt. Somehow, he kept up a businesslike patter as the senator walked him to the door when in his mind all he could think of was that he would see Melinda, hold her in his arms again.

"Oh, by the way," Roth added as Jack was shaking his hand good-bye. "If you've got a monkey suit, take it. There's going to be a wedding while you're down there and our people will be expected to make an appearance. It seems that Roca is actually going to get hitched to that movie star he's been boffing. Can you believe it? Have a good trip."

Somehow, Jack made it down the corridor and out onto Constitution Avenue. He tried swallowing huge gulps of air, but nothing helped. He felt like he'd been delivered a sucker punch to the solar plexus. Finally, giving in to the pain, he sat down on the curb, oblivious to the pedestrians stepping gingerly around the man in the nicely tailored suit crying softly to himself.

By the time he got back to the house on Thirty-first Street, Sam was already packing.

"Isn't it wonderful," she sang out until she saw his face. "Oh, Jack, I'm sorry," she amended, putting her arms around him. "I'm just so grateful that she's alive and all right."

"Me, too," said Jack, meaning it, hugging her back.

"I'm going down there tomorrow," she added.

"Me, too," said Jack again, eliciting from Sam a joyous shriek of disbelief, which was again tempered with a drop of sympathy.

"Roth asked me to go down as part of a delegation to supervise democratic elections. I said I'd go before I found out about the wedding. And by then, it was too late to back out without looking like a complete idiot."

"I'm sorry you have to go through this, Jack. But I have to admit, I'm not sorry you're going. I could use the company."

"Isn't Drew . . . ?"

"No," she said quickly, trying to make it sound purely practical, "he's staying with Moira. It's going to be pretty hectic."

He knew better than to ask more. "Isn't it funny," he said, "how you think things are resolved and you're fine, and then something happens and all your resolve goes up in smoke and you feel like shit?"

"Yeah," said Sam, "just hilarious."

But neither one of them was laughing.

From the sky, San Domenico did look like paradise. White sand beaches ringed the dense lush green island, leading into clear aquamarine water that looked like you could see right through to the bottom.

"Wow," said Sam, astonished by its extreme beauty, "if she's going to be first lady of somewhere, this is a great place to be first lady of."

"There's got to be an election first," Jack reminded her sourly.

"Is there any doubt of the outcome?"

"Not really. From what I've been told, he's either going to be democratically elected president or appointed God."

Sam took his hand. "This must be hard for you."

"A killer," he said and turned back to stare out the window.

Several limousines appropriated from the former president's fleet for the use of the people waited for the American delegation on the tarmac. They were met by some smiling but unidentified revolutionaries still dressed in camouflage, then shuttled directly to the presidential palace. There were still signs of the recent civil war: abandoned tanks by the roadside, buildings strafed with bullet holes, the occasional marker for a fallen soldier. But the tropics were quick to forgive, and flowers of peace were already beginning to sprout over the symbols of war. By the time the limousines had reached the walls of the presidential palace, there wasn't a single member of the delegation who wasn't already in love with San Domenico.

As they were ushered to a reception room to await an official greeting, Jack maneuvered himself toward the back of the delegation.

"You go ahead," he told Sam. "She'll want to see you first."

Too excited to argue, Sam let herself be pushed to the front of the group as they filed through the carved doors, and then she saw her sister. All ceremony was forgotten as the two sisters ran to each other, hugging and kissing, laughing and crying. There was an indulgent silence as the others stood back and couldn't help but be touched by their obvious emotion.

Then, hugging Sam for the eighth or ninth time, Melinda saw Jack standing toward the rear of the room. She let Sam go and started moving toward him, her arms outstretched, her eyes filled with tears again. He took a step to meet her, his heart already bursting with the joy of holding her in his arms before he even embraced her. But suddenly, there was a flourish at the door, and Diego Roca entered the room, flanked by his revolutionary council. They were all dressed alike in suits of army camouflage, but there was no mistaking who was the *commandante*. He stood out from the others by the dark intensity of his good looks and by the majesty of his demeanor. He had the dignity that comes not from pride of birth but from profound achievement. His appearance was of a world-class leader, but when his eyes locked with Melinda's, his face softened and was suffused with love. Jack did not know if any of the others had noticed, but from that moment, all doubt, all hope, for him was gone. He knew he had lost her.

Melinda was swept to Diego's side, and the American party filed past them in a single reception line. Introductions were made, and Jack could hear snatches of conversation and slivers of laughter. Because Melinda would not let her go, Sam had been wedged between her sister and a Roca deputy, and she was still standing there when Jack brought up the rear of the line. Melinda held his hands for a long moment.

"I saw your name on the manifest faxed from the White House. I couldn't believe it."

"I don't quite believe it myself," he said sadly, meaning a hundred things.

"Jack," was all she said, understanding.

"I guess it would be pointless, not to mention clichéd, to ask if you were happy?"

"I'm happy," she said, and he saw that she meant it and was genuinely happy for her.

"I would have preferred you closer to home," he said.

"This *is* my home now. I could never leave San Domenico."

"Like I said, the geography was just never right for us," he smiled. She hugged him, and he had instant total recall of the sweetness of her embrace.

He heard Diego Roca say, "Melinda?"

It was just her name, but he made it sound quizzical and commanding at the same time. She immediately pulled away from Jack and turned to him, introducing Jack as a special friend from home. Nothing particular was said, but for the first time, Jack sensed Diego's affability falter.

Speeches were made, plans announced, but Jack heard nothing except a quiet voice inside his soul that repeated over and over: *this time, she's really gone.*

During his tour of duty with the delegation, Jack saw little of Sam and even less of Melinda. There were few official dinners, since San Domenico was a small island nation recovering from war, and the ruling council had no interest in squandering what little remained of the treasury on the entertainment of foreigners, however benevolent. The women spent much of their time ensconced in Melinda's private quarters or walking the gardens of the presidential palace, talking, talking, talking. And at the one gala reception, provisions for which were supplied by the Americans, Melinda spent her evening at the side of Diego Roca, who, it seemed to Jack, kept a closer than necessary eye on her whenever Jack wandered in their direction.

The elections were a foregone conclusion. With no opposition to speak of and generally universal support for all Roca candidates in the newly created districts, there was little for the American delegation to oversee. But keeping with appearances, they set up ballot boxes, supervised the vote and the counting of votes, and announced to much cheer but no astonishment whatsoever that Diego Roca was the first truly democratically elected president of San Domenico. Only one last duty remained for Jack: to attend the wedding of President Roca and his bride-to-be Melinda Myles as an official representative of the United States of America.

The ceremony was to be civil. The revolutionaries had broken with the Church for failing to denounce Jorge Alvarro and his exploitation of the people. They were not the type to forget, and they were not yet ready to forgive. But the celebration was to be huge and public. It seemed the entire population had been invited to join in the festivities, and the wedding day was declared a national holiday.

With nothing to do but wait for the evening, the other Americans had gone to the beach. But Jack was too restless to relax. Assuming that Sam would be spending the day with the bride-to-be, he cajoled a Roca lieutenant who had already begun to celebrate and was in no condition to drive to let him borrow his jeep. With no particular direction he headed off toward one of the many dirt roads he had seen veering off from the main road into the jungle.

He had been driving for about two hours and had come to accept that he was thoroughly lost when he saw her. She was standing at the edge of a languid blue lagoon wearing a simple white cotton dress with brightly colored embroidery at the bodice that hung on her like raiment of the gods. It took Jack a moment to realize it was the traditional San Domenican costume for brides. In her dark curls someone had twisted dozens of white baby orchids, so fresh that the dew on their petals sparkled like diamonds in her hair. She heard the wheels of the tires crunching to a halt on the dirt, and as she turned to see who was there, he saw that the war had left a legacy of fear in her eyes. But the instant she realized it was him, her face lit up with such unmistakable joy that he would have stayed lost for the rest of his life just to bask in it.

"How did you know where to find me?" Melinda asked with obvious delight.

"I didn't," Jack said. "I don't even know where to find me. I'm lost." She gave him a sharp look, and he realized what he had said. "Well, that, too," he amended. "But what I meant was I was just driving and got lost."

"It's beautiful, isn't it?"

"Breathtaking. But why are you sight-seeing on your wedding day?"

She laughed. "I'm not. I guess I'm paying homage or something. This is where Diego and I . . ." she tapered off.

"Oh," he said, sounding as disgruntled as he was.

"You mustn't be angry Jack. Or sad."

"Why not? I mean, I know we parted ways more than once, but I never really believed we wouldn't get back together."

"That's funny. Me, too."

"So what happened?"

"I got kidnapped," she joked, although it was true.

"Damn," he said, playing along. "That'll do it every time."

They looked at each other for an unbearably long time. He longed to take her in his arms, to kiss her on the mouth, but he only reached for her hand. "I still love you, Melinda."

"I know, Jack. I love you, too. But it's different for me now. I feel as though I'm part of something that's much bigger than just myself. For the first time in my life, I'm not concerned with fame or money or acclaim. Words like *courage* and *freedom* and *loyalty* have become real to me, important. These people have changed me."

"I can see that."

"And Diego. He's a part of them. A part of me. I can't separate myself anymore."

"And me?"

"You're a part of me, too. The part that set me on the road that led me here."

"I see. I'm in the chapter on Melinda Myles: The Early Years."

She laughed. "You've always known what's really important Jack. When I wanted the glitz and glamour of Hollywood, you were working for the union. I know you tried to get me to share your values, but I wasn't ready. I needed to grow up."

"Growing up would have been okay. It's the growing away I object to."

"No. I didn't grow away. If anything, I grew into what you wanted. I just didn't do it with you."

There were tears in her eyes, and he saw that he was starting to upset her. He knew what he had to do if he truly loved her. He had to release her.

"Well, whatever you did," he said gently, "you did it beautifully. And I'm proud of you." Only then, because he saw her relief and knew that she had freed herself, he took her in his arms and kissed her. It was a long kiss, poignant and tender, that began with yearning, passed through desire, and ended in understanding. And when they separated, they both knew it would be a long time, if ever, before he could hold her in his arms like that again.

From the balcony of her room in the presidential palace, Sam marveled at the cavalcade of color. The sun had begun a slow fiery descent, and the sky was flushed with feverish pink. The courtyard had been transformed from a mortar-strewn battleground to a flower-filled sanctuary lined with deep emerald palm fronds interrupted by brilliant orange and purple birds-of-paradise. Many of the people who were gathering below had changed into the embroidered shirts and dresses reserved for festive occasions in San Domenico, their yellows, reds, and blues appearing like splashes of bright paint on the canvas of camouflage green SDLF uniforms.

As her sister's only attendant, Sam, too, was wearing an embroidered dress, hers in a pale peach that seemed to catch the copper highlights of her hair in its luminous folds. Just an hour in the San Domenican sun earlier that day had given her skin a tawny glow that in the fire of sunset made her beauty seem almost incandescent. Seen from below, she looked like Aurora's counterpart, a goddess of dusk, her radiance the motivation for the setting sun.

"It's almost time." her sister's voice woke her from her reverie and brought her back inside.

"I'm sorry," she said. "I should have come to you."

"That's all right. You wouldn't have found me. I was ready early, so I took a walk. I ran into Jack."

"Oh . . . And?"

"And it's sad, but it's good. I think I'm doing the right thing."

"Think?"

"I'm scared, Sam."

Sam went to her sister and hugged her. "Everybody's scared when they get married. I was. You can never know for sure if it's right. And even when you are sure," she added wistfully, thinking of herself, "you can never predict what will happen."

"It's not just Diego," said Melinda, "although that scares me too, I guess. He's so intense, so committed and passionate about so many things I'll never really understand because it's not my culture. But at the same time, I feel I owe these people something, and they expect something from me that I'm not sure I can give them."

"You're marrying a man, Melinda. Not a country."

But the cheer that arose from the crowd in the courtyard as Diego entered with his entourage, made up of his most trusted revolutionary advisors, told them it was not necessarily so. They watched together from the balcony as he made his way to the bower, where he would await his bride, and the people chanted, "Di—e—go! Di—e—go!"

He waved and smiled, his face reflecting the dark and powerful beauty that had first drawn Melinda to him. A small native band began to play a haunting refrain on the wooden pipes of the mountain people. Taut skin drums beat out a processional rhythm that marked his slow journey through the sea of his beloved *compadres,* who parted at his approach, only to engulf him again with hands reaching out to reverently touch him as he passed by.

"Are you sure?" Sam asked just once, needing to know for her own sake as well as her sister's.

And then, before Melinda could answer, the chanting from the courtyard changed, and they were chanting in one voice, "Me—lin—da! Me—lin—da!"

"Very sure," said Melinda quietly, her calling confirmed, and with her sister leading the way, she descended to her destiny.

A long narrow carpet had been laid the length of the courtyard leading to the altar of blossoms where Diego Roca awaited his bride. Sam took a deep breath and prepared to walk the distance, but Melinda held her back with a gentle hand on her arm.

"The last time we walked down an aisle together, I was your maid of honor," she reminded her sister.

Sam sighed. "I know. I hope you do better than me."

"I think you've done just fine, Sam."

"Oh, Melinda. I've made an awful mess of things. But this isn't the time to talk about it. You're about to get married."

"That's why this is exactly the time to talk about it."

Sam looked at her, confused. In their long talks, they had touched on what was happening at home, but Sam had avoided spoiling Melinda's happiness by dwelling on her own problems. It seemed a strange time for her sister to insist on dealing with it now.

Melinda laughed. "You didn't expect me to get married without a flower girl, did you?"

It was then that Sam saw them: the little girl with her mother's red curls and her father's blue eyes dressed in a miniature version of her own dress, running toward them chubby arms outstretched. And behind her, following at a more sedate pace but with just as welcoming a smile on his face was her father.

Tears filled her eyes as Sam stooped to hug her daughter. "Moira, my baby. Look at you. You're so beautiful," she cried, kissing her over and over again.

"Aunty Minna says I can be her fo-wa goo-wal," said the child, displaying her basket of petals, too excited to stay within the confines of her mother's arms for long.

Sam looked up, and there was Drew, grinning, as he reached to lift her up to him, to the long-deferred comfort of his embrace. He held her close and buried his face in her neck, breathing in her scent, more delicious to him than the jasmine wreath in her hair.

"Drew," Sam murmured, closing her arms around him, "we almost made a terrible mistake."

"I know, my darling. We have to promise each other never again. We're not going to make it without each other. It's a good thing your sister here was smart enough to see how stupid we were being."

Over her husband's shoulder, Sam looked at her sister. "You . . . how . . . why . . . ?" She couldn't even phrase the question, but it didn't matter.

"Myles Militia forever," Melinda answered, smiling. "I knew."

"Can I be the fo-wa goo-wal now?" Moira demanded impatiently, making them all laugh.

"You better be," said Melinda. "I've got to get married, and I can't do it without my flower girl."

"Mommy?" Moira reached out her hand to her mother, suddenly too shy to go down the aisle alone. Drew kissed them both, and they began their procession. On both sides of the aisle, the San Domenicans chuckled with delight. To them, nothing enhanced a celebration more than the participation of children.

Stationed near the presidential palace gates, Jack

watched the family reunion from a distance. He thought about how his life had become inextricably tied to these two sisters and how their happiness had come to mean so much to him. But as the crowd grew quiet, watching with love and reverence, and the woman they had adopted as one of their own made her way to the side of the man they revered, there was an ache in his soul that threatened to suffocate him.

"Looks like a fun place. Wish I didn't have to go back right away," said a man in American-accented English to no one in particular as he made his way past Jack and out the gate.

"Excuse me," called Jack, hurrying after him, "where exactly do you have to get back to?"

"Washington," came the quick and friendly response. "I just flew Mr. Symington down with his little girl. I was hoping I could stay awhile, catch some rays, party a bit, you know. But I got word the plane is chartered as of tonight, so I won't even have time to see the wedding."

"Can I come with you?" asked Jack. "I'll pay . . ."

"Naw, it doesn't matter. I've got to go back anyway. But don't you want to stay for the wedding? I hear there's going to be some party after. And . . ." he hesitated, looking around Jack to see if there was any wifely presence in the vicinity before continuing, "these San Domenican women are really something in case you haven't noticed."

Jack shrugged. "Weddings make me nervous."

"Suit yourself. Actually, I wouldn't mind the company."

No one noticed the two men slip away as the bride made her way down the aisle to the lilting harmonies of native music.

Diego Roca watched his bride float through the sea of people, her grace and beauty touching them all like the warm gold threads of light from the setting sun. She was beautiful, his Melinda, and noble and good and compassionate. And she was strong, he knew, strong enough to stand by his side while he led his nation out of their years of restriction and into the inevitable hazards of sudden freedom.

"I have always known what it is to dream of justice," he told her when she had reached his side and placed her hand in his. "But until I met you, I had never known what it is to dream of love. I dreamed of satisfaction for my people but never my soul. I acknowledged the spirit but denied the heart. You have taught me that true fulfillment comes only when we can love one person as much as we love an entire nation. Before, I had ambition, now I have desire. Before, I had commitment, now I have understanding. Before, I was proud to be a leader; today, I am proud to be nothing more than your man.

"Will you have me and keep me, stay by my side, serve the people as we serve each other, honor our nation as we honor each other, love our country as we love each other?"

For a moment, a droning buzz muffled Diego Roca's words. Drawn by the sound, Melinda looked up for a moment and saw a small, low-flying plane that seemed to hover above them.

Sitting next to the pilot, peering out the side window, Jack Bader could see the fortified wall of the presidential palace holding in its confines the splotches of color that signified the crowd. At the head of the white thread of carpet that divided the courtyard in half, he thought he could make out the arbor of flowers and beneath it the light and dark of the bride and groom.

"I hope you're happy," he whispered, aware that no one could hear. "But if you're not, I'll always be here for you," he promised, making a wedding vow of his own.

"I can't go any lower, Jack," the pilot interrupted his passenger's muted oath.

"That's okay," Jack said softly. "It's over now."

On the ground, Melinda caught her breath as she saw the plane, the orange ball of the setting sun reflected on its side, ascending to the horizon like a star on fire, blazing its way to another galaxy. For a moment, something pressed against her heart, and she could not speak. Then, abruptly, it let her go.

"I will," said Melinda, promising herself to both Diego Roca and the people of San Domenico.

A cheer went up from the crowd. Moira reached for her mother's arms, confused and a little startled.

"Is it over?" she asked as Sam scooped her up.

Sam looked at Melinda and Diego, waving and smiling as they made their way down the aisle, the president of San Domenico and his new wife. She looked at Drew, standing beside her, one arm reaching around both her and their daughter, loving and resolute. None of them would have guessed what it would cost in pain and perseverance to bring them here. None of them could know what toll the future would exact. But all of them, she was certain, would agree that it was more than worth the price.

"No, sweetheart," said Sam, knowing she spoke of much more than a wedding. "Just the first part is finished. We're still going to have a lot more fun before we're through."

ANOTHER SUMMER OF L♥VE TRILOGY
by Leah Laiman

MAID OF HONOR
(available)

THE BRIDESMAID
(coming mid-July)

BRIDE AND GROOM
(coming mid-August)

POCKET BOOKS

1085-01

Pocket Books
Proudly Presents

The Second Title in Our
Another Summer of Love Trilogy

THE BRIDESMAID

LEAH LAIMAN

Coming from
Pocket Books
mid-July 1995

The following is a preview of
The Bridesmaid. . .

"Are we rolling?" asked Barbara Walters, looking into the red eye of the camera. "Are we? What's happening guys?" Her smile never faltered, but a hint of irritation was discernible in her voice. "I'm sorry, Mrs. Roca, we seem to be experiencing a little confusion. I'm sure they'll have it straightened out in a minute. Thank you for being so patient."

Melinda Myles smiled and said, "Not at all."

She had been married for two years, but hearing someone call her Mrs. Roca—especially the way Barbara Walters pronounced it, not quite Woca the way she was mercilessly mimicked, but not with the rolling *r*'s that the San Domenicans used either—was still strange to her ear.

Melinda stayed where she had been positioned beneath the flowering arbor in the garden of the presidential palace as Walters went to consult with her crew. The two women were a contrast in styles with Barbara in a blue Chanel suit, blond hair perfectly coiffed, makeup expertly if generously applied, and Melinda in a simple white lace dress, mane of chestnut hair pulled casually off her face, hazel eyes, and perfect cheekbones unenhanced.

Clear blue skies and a brilliant afternoon sun warmed the air, which was redolent with the smell of jasmine. Although the pink palace was still pockmarked by the bullets of the revolution, its terraces and balustrades embellished with wrought iron latticework still made an imposing backdrop.

"It'll just be another minute," Barbara called apologetically.

"That's fine," Melinda said graciously. "You forget I was once in show business myself. I know all about waiting."

They laughed, grateful that the wife of the president of San Domenico was so cooperative. Seeing her so poised and reserved, the picture of respectful propriety, it was hard to imagine her as the impetuous movie star she had once been. Even Melinda, her Academy Award sitting neglected on a mantle in her palace bedroom, had almost forgotten what that life had been like.

"We're ready now," said Barbara as she joined Melinda and squared her shoulders to camera, looking like the world-class journalist that she was.

"Five, four, three, two, . . ." came the drone, and then a finger pointed in their direction, and they proceeded to walk slowly as though on a casual tour of the gardens.

"The island nation of San Domenico," Barbara Walters began, looking into the camera, "is often called a natural paradise, and with its lush jungle vegetation pressed between white sand beaches, it would be hard to dispute that claim. Adding to its allure is the glamour of its reigning couple: the mesmerizing president, Diego Roca, and his beautiful wife, the former Academy Award-winning movie star Melinda Myles, with whom we are talking this gorgeous afternoon. Thank you, Mrs. Roca, for speaking with us."

"You're very welcome, Barbara," Melinda laughed. "And I'm sure my husband will be intrigued to hear himself described as mesmerizing."

"Well, he is, don't you think?" asked Barbara conspiratorially.

"Of course I do," Melinda shared in the moment of bonhomie. "But I'm not sure he considers that his most salient attribute."

"Still, yours is a rather fairy-tale-like story. A beautiful actress from Hollywood gets caught in a revolution and ends up marrying the handsome rebel leader who deposes both a tyrannical dictator and the military junta and becomes the first democratically elected president of San Domenico."

Melinda smiled indulgently. "When you put it that way, it does sound rather like a fairy tale. But the true story, like all realities, is much tougher and less picturesque. Many lives were lost in that revolution, and the country's recovery from years of exploitation and deprivation has not been an easy one, as you know. My husband and I are both committed to making San Domenico as appealing for its quality of life as the quality of its flora and fauna. But there are many hardships to be faced along the way."

"I'd like to talk about that, with both you and the president, who will be joining us later in the program. But, for now, while we are alone, Mrs. Roca, I'd like to touch on your own remarkable personal story. You began as a small-town American girl, had a meteoric rise to stardom in Hollywood, which, forgive me for adding, did have an added element of scandal, and then gave it all up to become first lady of an emerging nation. How have you dealt with these enormous changes in your life?"

"First, let me say that my life in Hollywood, which I must admit was not always exemplary, was the easiest link to sever. I did enjoy working as an actress. But as I learned very quickly, the values promoted by that system were ultimately not fulfilling for me. I am still a small-town American girl, and my family in Oakdale, Illinois, is very important to me. But seeing the courage of the people of San Domenico, joining them in their fight for freedom, changed my priorities forever."

"And would you say falling in love with Diego Roca, the dashing rebel leader, exerted a powerful influence as well?"

"Barbara," Melinda laughed good-naturedly, "you are determined to turn this into a romantic adventure."

"Well, it is very romantic," asserted Walters with a smile. Then turning full into the camera, she added, "We'll get the president's perspective on this when we return."

The camera was turned off and for a moment, there was a visible reduction in tension. Then, Melinda heard a hum, and the air seemed to charge with electric current. Without even turning her head, she knew that her husband was approaching. Walters jumped up to greet him.

"Mr. President. Thank you for giving us your time."

Diego Roca took Barbara Walters's hand in his and held it there. His dark eyes, flecked with fires of gold, seemed to search hers. "Barbara, I hope you are not going to embarrass me by making me sound like the hero in a soap opera," he said with evident humor.

Melinda had to smile as she saw Barbara Walters melt. She wasn't surprised. Diego had always had the ability to capture attention. Mellowed in the two years they had been together by both his political and personal security, he had learned to capture hearts as well.

"Well, Mr. President. You and your wife make a striking couple, and there's no denying the circumstances of your meeting are the stuff of many a fantasy. Are you willing to talk about it on the air?"

"I most certainly am, providing we can also talk about some of the substantive issues that concern my country." Still holding Barbara Walters's hand, he glanced over her shoulder at his wife and saw an almost imperceptible nod. When the request had come for an interview, they had both been hesitant. Melinda had experienced the power of the media firsthand, and Diego, having evolved from a skilled warrior into a consummate politician, knew the advantage of being able to control the spin on the situation. The opportunity to publicize the plight of San Domenico, caught in a vise of rising inflation and declining tourism, was too good to pass up. So they had agreed to let Barbara Walters into their home and their lives. But not without a clear understanding that they had an agenda beyond titillating the insatiable curiosity of the American public for the private thoughts of people with a modicum of celebrity.

The cameras were rolling again. "We are so pleased to have you join us, Mr. President," Barbara Walters intoned unctuously. "Your wife is trying to demythologize your union, but it's hard for us in America to see your situation as anything but a dream come true."

"You are right, Barbara. My wife is modest. But, in fact, she is not only my personal dream come true but San Domenico's as well. Her obvious beauty is only surpassed by her compassion and kindness. Your countrymen think of her as a movie star, but mine know her as a champion of their cause. We could not have won the revolution without her courage, and I could not govern without her encouragement. If I am the arm of the people, she is the heart. And not a day goes by that I don't thank God that she is beside me."

There was an almost reverential hush as Diego stopped talking and looked at his wife. They did not touch; they did not need to. The connection between them was so strong and so visceral it seemed almost visible.

When Barbara spoke, there were tears in her eyes. "That was a very beautiful speech, Mr. President. And I'm sure there isn't a woman in the world who doesn't wish you had been speaking about her."

They laughed and Diego said, "Now, Barbara, you promised not to embarrass me."

"I'm sorry, Mr. President. I'm a journalist and I have to speak the truth. Does it ever worry you, Mrs. Roca, that your husband has become the matinee idol of the diplomatic world?"

"You heard him," said Melinda affably. "Would you worry?"

"I guess not," chuckled Barbara as the camera zoomed in on Melinda and Diego, sharing a smile. "At least not about his being a good husband."

"He is also a good president," said Melinda quickly, sensing, before anyone else, a change in the tone of the conversation. Her media senses were still honed enough to recognize the sound of impending danger.

"We would like to believe that," said Barbara with an abundance of sincerity, "but there have been rumblings."

Melinda looked at Diego. It was immediately clear to her that he was not worried. He had been expecting this, and he was prepared.

"There are always rumblings, Barbara. That is the nature of democracy. People are allowed to speak their minds, and it is impossible to have one hundred percent agreement."

"With all due respect, Mr. President, it is said that the freedom promised by the revolution has not come to pass. They say your government is restrictive and not truly democratic."

"Well, the fact that you have heard these things and that

people are allowed to say them should tell you something, Barbara. As for the promises of the revolution, unlike American politicians, I did not campaign on promises. Yes, we had hopes and still do. But under the dictator Jorge Alvarro and then the military leader Raul Guzman, San Domenico was pushed into third-world status. Bringing a nation back from the brink of ruin is no easy task and requires many sacrifices. Unfortunately, not all people are willing to relinquish their individual comforts for the sake of the community. So, there are, as you say, rumblings."

He looked to Melinda, and she knew it was her turn to speak. "Let me add, Barbara," she moved in smoothly, "these people are in the minority. The vast majority of the people in San Domenico understand that change takes time and are willing to do whatever is necessary to see it happen. Believe me, no one wants to go back to the way it was."

Diego smiled at her. She'd done well. Impulsively, but not unaware of the effect, she leaned lovingly against him and was rewarded with a grin from the cameraman, who, relishing the moment, motioned furiously for them to move to the right and stay in the shot. With the instinct of the actress she was, Melinda stepped to the right, blocking Diego for an instant until he could position himself beside her again.

It came in that instant: a pop, barely discernible above the whirr of the camera. Melinda felt a sting. There was another pop, and someone shouted, "He's got a gun!"

Then, burly men, security guards, were pushing them to the ground, their own guns drawn, and the screaming began in earnest.

Melinda wondered why everyone was looking at her instead of at the disheveled man who was being tackled by the guards. She followed their eyes and saw a crimson stain spreading over the white lace front of her dress like a valentine gone wild.

Only when she felt Diego's arms close around her and heard him crooning, "Melinda, *mi amore, mi amore,*" did she understand that she had been shot.

"Oh my God," she heard Barbara Walters say, "are we still rolling?"

And then she passed out.

"This is it?" asked Sam, disappointed, as they approached the nondescript, government-issue quarters of the State Department in the Foggy Bottom district, not far from the Lincoln Memorial.

In the two years since they'd been living in Washington fulfilling a contract to supply vehicles for the military, Andrew Symington, heir to the D'Uberville Motor Company fortune, and his wife, the beautiful Samantha Myles Symington, had been invited to a number of receptions and galas. Even Sam's highly publicized sexual harrassment suit against the once up-and-coming Senator Amos Kilmont hadn't dimmed their social luster. But no event had piqued Sam's interest quite as much as this formal dinner for five hundred given by the secretary of state to celebrate a new Franco-American cultural exchange. Now, after being directed to the elevators by a stony-faced receptionist in the severe Twenty-third Street lobby, Sam wondered if perhaps she had been anticipating too much.

"Do you think I'm overdressed?" she worried aloud.

Drew eyed his wife. She was wearing a deep ruby red strapless gown, it's shimmering folds ending in a train that swept behind her. Her copper curls, reflecting fiery highlights from her dress, had been swept up, emphasizing her long neck and the expanse of perfect honey-toned skin exposed by her daring décolletage.

"You look perfect," Drew said simply, but his voice had the hush of reverance reserved for the sight of miracles and objects of sublime beauty.

A moment later, the elevator doors opened on to a crystal-chandeliered corridor with marbled pilasters, and all doubt was gone.

"I didn't expect this," whispered Sam as they made their way through the entrance hall that looked like the drawing room of an eighteenth-century house.

A little awed, they proceeded down a hallway framed by

Palladian windows and lined with American Chippendale and Queen Anne furniture. Following a gathering crowd, they moved into the John Quincy Adams State Drawing Room, where a reception line stood to welcome the dinner guests. A trio of crystal chandeliers illuminated the yellow-and-red damask-covered eighteenth-century furniture, fine paintings, and precious Oriental rugs as they passed through the line and into the Thomas Jefferson State Reception Room with its celadon walls and restrained neoclassical motif. At last, they came to the Benjamin Franklin State Dining Room, where large round tables elegantly laid out to accomodate the five hundred expected guests filled the space under the seal of the United States carved into the ceiling. Eight chandeliers threw brilliant sparks on the walls bordered by faux marble columns, topped with gilt Corinthian capitals.

"Here comes Jack," Sam said, pointing at the handsome blond lawyer in the elegant tuxedo striding across the room.

They watched as he made his way toward them, stopping every few steps to bestow a dazzling smile, shake an outstretched hand. Sam smiled, remembering how not so long ago, he'd been a ponytailed stranger working on the assembly line beside her. Only her need had made him finally acknowledge the law degree that he'd kept secret for fear of getting sucked into a lifestyle he couldn't and wouldn't tolerate. They'd left the line together and worked their separate ways up, Sam to designing her beloved cars under the auspices of a husband she adored, Jack to his position as a union advocate even though it meant giving up the love of Melinda, Sam's sister. Then, two years ago, again responding to an appeal by Sam, he had made his appearance in Washington, representing her in her case against Senator Kilmont and ultimately discovering the evidence that forced Kilmont to concede defeat. Sam had expected him to return home to Oakdale and the auto union after that, but he'd been offered a job at the State Department, and the challenge of a new adventure had been too compelling to refuse. In the two years since, he'd had a rapid rise both professionally and socially, as nothing quite caught the eye of Washington's aristocracy as a handsome, eligible, well-connected bachelor.

"Aren't you two the glam couple," Jack greeted them.

"What's up, Bader?" smiled Drew as Jack hugged Sam and she kissed the air beside his cheek.

"Funny you should ask," Jack said, striking a deliberately casual note.

But it was no use. They knew their old friend too well not to recognize the timbre of alarm, no matter how faint.

"What?" was all Sam said quietly, clutching at her husband's arm and Jack knew what she was asking. Since Melinda had married Diego Roca and become first lady of San Domenico, they had relied on Jack's connections with the State Department to give them advance notice of any rumblings, favorable or not, in the small island domain.

Jack took a breath. "Okay," he began, "let me start by telling you right off everything is fine."

"Why shouldn't it be?" Sam said peremptorily, perferring to hear the real news instead of the reassurances.

"Barbara Walters went down to do an interview with Melinda and Roca in San Domenico."

"I know that," Sam interrupted, impatient.

Jack saw it would be best just to tell her the whole story and be done with it. "During the interview there was an assassination attempt. Some nut with a gun and a silencer, so he got to shoot a couple of times before they dropped him. No one was killed, but Melinda was wounded. But she's all right."

The blood drained from Sam's face.

"She's all right," Jack repeated forcefully. "She got hit in the chest, but the bullet missed the heart or any major arteries. They operated on her immediately, took it out, and she's recovering."

"When did all this happen?" Drew asked while Sam caught her breath.

"A couple of hours ago. Because I left the office early to dress for this stupid shindig, I wasn't there when the information came in, and it took the guy who was covering a while to figure out where to direct it. I just found out myself on the way over here. I tried to call you at home, but you'd already left. It'll be on the news tonight."

Drew looked at his wife. They had heard the phone ringing as they left the Georgetown house, but because she'd been so excited about the evening ahead, they'd decided to let Mrs. Halsey, the baby-sitter, answer.

In spite of all Jack's assurances, Sam's eyes were filled with tears.

Again, he tried to reassure her. "Soon as I heard about it, I went to my office and called our rep down there. All the reports are positive. She's in stable condition."

"But you're always saying that it's getting harder to get verified reports from San Domenico," Sam pointed out.

"Well, as a matter of fact, I figured you might worry about that. So I got an aide to stay on the horn and try to make contact with Diego Roca himself on your behalf. I told him to come and get you here when he gets through."

"Oh, Jack." Sam threw her arms around him, grateful for his foresight and thoughtfulness. Suddenly, she stepped back, worried again. "How's he going to find me? Maybe I should go to the office now and wait there."

Jack laughed. "First of all, I just told him to look for the gorgeous redhead. Second, it's just been two years since your face was splashed all over the front page. People in Washington forget, but not that fast. Third, I gave him the seating plan, so he knows where your table is. And fourth, there's no telling how long it's going to take, so you might as well eat. Or at least drink. They're pouring some exceptional wines tonight, and it wouldn't hurt to get a little snookered, if you know what I mean."

"Thank you, Jack," said Drew fervently, speaking for both of them.

"I've got to mingle," he said. "It's my job. But I'll keep checking in with you. And don't worry," he added, looking at Sam's still-stricken face. "She's all right. We'd know it if she wasn't, wouldn't we?"

Sam rewarded him with the first smile since she'd heard the news. She and her sister had a visceral bond that extended over time and space. If something were really wrong with Melinda, Sam was sure she'd feel it in her heart. After all, they were the Myles Militia.

"You're right," she told Jack, meaning it. "Go circulate. We'll find you when we get the word."

Feeling more unsettled than he knew he should, Jack took his leave and moved through the crowd. He grabbed an unidentifiable cocktail from a passing tray, downed it, and took another. He hadn't eaten all day, and the drink was stronger than he had expected, which was just as well, since he felt he could use a little of the numbing he'd recommended to Sam.

It had been four years since he and Melinda Myles had parted ways, as certain of their love for each other as they were of their inability to live together. It was ironic that Jack's refusal to leave the simplicity of life in Oakdale and Melinda's determination to taste the glamour of Hollywood had driven them apart. And here was Jack, wandering through the elegant corridors of the Washington elite, while Melinda languished in the spare conditions of an emerging nation. Still, being the wife of Diego Roca was not without its own high profile, and for all Jack's advancement in the State Department, it was still an elementary existence he craved.

"Which means," he said to himself, hardly aware that he was speaking out loud, "you're an idiot for still thinking about her. Get over it!"

"Talking to the most interesting person you could find?"

"What?" Embarrassed, he whirled around to see who had caught him.

Almost as tall as he was and sliver thin, she was what had once been described as a long drink of water. Barely combed, her hair was the white blonde of movie stars in the thirties, but it hung straight and long, like platinum strands brushing her pale white shoulders. She was dressed in a slip of a dress, cut on the bias, clinging to the contours of her body, an intriguing juxtaposition of angles and curves. The dress, too, was white, and for one irrational moment, Jack was reminded of the childhood pleasure of licking icicles.

"I have to admit," she said, "the crowd is more boring than usual."

"Present company excluded, I assume," he said, playing along.

"That remains to be seen," she answered. "Let's get out of here."

She reached for his hand and swayed a little, and he saw then that she was a bit drunk. He moved to steady her, wavering somewhat himself, and realized with a laugh, so was he.

"Where are we going?" he asked.

"Does it matter?"

He looked at the swell of her ample breasts rising above the scoop of her neckline, then raised his eyes to her face. Her mouth was full and turned up at the edges in an ironic smile that didn't quite eliminate the sensual pout. Her slate gray eyes seemed to mock him or herself, he wasn't sure. He was sure that she was beautiful, and the involuntary rise of sensation he was beginning to feel told him she was desirable as well.

"No," he answered, letting himself be led, "I guess not."

"Then shut up and come with me."

She started pulling him through the large reception room, moving swiftly. He followed, keeping his eyes averted from the people they passed, feeling an urgent need right now to avoid contact with anyone except the mysterious stranger who was taking him away.

"Jack!" someone called. He tried to ignore it.

"Jack!" again, and he recognized Sam's voice. He stopped short.

She looked at him, her lopsided grin revealing perfect white teeth. "So you're Jack," she said and it sounded almost like a taunt.

Before he could respond, Sam was at his arm. She was too overwrought to even notice he was not alone.

"Your assistant found me. As soon as he puts me on the phone, they're going to connect me to Diego Roca. Are you coming?"

Automatically, he went to follow, turning momentarily to the woman beside him to proffer his apologies. She was watching him with downcast eyes, a seductive smile playing on her lips. She was exquisite. He heard his own words come back to him like instant replay. *Get over it!*

"Listen," he said to Sam. "you're his sister-in-law. I'm

just . . . just . . ." He didn't even know what word to put on it.

"Okay," said Sam, understanding. "I'll let you know. I'm going to take it in your office, okay?"

"Of course," he said and watched as she hurried off. For a moment, he wanted to run after her. Then he forced himself to take hold of the blunt reality. Melinda was going to be fine. He didn't need her husband to tell him that. *Get over it,* he repeated to himself like a litany.

"Well?" the woman said. He wondered at her uncanny ability to make everything she said sound like both an insult and an invitation.

He grabbed another drink off a tray and threw it back, relishing the fire as it went through his body and rekindled his desire.

"Let's go," he said and blindly trailed as she pushed through a door and out of the light and the din.

"What have we here?" she breathed excitedly as their eyes adjusted to the gloom.

"The James Madison Dining Room."

"Aren't you knowledgeable?" she said, and he wondered why he found her derisive tone so enticing.

"I work for State," he said, instantly regretting he had given her so much information.

"Well, Jack, who works for State, see anything you'd like to dine on?"

And with that she kicked aside one of the sixteen Sheraton chairs and positioned herself on the edge of the table, letting the strap of her dress slip just enough to reveal one round and rosy nipple.

He moved to her, wondering for a moment what he was doing. But he knew the answer. She was everything Melinda was not. An anonymous, careless, emotionless fuck. And even if it would only last a minute, it would be one minute less that he would be aching for the woman he had loved and lost.

"Listen," he said, still needing to be fair. "I'm not—"

She covered his mouth with her hand, interrupting.

"Neither am I."

She opened her purse and extracted a condom, handing it

to him without a word. He pushed her back against the eighteenth-century mahogany table and, without comment or criticism, accepted her for the gourmet offering that she was.

Look for
The Bridesmaid
Wherever Paperback Books
Are Sold
mid-July 1995